Smart M♥ve

OTHER BOOKS AND AUDIO BOOKS
BY MELANIE JACOBSON

The List

Not My Type

Twitterpated

Smart M♡ve

a novel

Melanie Jacobson

Covenant Communications, Inc.

Cover image: *Smart Move* © McKenzie Deakins

Cover design copyright © 2012 by Covenant Communications, Inc.

Published by Covenant Communications, Inc.
American Fork, Utah

Printed in the United States of America
First Printing: October 2012

18 17 16 15 14 13 12   10 9 8 7 6 5 4 3 2 1

ISBN 978-1-60861-568-1

For Eden,
who loves stories but, more importantly, loves others.
Stay beautiful inside, sweet girl.

Acknowledgments

WITHOUT KENNY, I COULDN'T WRITE books. You, first and foremost, make it possible. You believe in me and then back up your encouragement by serving as a sounding board and brainstorming partner; you never begrudge the time I sometimes have to steal from other places in our lives to get this writing done. Thank you to Amy Lou, my first and most honest critic. Thank you to my patient critique partners—Aubrey Mace, Kristine Tate, Brittany Larsen, and Krista Jensen—who batted clean-up. Thank you to the friends who read rough drafts and told the truth: Josi Kilpack, Susan Auten, Rachel Gillie, DeNae Handy, Karen Peterson, Dedee Freestone, and Jen Schumann. Thanks to my awesome editor, Samantha Van Walraven, who has yet to be fazed by one of my freak-outs. Finally, thank you to all of the friends who demand, "When is your next book coming out?" and ask it like they really care. It feels good every time I hear it.

Chapter 1

SANDY TAPPED THE TOE OF her high-heeled boot as she considered its sharp point and where it would do the most damage to Jake Manning.

Jasmine leaned over her desk, peering at the paper Sandy had slammed down moments earlier. "What is it? It's El Diablo, right?"

"That's not a strong enough name for him, but I can't think of any better ones that don't involve swear words," Sandy said.

"Yeah, that's El Diablo," Jasmine said with a nod then settled back into her seat. "He's a jerk."

Even *jerk* was too mild for the attorney bent on making their jobs a living nightmare.

"This is your fault," Sandy grumbled.

"My fault that I got promoted? I'm so sorry."

"You should be," Sandy said, smiling. "I can't believe you're leaving me for New York."

"You're right. It's very selfish of me to try to move my kids back near my gigantic family and make my kids' lives easier."

"Just sayin'." Sandy ducked the paper clip Jasmine sent sailing her way.

"Stop complaining," Jasmine said. "I'll be here for a couple of months until they're done with school. That's plenty of time to teach you how *not* to run this place into the ground."

"I'm not worried about that part. I'm mad I got put on Jake Manning duty. There are two dozen people in this office, and I'm the lucky one who gets stuck with him. As if my sixty-hour work weeks weren't enough while I try to figure out how to even do my job."

"You know why it has to be you."

"Yeah," Sandy sighed. "I do." She'd been recruited to take over the deputy director position at the New Horizons Washington DC headquarters, and that meant handling their major headaches.

"Your only escape is to be less awesome."

"Wow. I'd thank you for that compliment if it weren't for the sarcasm."

Jasmine grinned. "I wouldn't dish it if you couldn't take it."

Sandy grimaced, and Jasmine laughed again. Sandy straightened in her chair. "He filed an injunction to stop our zoning permit."

The persistent lawyer represented a neighborhood group trying to block them from opening an outreach center in their community.

"I told you that was coming."

"I know. That doesn't make it less aggravating." Sandy crumpled the copy of the injunction into the tiniest ball she could make. "It wouldn't be so bad if he weren't so arrogant every time I talk to him. He told me the River Oaks people were concerned about a project from a bunch of 'bleeding-heart liberals.' He made me slam down the phone again. Me! The nicest girl in the whole wide world!" She threw the paper wad into her trash basket, feeling slightly better when she nailed the shot.

Jasmine laughed. "Nice until Jake Manning enters the picture."

Sandy groaned and dropped her head back on her chair. She wondered if it was possible to drown in all the paperwork he'd filed against them with the zoning commission. His third request for an injunction, the one she had crumpled, had come in only a few minutes earlier.

"I feel for you. I think he could make the pope mad enough to spit," Jasmine said.

"You sure you don't want to stay and deal with him?"

"No way. I miss Brooklyn. My kids can't wait to live by their grandparents again."

Sandy nodded in understanding. Jasmine had been a single mom for four years, which fueled her desire to help other women who were trying to pull their lives together for the sake of their kids. She worked hard and deserved the promotion, but Sandy hated to see her go.

A soft chime announced that the center had a visitor. A girl, barely more than a teenager, walked in with a toddler on her hip. Her worn T-shirt looked as if it would dissolve with one more washing, and it hung from her thin frame. The dark circles beneath her eyes put Sandy on high alert. Sandy straightened and smiled. "Hello."

"Hi," the visitor said, her voice soft and uncertain. "My friend Lacey sent me here . . ." She trailed off and stared at the ground. The wan little girl she held hid her face in her mother's neck. "I heard you help people get jobs," she said. "Can you help me?" She stole a quick look up to meet Sandy's eyes but then dropped her gaze again.

"We'd love to try," Sandy said, her voice warm. "I'll need to ask you some questions to know for sure though. Why don't you take a seat, and you can start by telling us your name." She and Jasmine exchanged knowing glances. Time for them to do what they did best.

Gently, Sandy guided the young woman through the questions to assess whether she was a good candidate for job retraining. Sandy loved this part, the part where hope sparked in a client's eyes when she realized a whole new set of possibilities was opening up for her; it made every last second of overtime worth it. It was the kind of job Sandy had dreamed of since high school: the kind that made a real difference for others. Even El Diablo and all his schemes couldn't dampen her spirits when confronted with someone like this new client—Kayla, she'd found out from the questions—someone who deserved the second chance the center was about to help her take.

When Kayla finished the simple survey, Sandy read it through and smiled, her heart doing a happy skip. She glanced up to catch anxiety flickering in Kayla's expression. "Kayla, I think you're perfect for New Horizons. You're going to be so great."

It felt awesome to put a huge grin on someone else's face. New beginnings for the women everyone else had given up on—that's what it was all about. *Take that, stupid Jake Manning.* No way would New Horizons back down.

* * *

The slap of leather against wood sent Larry the cat flying out of the kitchen to investigate. The cat must have realized it was only its owner's purse hitting the foyer table because it slunk back to whatever havoc it'd been wreaking.

Sandy shook her head. "I got you so I wouldn't need roommates," she called after the cat. "You're supposed to keep me company." Her only answer was Larry's gray tail disappearing around the corner. "My mother warned me you'd be antisocial."

Her downstairs neighbor Brooke said Larry's bad attitude was because she resented her name and wanted to be a Sheba or a Nefertiti. Maybe Brooke was right, but Sandy had named her after the nice man at the rescue shelter, and he was most definitely not a Sheba or Nefertiti. He was a Larry.

"It's a good name," she said aloud to Larry Junior, who walked back into the room but continued to ignore her as she plopped down to clean herself. "Too bad you didn't get his sweet disposition." Larry's only response was to turn her back and clean from a different angle.

Sandy's mother's anticat stance had been the deciding factor in Sandy adopting the ornery Larry. If Magdalena hated cats, then the cats must be doing something right . . . even if Sandy still hadn't figured out what that was after cohabiting with her furry houseguest for several weeks.

It was as if thinking of her parent had summoned her; Sandy's phone blared "Crazy Train" to announce that Magdalena was on the line. She sighed but knew that ignoring the call would only provoke her mother to bombard her voice mail with increasingly hysterical demands to call her back. Magdalena called a minimum of three times a day, and at least half the time, she was in a state of dramatic emergency. She claimed it was due to her highly sensitive nature. That was one way to put it.

"Yes, Magdalena?" Sandy said by way of greeting.

"I wish you would get a home phone. It can't be good to spend all that time on a cell phone," Magdalena said, her tone fretful. "I was reading an article the other day—"

"In *New Age Mumbo Jumbo Monthly?*" Sandy asked, irked that her mother's call had started with a lecture. "Science says talking on cell phones doesn't give you ear cancer."

"Honey, that's what the media companies want you to believe," Magdalena scolded. "I'll send you the article, and you'll see."

"Really, don't worry about it." Sandy stifled another sigh. She briefly considered buying a bird so the stream of photocopied articles from her mother could serve a useful purpose as cage lining. Eyeing Larry, who forced Sandy to step over her en route to the refrigerator, she wondered if a talking bird would make up for the cat's social deficits. "Did you need something specific?" she asked her mom while she dug through the veggie drawer.

"There's a seminar in Taos this weekend that I want you to come to," her mother said. "It's called 'Shedding Your Virtual Skin,' and the facilitator, Guru Lalan, is fantastic."

Sandy stuck with a polite, "No, thanks." It was her standard response to pretty much all of Magdalena's invitations to explore further enlightenment.

"Oh, but Guru Lalan is one of the West's foremost experts in meditation and transcendentalism," Magdalena gushed. "I can get you in even though the registration deadline has passed, and I can book a plane ticket for you in two seconds flat."

"Using the Internet? That doesn't sound like shedding your virtual skin, Magdalena." Under her breath, Sandy added, "Actually, the whole workshop concept sounds suggestive."

"I heard that, Sand Dollar."

Sandy flinched at the use of her given name. Never mind that she had gone by Sandy since she was four and had legally changed her name when she was twenty. Magdalena insisted on using her birth name as if, at age twenty-seven, Sandy would suddenly decide to embrace it.

"Don't be so disrespectful," her mother continued. "I'm trying to help you maximize your aura. It's been so dim."

"How do you know? You haven't seen me in months," Sandy said.

"Is that my fault? You won't accept any of my invitations to visit."

"That's because they're always attached to some kind of purification ritual or cleansing ceremony or guru summit in podunk towns I've never heard of. I'm happy with my church, Mother." She got so tired of repeating herself.

"Are we on that again?" Magdalena sighed. "I thought you'd finally seen the light and left organized religion behind you. Why are you going back?"

"I took a short break," Sandy conceded, not sure if three years of inactivity would count as short in the minds of never-take-a-break Mormons. "But I'm back, and I wish you would respect that."

"Like you respect my spiritual choices?" Magdalena asked.

"At least I'm not constantly trying to talk you out of them."

"No, you settle for ridiculing them instead," her mother snapped.

Sandy felt her temper rising. "It's no different from your implied criticism of Christianity every time you ship me a crystal or a moonstone," Sandy said and then delivered herself a mental slap for engaging in the tired, old argument that neither of them ever won. How did she keep getting sucked into this crazy debate?

"I'm your mother"—*Oh, yeah. That was how*—"and it's my place to help you redirect when your life is going off track."

"Magdalena! I'm working in the nation's capital to help women in poverty. I'm financially independent, healthy, and happy. A lot of mothers would be thrilled to say the same thing about their daughters. Why can't that be enough?" She hated that she even wanted her mother's approval. Some things you never grew out of. "I figured you of all people would appreciate raising a bleeding-heart liberal." Jake Manning's parting insult from the afternoon still tasted bitter on her tongue.

"Liberal? *You?*"

"Forget it."

"If you say so. As for your job, I know your heart is in the right place, but you're only focusing on improving those women's minds. What about their spirits? What about *your* spirit? Are you practicing your yoga?" Her voice dropped to a strangled whisper. "Don't you care at all that your chakras are suffering?"

Sandy lifted the phone from her ear to pound it lightly against her forehead. Taking a deep breath, she addressed her mother again. "Thank you for the invitation, Magdalena, but I already have plans this weekend. I can't meet Guru Lalan."

Magdalena seemed to stew on that for a minute. "What kind of plans? It's not from that hookup site, is it?"

Sandy rolled her eyes. "It's Lookup, not hookup."

"You go on there to meet boys," Magdalena pointed out. "How is it different?"

Deciding to retreat from another losing battle, Sandy fumbled for an excuse to end the phone call. "I have to work. Lots and lots of hours. And Larry's hungry, so I need to feed her. I better go." She reached under the sink and grabbed the cat food, crinkling the bag so her mom could hear it.

"Fine," Magdalena said, her sigh long-suffering. Her tone said she didn't buy the excuse. "Go feed your cat. But a dog would be less demanding and far more appreciative."

"You don't know many dogs, do you?" Sandy asked, shaking out some dry food for Larry, who promptly turned her tail on the premium kitty kibble in her bowl. "I'll call you later." She hung up then turned to her cabinets and the impossible task of finding her finicky cat an acceptable meal.

After Larry finally condescended to eat some canned tuna and Sandy had changed into her favorite yoga pants, she pulled her laptop out and accessed her LDS Lookup account. Despite her mother's misgivings, she had every intention of seeing if anyone new or interesting had joined in the last couple of days. Especially anyone male and extremely good-looking. Even though there was a large-ish population of young LDS singles in the DC area, Sandy had met only the people who attended her ward. Who knew what cool guys were floating around unattached in one of the other two singles wards? LDS Lookup was a great way to find them.

She'd discovered the site well over a year ago while trying to find a dating site for her old Seattle roommate, Jessie. Jessie had been so stubborn in her refusal to socialize that Sandy had taken matters into her own hands and set up an account for her without Jessie's knowledge. She grinned at the memory of Jessie chasing her around the house with a yoga mat when she'd discovered Sandy's trick. She smiled even bigger when she saw a message in her inbox from Jessie, reminding her to get her bridesmaid gown fitted in time for Jessie's wedding to Ben in six weeks. That Lookup experiment had gone well.

Eventually Jessie had coaxed Sandy back to church, saying she was returning the favor. It felt strange to sit in the chapel after a three-year absence . . . but somehow right. Once Sandy had embraced activity in the Church, things had changed at a dizzying pace. It was without doubt the Lord's hand in her life. No sooner had she begun to pray again and ask for direction than Roberta McGinnis, the founder of New Horizons, had contacted her. Roberta had been so impressed with the mentoring program Sandy had set up between the Macrosystems corporate office and the surrounding community that Roberta had recruited her to New Horizons with an aggressive help-make-a-difference campaign. Sandy had felt prompted to take the offer on the opposite side of the country and was ready to be a part of something that mattered more than a lifeless corporate machine.

When she had returned to church activity six months ago, she'd made the change from meeting guys while out clubbing with friends to sticking with LDS guys. Lookup helped, and she'd had a steady stream of dates since joining. It was even better in DC, where the dating pool ran deeper than it did in Seattle.

She clicked through her messages, bookmarking a couple of interesting possibilities. She deleted the usual handful of e-mails that pretty much amounted to "Ur hot. Wanna make out?" She appreciated compliments as much as the next girl, but she'd grown annoyed years ago with the same old comments about her looks. When her senior class voted her Best Hair and Nicest Eyes, she had smiled and said thank you but had inwardly wished she'd been voted Future President instead. When a guy could see past her face, she took notice. Any Lookup e-mail that referenced only her picture and not all of the information she included in her personality profile was an automatic delete.

She returned a message from Evan, a Lookup contact from the Colonial singles ward, confirming a second date. He worked too much for her taste, but he could keep a conversation going. Not a bad way to pass a Friday evening. She folded away her laptop and reached for the TV remote. Very few things from Magdalena's New Age gobbledygook stuck with her, but yoga had. She cued up her DVD and began the demanding stretches, feeling the tension over her mother's phone call and her growing Jake Manning problem slowly melt away. They were nothing she couldn't handle.

Chapter 2

"I CAN'T HANDLE IT!" SANDY cried in frustration, tangling her hand in a shock of her red curls. She glared at the phone on her desk.

She heard Jasmine snort. "Jake Manning?"

Sandy yanked her hand back out, wincing when one of her newly manicured nails managed to snag a stray curl and pull a strand loose. She waved the orphaned hair at Jasmine and glowered. "Even this is his fault."

"Pace yourself, or you'll go bald inside of a month dealing with him," Jasmine said. She held up her own ragged fingernails. "I quit getting my nails done after I lost count of how many times El Diablo made me chew them off."

"He's unreasonable," Sandy said.

"What happened now?"

"After I left *eight* messages for him about meeting to discuss his clients' concerns, he finally calls me back to say he already explained it all to you and he saw no reason to explain it all again to me. Oh, and he called *our* clients a 'criminal element.'"

Jasmine's eyes sparked with anger, but she looked unsurprised. "I know he didn't leave it at that," she said. "What else?"

"I offered to show him this center and the plans for the annex. I figured it wouldn't hurt for him to see what his group is opposing. You know, resolve some concerns. But no. He ranted on about private citizens' rights and how we're going to drive their property values down. He won't even come see for himself if there's really anything to worry about."

Jasmine nodded. "He's not even in DC right now. His firm has several offices, and I get the impression his isn't here."

"Why is he representing such a small group on such a small issue if his firm is that huge? That doesn't make sense," Sandy mused, feeling her blood pressure finally returning to normal.

"I don't know," Jasmine said. "You saw yourself that it's hard to get very far with him. And I didn't mean it was *his* firm. I meant the firm where he works."

"Yeah, I figured that out when I didn't see 'Manning' in the Booker, Hughes, Pennington, and Washe letterhead he sends me with every stupid motion he files," Sandy said drily.

"It'll be there before long," Jasmine warned her. "He's ambitious. And worse, his assistant mentioned something last week about him relocating here soon. You may be wishing he'd stayed too far away to visit if that happens."

"Maybe," Sandy said. "But I know I could make some progress with him if I could get him down here to take a look." She got up and headed toward the office minifridge.

"At you," Jasmine said, her grin wicked.

"Excuse me?" Sandy asked over her shoulder.

"You mean, you think you can twist him around your pinky finger if he could get a look at you and your sassy little walk," Jasmine teased. "Don't deny it, girl. If I had a body like yours, I'd wear pencil skirts and stilettos too."

"Spanx," Sandy said.

"You're welcome."

"No. *Spanx.* You know, that super-suck-you-in Lycra stuff? That's how I can get away with a fitted skirt."

"No way," Jasmine said. "I don't believe it."

"Believe it," Sandy retorted. "If I don't watch everything I eat and work out five times a week, these dangerous curves become dangerously squishy. If I gain even ten pounds, I go from curvy to lumpy." She shuddered and waved the light yogurt she had retrieved from the fridge to reinforce her point.

"What size do you wear? A six?"

Sandy nodded. "Barely. With really, really hard work." She knew Jasmine was trying to distract her, and she appreciated it.

Jasmine laughed. "You need to find a good Puerto Rican. We think a size ten is too skinny."

"Do they like redheads?"

"Just the curvaceous *mamacitas* like you."

"Sounds like my kind of guy." She stared into her yogurt, stirring the fruit and thinking about how to solve their zoning problem, which meant solving their Jake Manning problem. So far, he had resisted solving, and she had to fix that.

"You look like you're trying to read the future in that thing," Jasmine said. "It only works for tea leaves, not"—she squinted at the carton for a minute— "not Tropical Medley Cream."

Sandy set the yogurt down. "Maybe it's not a bad idea."

"What isn't?"

"At church we have this joke that sometimes you have to flirt to convert. I hate to say it, but Jake Manning's voice is kind of sexy. All deep and smooth—"

"No!" Jasmine nearly shouted. "Don't even think about it. No flirting. No even being *nice.*"

Sandy laughed at how easily Jasmine had taken the bait, but when the door chimed, she turned in relief to greet Kayla. She had almost mentioned the strange shudder his voice had provoked from her. Twice. Saved by the bell. Jasmine waved Kayla into a chair. "Hey, girl. I'll help you finish your paperwork. Sandy's going to go find her brain, and then she'll do an advanced skills assessment with you, okay?"

Sandy took a quick moment to finish her yogurt and load the aptitude test they gave all their new prospects. When Jasmine escorted Kayla back to the computer lab, Sandy greeted her with a smile and showed her how to take the test about her strengths and preferences. Like most of their new clients, she looked intimidated by the rows of computers lined up like sleek black soldiers. Sandy spent several minutes settling her in and helping her navigate the programs. Once Kayla seemed more sure of herself, Sandy introduced her to their tech assistant, Geneva, and then left Kayla to complete orientation at her own pace.

As Sandy made her way back down the hall, Roberta poked her head around her office door and beckoned Sandy in. Sandy loved Roberta's office. Rich browns and soft gold accents in the small but well-appointed room conveyed both femininity and professionalism, much like its occupant.

"How's it looking with the new client?" Roberta asked once Sandy had settled herself in a chair.

Sandy nodded. "Kayla's a good fit. She only has her high school diploma and a couple of semesters at a community college, but she seems stable enough. If anything, she's really shy. Self-esteem issues, I think."

Roberta looked unsurprised. "It's amazing how many different ways low self-esteem manifests itself, isn't it?"

Sandy could only agree. Sometimes a client walked through the door looking like she was dressing for the world's oldest profession rather than an office job; sometimes she came in like Kayla, with little to no care for her outward appearance; and other times she was everything in between. Whether their insecurities were buried under pancake make-up and smudged eyeliner or written all over their faces, the women all shared the same fears and false beliefs about themselves. Part of the retraining New Horizons offered focused on teaching these women to substitute those negative messages for new ones that empowered them. It was the major reason Sandy had accepted the assistant director job.

"At any rate, I'm glad to hear we'll be able to help her," Roberta continued.

It wasn't always the case. Sometimes the women who came to them needed help getting their basic needs met, like food and shelter, which wasn't what New Horizons did. They took on clients that had those pieces of their lives already in place but didn't know how to move to the next level.

"But that's not what I wanted to discuss with you. How is the annex going?"

"Fine," Sandy said, unwilling to admit that it was stressing her out. Or, to be specific, that Jake Manning was stressing her out.

Roberta rifled through a small stack of papers on her desk, found the one she was looking for, and handed it over to Sandy. "I was waiting for you to acclimate to the center before moving Jasmine out, but you picked up even faster than I'd hoped you would. You can do this."

Sandy glanced down at the paper Roberta had handed her. It was a long-term contract. She looked up in surprise.

"I know I said we'd do a three-month probationary period, but I don't need it," Roberta explained. "You're right for this job. I figured I better make it permanent before you wise up and run off."

"Because of Jake Manning?" Sandy asked with a half smile, keeping her sigh inside.

"And the people he represents, yes." Roberta studied Sandy with a practiced eye. "I recruited you because of your human resources background. You may be wondering what that has to do with zoning permits, but I promise you, your people skills will be infinitely more valuable than anything you might know about city ordinances." She pushed away from her desk, walked around it, and perched on the edge, then studied Sandy. "If ever there was a time to establish a connection and create some dialogue, this is it. We need to settle this soon. Can you handle it?"

"I can," Sandy reassured her. Roberta had won them a fantastic grant, but they would lose it if they didn't use it for technology upgrades and expansion, and the expiration on the grant was ticking down. There was no time to go through the incredibly time-consuming processing of finding and vetting a new location before their funding evaporated. Turning over the River Oaks expansion to Sandy signaled a huge vote of confidence. She knew Roberta would rather oversee it herself, but she needed to spend the bulk of her time on raising funds to keep New Horizons growing. Between grant applications and schmoozing with lawmakers and corporate bigwigs, Roberta had a full agenda.

"I'll be hiring a new associate soon. That should help spread the workload more evenly. Is there anything else you need from me to go forward on this?"

"Not yet. I'll be sure to let you know if something comes up."

"Good. Now go make Mr. Manning regret he ever picked on us."

* * *

"New Horizons, Sandy Burke speaking."

"Please hold for Mr. Manning," ordered a crisp voice on the other end.

Resisting the urge to stick her tongue out at the receiver, Sandy waited for the lawyer's voice to come on the line.

"Ms. Burke?" Jake inquired politely. Even though she'd only been teasing Jasmine about flirting with him to further their cause, his voice really was kind of sexy. Dang it. Too bad his personality was so off-putting.

"Call me Sandy," she said, hoping to establish a rapport.

"Of course," he said. "I understand that you wanted me to return your *several* messages?"

She ignored his barb. "Yes, thanks for calling back. I wondered if you've had an opportunity to consider my earlier invitation to tour the center."

"It wouldn't serve a purpose," he said.

"I disagree." She was careful to keep her voice neutral. "I think we'd both find it invaluable to meet face-to-face to discuss the plans New Horizons has for the River Oaks property."

A note of impatience crept into his response. "I know exactly what the value of that would be. At six hundred dollars an hour, it would cost my clients nearly a thousand dollars for me to take a little field trip to your office."

Heat crept up the back of her neck, a warning sign that she was close to fulfilling every stereotype about redheads and fiery tempers. Man, he was arrogant. "I'm sure your clients would support you in doing your due diligence in a case like this. Isn't it merely responsible to take a look at what you're opposing?"

"My responsibility is to help my clients get what they want," he answered coolly. "They don't want your center or its baggage."

Sandy ground her teeth and drew another deep breath. "Mr. Manning, *my* responsibility is to get *my* clients what they *deserve*, and that's a fair shot. We're not backing down."

"Good luck with that," he said, sounding amused. "You don't need to wish River Oaks the same. They've got me." And he hung up.

Sandy replaced the receiver and stared at the phone. "Define justifiable homicide," she said, startling a laugh out of Jasmine, who had been listening to Sandy's end of the conversation.

"Whatever you're thinking, stop," Jasmine ordered. "If you don't, you'll get nailed for premeditation. When you kill Jake Manning, do it in the heat of anger. Not only will you get a lighter sentence, but they'll probably drop the charges and write you a thank you card too."

Sandy leaned back to study the purple painted nails peeking out from the peep toe of her zebra-striped heels. "Jake Manning is going to be so, so sorry he ever heard of New Horizons."

Jasmine lifted her eyebrows and studied Sandy's intent expression. "You are scary," she said.

Sandy plucked an emery board out of her desk drawer and buffed her fingernails with brisk, precise strokes. "Don't worry," she said. "I'm sharpening these claws just for Manning." Then she smiled.

Chapter 3

MUFFLED THUMPS SOUNDED FROM DOWNSTAIRS. What were the girls up to? Sandy rented the entire top floor of an old Georgian house in Arlington. Most of the young LDS singles working in DC did the same; the city was for work, but Virginia was for play. Her kitchenette and separate entrance gave her a sense of privacy, but she could wander down and join the constant party the girls below seemed to throw at any given time. In the weeks she'd lived above them, she had yet to see an ebb in the traffic that flowed in and out. She'd met half of her ward by hanging out in their living room.

She liked the arrangement. She enjoyed the easy access to company and entertainment, but she appreciated the retreat of her upstairs haven after her long days at work. As much as she had liked living with Jessie in Seattle, she loved having her own place to imprint with her style. Sandy had spent most of her Saturday mornings since she moved either scouring consignment shops for interesting furniture pieces or haunting the Ikea in Woodbridge. Slowly, her place was coming together with an eclectic mix of vintage and chic that reflected her perfectly. Sometimes she liked to sit on her corduroy sofa and enjoy *her* space in blissful peace and quiet. Still, in case it ever got too quiet, she had Larry to make up the difference.

She glanced at her cat, who sat cleaning herself on the windowsill with supreme disregard for her audience. Hmm.

Larry was probably her only misstep in this new life adventure. Even with the zoning issues at work, everything else about this new job and new city had proven to be exactly what she needed. Her life had been fine in Seattle. She was busy and successful, and all the way up until one fateful night at The Factory—her favorite hangout, she had been content with it. Pretty much. If she had ever felt a slight emptiness, she had dragged a friend out and played until the feeling went away. It had worked well.

Mostly.

She thought about that night for the millionth time. It was funny that a chance meeting anyone else would chalk up to another night on the town had ended up being life-changing. All because of a guy, of course. A guy who had captivated her from his first hello until the club closed down in the early hours of the morning, forcing their conversation to end.

He'd been different. He'd been sober, for one. Completely out of place in The Factory and yet totally comfortable in his own skin. Seriously hot too, but . . . more. Funny. Smart. They'd laughed first about being the only eligible designated drivers in the whole club and then kept finding things to laugh about. She had connected to him instantly, wondering if he was the spark she'd sensed missing.

She couldn't wait to tell Jessie about him the next day. The wild giddiness had reminded her of a high school crush, and she hadn't cared when Jessie teased her about love at first sight. She had waited all day, tingly and excited, for him to call. But he never did.

That hadn't happened to her before. At first, it had made her mad. Then she had doubted herself, wondering if she had imagined their connection and how she could have felt so drawn to him when he hadn't felt anything at all—if her silent phone was any sign.

She had resolved to forget about him, but weeks went by and everything around her felt flat. Over the next few months, Sandy had found herself skipping a stream of party invitations and trying to fill the time with other things. It had made her painfully aware that despite a high-powered career and an active social calendar, gaps riddled her life. She had watched Jessie and Ben's relationship blossom and fought a creeping melancholy that she had never experienced anything similar for herself.

She'd shanghaied Jessie into helping her with a life makeover, trying one new thing after another to recapture the spark from that night at The Factory. She'd learned some useful lessons, like that she'd rather die than camp ever again, and she would not be flooding the Red Cross with her poorly attempted knit blankets for disaster victims anytime soon. She took up vegetarianism and volunteer work, which stuck. She tried rock climbing and cooking, which didn't.

A road trip to Jessie's hometown had provided the real turning point. After a conversation with Jessie's mom, Sandy had decided to look at what she could do for others instead of for herself. She returned to Seattle and set up the volunteer tutoring program at her massive software firm, ultimately capturing Roberta's attention. Between Roberta's job offer and Jessie's gentle nudges back toward church, Sandy'd had one of those rare instances where she could recognize promptings when she heard them. She'd taken the job, moved across the country, and hadn't looked back.

Except for sometimes when she thought about that night.

Another thump sounded from below, and Sandy wandered downstairs to investigate. She found Brooke and Shannon straining to relocate a sofa in the living room.

"What are you guys doing?" she asked.

"We're hosting a big dinner tonight," Brooke explained. "But word got around, and now it's going to be even bigger than we thought, so we're trying to make room for everyone."

Almost every Sunday brought an invitation to one house or another for a family-style meal. Everyone showed up with a dish in hand, ate their food, and then got down to the serious business of flirting.

"Did I know about this and space it?" Sandy asked.

"No, it came up last night," Shannon reassured her. "You coming?"

"Sure," Sandy said. "I'll bring a salad. Can I help you get ready?"

Brooke gestured to the sofa. "Maybe you could help us push it out of the way?"

Sandy helped shove the behemoth the rest of the way to the wall then turned and collapsed on the worn but comfy cushions. "Two hours until church. What next?"

After another hour of rearranging, Sandy headed up to get ready. She loved her curly hair, but the East Coast humidity had been playing games with it for weeks. She scrunched in the cocktail of products that tamed it then turned to her closet. The large walk-in was the most attractive thing about the house when she'd found it on an LDS housing message board. Well, the closet and the four cool girls living downstairs.

She picked her way through the piles of laundry strewn across the floor and decided she had too much stuff. Time to organize a clothing drive for the center. She had some great business pieces she could donate. Ooh, and she could have some of the girls at church teach a dress-for-success type of workshop one night and—

"Ten minutes!" Cami's voice called up the stairs.

Sandy flipped through her hangers and considered her choices. Still not quite warm enough to break out the spring clothes. She settled on a brown pencil skirt and an aquamarine cashmere fitted sweater a few shades lighter than her eyes. And heels. Very high heels.

She rode to church with two of the downstairs girls, Cami and Leah. They were young and silly, and she liked their company.

"How did your date with Evan go on Friday?" Leah asked once she had merged with traffic.

Sandy shrugged. "Fine."

"That's not good," Cami said. "That's like saying it was interesting."

"I wish it had been. He's a nice guy, but he's too intense for me."

"Too bad," Leah said. "I saw him walking you out to your car. He's pretty cute."

"You want dibs?" Sandy asked. "He's on Lookup. You could send him a note or something."

"You don't mind?" Leah asked, surprised.

"Nah." Sandy half wished she did. Jessie had often teased her about being heartless, but she didn't mean to be. She just got an itchy feeling and needed to move on. She'd hoped that would change when she switched to dating LDS guys and the difference in her standards was no longer an issue, but she still felt the same discontent she always had. No one had truly held her interest since—

Grrr. Never mind.

Leah pulled into a parking space at the church building with five minutes to spare. They walked in to find the chapel still only half full. It would be packed through the overflow by the time the sacrament ended.

Sure enough, by the last amen, the chapel was brimming with young single adults.

After sacrament meeting, Sandy didn't even make it up from her pew before an excited Shannon pounced on her. "Did you see him?" she demanded.

"Who?"

"The new guy. He is *hot*."

"I still can't tell all the new guys from the regular ones," Sandy said. "Give me another couple of weeks."

"There's no missing this guy. Dee-lish," Shannon said.

"Go get him, then," Sandy teased her. "Sounds like you better move quick."

"No, he's too old for me. But he'd be perfect for you."

"So he's midfortyish?" she joked, deciding not to take offense that in her neighbor's mind, there was a huge gulf between twenty-two and twenty-seven.

"No! Thirty, tops. You know me, I like the unsuspecting fresh RMs. Seriously, you have to see this guy." Her eyes widened for a split second as she stared past Sandy's shoulder. "Here he comes."

Before Sandy could turn, a deep voice hit her from behind. "I don't believe this. I know that hair. Sandy?"

It was the same voice that had sent shudders down her spine twice that week. Feeling a dip in the pit of her stomach, she knew that through some bizarre twist of fate, when she turned around, she'd find Jake Manning standing there in *her* chapel. She turned to face him and gasped.

She knew that face too. She'd seen it way too many times in her memory of that night at The Factory.

Chapter 4

"You!"

"Me," he agreed easily.

"*You're* Jake Manning?" She narrowed her eyes. "Fan-freaking-tastic. It's not enough for you to tick me off all week. Now you're *here*?"

"How did you know my last name? And how did I tick you—" He broke off, and disbelief washed over his face. "Wait, you're Sandy *Burke*?"

"What's going on here?" Shannon asked. "You two know each other?"

"I didn't think when I met you in a bar that the next time I saw you would be in a chapel." He smiled to let her know he was teasing her. She didn't smile back.

"You met in a *bar*?" Shannon's eyes bugged ever so slightly.

Sandy shot Jake a cool look completely at odds with the tumult inside her head. "It wasn't a bar," she said. "It was a dance club."

"Where? In Seattle?"

"Yes, Shannon. In Seattle."

"Well, this is kind of a neat coincidence, right?" Shannon asked. Neither Sandy nor Jake said anything. After an awkward silence, Shannon cleared her throat. "Uh, I'm going to go find . . . someone," she mumbled and scurried away.

Sandy crossed her arms because she didn't know what else to do with them. She was freaked out but didn't want to show it. Jake Manning, the guy who had driven her crazy all week, was the same Jake she'd spent an amazing evening with a year ago and then . . . had never heard from. *That* Jake had been warm and funny. *This* Jake . . . she couldn't stand.

But he was the same guy.

"Why are you here?" Sandy asked.

Breathe. She didn't know who had taken over her brain the second she clapped eyes on Jake, but she needed the real Sandy to come back. What would the real Sandy do?

Flirt. Definitely flirt in a you-can't-have-this kind of way until she could figure out what was going on. It was the only thing she could think of to knock Jake off balance too.

"I think this is supposed to be my ward," he said, answering her question.

"Isn't your ward in Boston?" she asked. That's the hometown he'd claimed at The Factory.

"It was. I'm relocating to the DC office."

"Ah. Lucky us." She gave him a warm smile, hiding her consternation.

Jake slid his hands into his pockets and rocked back on his heels. "I'm sorry I didn't call you after that night at The Factory. I assumed you weren't LDS since we met at a nightclub. It wasn't personal."

She waved her hand to dismiss his apology. "Not a big deal," she said. "I'm more worried about why it took so long for you to call me back this week about the New Horizons stuff."

"Business," he said, waving his hand in imitation of her. "So this is strange, right?"

"What is?"

"Bumping into each other a year later on the other side of the country and finding out we're both Mormon. It's a crazy coincidence."

It was crazy, all right. She had no idea what to think. At least the shiver his voice had given her over the phone made more sense, but it made her mad too. Jake-from-The-Factory, she could manage to ignore. El Diablo, she had to humor. Unfortunately.

She let none of that show on her face. "Yeah, it's pretty wild. Enjoy the rest of your Sabbath, Jake. I need to do the Sunday School thing." She bit back a smile at his look of surprise. It might be kind of fun to keep him off balance. Call it payback. Before she could sidestep him and head down the hall, Shannon popped back in.

"Everything good?" she asked.

"Yeah," Sandy said. "It's fine."

"Oh, cool. Did Sandy invite you to our dinner party tonight?" she asked Jake. Sandy wanted to kick her.

"I'm sure she was getting to it," he said.

Sandy flashed her most flirtatious smile. "Definitely. You should totally come. You can meet all kinds of people from the ward."

"Sounds good," he said. "Maybe we can catch up on old times tonight."

"Maybe," she agreed. "But don't feel bad if it's maybe not. These dinners get so big and loud you can't hear yourself think, much less carry on a conversation."

"Funny, I would have thought the same thing about The Factory until you showed up. I must have wanted to listen." He smiled, and it might have been charming if it hadn't been so practiced.

"Too bad you're not up for listening now," she said. "I wonder how many calls it will take for your assistant to put you on the phone next time." It was her turn to smile when his eyes narrowed. She turned and sauntered away, infusing her good-bye walk with as much "You wish" as she could muster—which was a lot.

Chapter 5

LEAH AND CAMI LEAPED FROM the car as soon as it stopped, rushing to get ready for the dinner crowd that would soon invade. Sandy took her time. She pulled on her favorite pair of Joe jeans and a fitted cardigan. She touched up her make-up, applying her lip gloss generously, which triggered good memories. She liked to think she left Jessie with two enduring legacies: Jessie's marriage to Ben and a conversion to MAC Lipglass. There were few superficial wrongs that hairspray and lip gloss couldn't right.

In the kitchen, she tossed some nuts and apricots into her spinach salad and wondered if Jake would really make an appearance. After the seismic ripple he'd sent through her universe a year ago, it was too bizarre that she'd found him standing in the chapel at church. It didn't make sense.

Her phone erupted into "Crazy Train," and she stabbed the ignore button. She'd already had four lectures in as many days from her mother about her lifestyle choices and didn't need another dose of Magdalena, but she did need to talk to *someone*. She dialed Jessie.

"Sandy!" Jessie cried, sounding delighted.

"Guilty!" Sandy answered back.

Jessie laughed. "I've been meaning to call you for a week, but it got nuts with the caterers and—"

"You don't need excuses, lady. I know the wedding thing is running you ragged. Is it all coming together?"

"I think it is," Jessie said. "Ben's sister-in-law has been a huge help. There're some fires only I can put out popping up every two days, but I'm hanging in there."

From her voice, Sandy could tell her former roommate was more than hanging in there. She sounded downright happy.

"Cross me off your list of things to worry about," Sandy said. "I ordered my dress, and it'll be here soon."

"Oh, good." Jessie sighed. "You wouldn't believe how long it took me to find bridesmaid dresses that didn't look like I was trying to punish you guys."

"You did good," Sandy said. "I can wear the color, and the dress doesn't have any large bows that are going to try to wear me."

"So I know you didn't call to give me a dress update," Jessie said. "What's up?"

"I have an insane story to tell you."

"My favorite kind."

Sandy settled onto her sofa, tucking her legs beneath her. "Do you remember that guy I met at The Factory and then never heard from again?"

"How could I forget? What was his name? Jack?"

"Jake," Sandy corrected her. "Remember how annoyed I was when he never called me later?"

"Annoyed? He kicked off your quarter-life crisis."

"Glad you find it funny, Jessie."

"Oh, lighten up. You survived it."

Barely, Sandy thought. It sounded so corny to say, but that night with Jake had felt like a moment out of time. He'd leaned in close to introduce himself and his breath held the tiniest whiff of cinnamon but no hint of alcohol.

They'd drifted over to a quieter part of the club, and even as she'd drowned in his root-beer eyes, she couldn't make herself come up for air. She felt like it had taken months after he'd dropped off the radar before she'd drawn a deep breath again.

Realizing Jessie was waiting for the point of her call, Sandy shook off the memories and picked up her story. "I survived it. But guess who just showed up in Virginia?"

"Jake?!" Jessie nearly shouted. "Shut up! Details. I want details now!"

Sandy laughed. "Do I shut up or talk?"

"Tell me how on earth you ran into him again. I thought he was from Boston."

"Here's where it gets really weird. He was, but his office is transferring him here. And get this—he's Mormon!"

"No! How did you not know that before?"

"I don't know. I guess the one time I met him *in a club* didn't make me think to ask him which church he went to. But he's moving into my ward."

"Holy cow."

"It gets better."

"It can't. This is already too good."

"Oh, you'll love this. Jake Manning is also El Diablo."

Jessie gasped and then burst out laughing. "This story is making me so happy right now."

Sandy rolled her eyes. "You're not supposed to kick me while I'm down."

"Sweetie, you've never been down. This is awesome."

"Awesome? The only guy I ever wanted rejected me, and now he's my arch-nemesis on the biggest project of my professional career. Nice, Jessie."

"Arch-nemesis? You don't see the potential here."

"I see huge potential for losing my mind *and* my temper *and* shoving his next motion to dismiss our zoning permit down his throat."

"Nah, think of it as closure. Now you can find out why he didn't call you."

"He already told me. He said it was because he thought I wasn't Mormon."

"Okay, but there's another upside to this. Tell me it wouldn't be fun to make him pay for all that time you spent cursing your cell phone for not ringing."

"Don't think I'm not already plotting."

Jessie laughed again, and Sandy grinned, knowing she probably deserved it after the teasing she had done when Jessie had first started dating Ben. "All right, Sandy. Truth or dare."

"Truth," Sandy said.

"Is this payback plot an excuse to find out if there's still some kind of spark with Jake?"

Sandy wrinkled her nose. "I changed my mind. Dare."

"I dare you to find out if there's still some kind of spark with Jake."

Exasperated, Sandy ignored the bait. "You have a one-track mind. Go focus it on some more wedding planning."

"I should," Jessie said. "I like your suggestion of giant dress bows."

"Evil," Sandy said.

"Right on the back where it'll really draw everyone's eyes . . ."

"I have to go now before you veer toward princess puffy sleeves."

"Good luck with Jake," Jessie said before hanging up.

Sandy headed downstairs to find out exactly how her luck was running.

* * *

She was trying to listen to Lee, another newbie in the ward, but it was hard to hear him over the music the girls were blaring from their hot-pink iPod dock.

Sandy smiled apologetically. "Sorry," she said for the fifth time. "I didn't catch that. What do you do?"

Lee shook his head at the iPod and then pointed outside toward the porch, his expression inquisitive.

Nodding, Sandy stood and followed him to the old sofa that sat out front. Despite being chilly, it was at least quieter.

Lee smiled when Muse managed to leak through the pane of the closed window. "I guess this is still an improvement," he said.

"Definitely," she agreed and then shivered with the slight gust of wind.

"Let me grab my jacket for you. It's in my car. I parked a couple of blocks over, but I'll hurry."

Another shiver shook her, and she nodded. "Thanks." She would have run up to grab hers, but it would take an archeological dig to excavate it from whichever pile of clothes it was hiding in.

He set off at a brisk pace. They hadn't had much of a conversation with all of the noise and commotion in the house, but he seemed nice enough.

Eyes closed, she leaned her head back against the sofa to savor the momentary break. Within a minute, the scuff of shoes on the walkway alerted her that Lee was already back.

"That was fast."

"Thanks, I think," he said. Only it wasn't Lee's voice. Her eyes flew open to find Jake standing there. She'd begun to think he wasn't coming. Well, well. Let the games begin. "Hi. You missed dinner."

"I didn't have anything to bring, so I ate at home."

"Good manners. I'm impressed, but most people come for the food, you know."

The front door opened, and a couple dressed in light jackets for a walk stepped out with hands clasped. They moved down the sidewalk without even noticing Sandy and Jake.

"The food?" he asked as he stared after the two people wrapped up in each other. "I doubt it."

"Then why are you here?"

"For you."

He said it to provoke a reaction, and she refused to give him anything more than a Mona Lisa smile. "What can I do for you?"

"I was hoping we could finish our conversation from this afternoon," he said.

She nodded toward the front door. "I'm busy now; feel free to go in and help yourself to some brownies."

He smiled, only half of his mouth curving up. She remembered that same smile from the night at The Factory. She'd gone out of her way several times to provoke it, loving the way she could tug it out of him. She brushed the memory aside.

He climbed the remaining couple of steps to the porch and joined her on the sofa. "I really didn't come here for the food," he repeated.

Before he could say anything else, Lee headed back up the walkway. "I knew I shouldn't have left you alone," he joked.

"Because of Jake here? Don't worry about him. He's leaving." She pointed to the jacket over Lee's arm. "Is that for me?"

He climbed the steps to give it to her. Outmaneuvered, Jake relinquished his spot on the sofa. Lee handed her the jacket and sat down.

"Nice coat, man." Jake's tone was mild. "But she probably has five inside."

Lee bristled, but Sandy pulled the jacket's collar closer. "None of them smell like Lee." Jake's eyes narrowed, and she was pretty sure Lee's nearly crossed. Sandy gave Jake a small wave. "Enjoy yourself inside."

His lopsided smile flashed again, but he only said, "I'll catch you later," before disappearing through the front door.

Lee arched an eyebrow. "Will he?"

"He wishes," she said.

Lee looked concerned. "Am I stepping into the middle of something? I just assumed when I saw you on Lookup that you weren't in a relationship."

"I'm not," she said. "We work together. Or more like against each other," she amended. "It's nothing."

"Good," Lee said, sounding a touch shy. "Where were we?"

"You were about to explain to me what you do," she prompted him.

He grinned. "The fascinating world of international finance."

She clasped her hands beneath her chin and batted her lashes at him. "Tell me more."

He laughed and explained his work with microfinance in developing nations. Genuinely interested, she pushed thoughts of Jake aside and concentrated on learning something new.

* * *

An hour later, she found herself in the kitchen facing down Cami, resident baker and diet wrecker, who waved a hot, gooey brownie under her nose. "I pulled them out of the oven a few minutes ago, and they're delicious. Have one."

Sandy crossed her arms and thinned her lips, determined to resist the chocolate seduction. She glared at the brownie and shook her head.

"Come on! You'll love it!" Cami said. Her Georgia roots made her genetically incapable of resisting the urge to feed everyone who crossed her threshold.

Sandy backed up a couple of paces to create some distance between her and temptation and bumped into a solid wall of muscle. A pair of large hands settled on her shoulders. The tingle down her spine told her who it was.

"Imagine running into you here," Jake said, and she felt the vibration of his words against her back. She took one step toward the lesser evil of the brownie and turned to face him, reluctantly noting that his eyes were the same rich brown as Cami's dessert.

She offered him the enigmatic smile she'd been teasing him with all night. "Do you need something? Because Cami and I were discussing—"

"Nothing important," Cami interrupted. "I have to go do a thing in the other room." She dropped her brownie back into the pan and scooted out.

Subtle, Cams, Sandy thought, but she didn't say anything. She glanced back at Jake and found him giving her a long, searching stare.

"It's surreal to see you standing here," he said.

"I live here. What's the confusion, counselor?"

"You aren't going to cut me any slack, are you?" he asked, smiling.

"I'll tell you what," she said, slipping nearer and resting a hand on his chest. She tapped her manicured finger against it slowly while pretending to consider the question, "I'll cut you as much slack as you've cut us over the new outreach center." Her hand dropped away. "Ooooh, too bad. I guess that means I won't be cutting you any at all."

He laughed. "Fair enough. I'm prepared to wait."

"For what?"

"For you. I don't think we remember that night at The Factory the same way," he said.

"Why do you say that?"

"How about I tell you what I remember, and you tell me if I got it right."

She leaned against the counter behind her and absentmindedly grabbed a brownie to pick at. "I can't stop you." And not a single part of her wanted to. Not that she'd show it.

"I had no idea that week of court in Seattle would end with meeting you. I can't believe I almost didn't let my coworkers drag me to their victory celebration. They said it didn't matter that I don't drink; they wanted to show me a night on the town. They said the soda was on them and that I couldn't refuse."

She faked a ladylike yawn.

"Be patient," he countered. "I'm not a nightclub guy or a dance club guy or even a sports club guy. Sometimes there's a certain expectation from my clients and business associates that sends me to those places, but I don't enjoy them. The more the liquor flows, the dumber the conversations get. Add in women, and it's a whole different mess of trouble."

"Wow," Sandy said, deadpan. "It must be so exhausting to fight them off all the time."

"Thanks for thinking that's what I meant," he said with a grin. "But I'm talking more about how it's a dating wasteland."

"The Factory always has lots of hot girls," she pointed out.

"Yeah, if you're into sloppy drunks and exhibitionists."

"That's an overstatement."

"Not by much," he said. "You may be the only girl I've ever met in a place like that who either didn't expect me to buy her a drink or didn't smell like alcohol when she said hello. That caught my attention. Right after that turquoise dress you were wearing," he added.

She was surprised he could recall her outfit over a year later. "It's a pretty great dress," she said to make him laugh, and he did. "And I don't drink. I never have."

"I kind of figured when I saw you at church today," he said. "When you were in the club, I assumed something different."

"Then why did you come up to me that night in the first place?"

"You said it yourself. It was a pretty great dress."

She pinched another piece off the brownie and grinned at him.

"Seriously, though, when we talked, it was . . ." he trailed off, at a loss for words.

"Yeah," she said, "it was."

He watched her, and his gaze stilled. Time to get her game face back on. She turned away as if in search of more dessert, a handy excuse to break their connection.

"I remember all of that," she said after swallowing a convenient piece of brownie. "Why would you think I didn't?"

He tilted his head and measured his words. "The second I saw you again, I was right back at The Factory a year ago. I wanted to grab you and hug you. You seem more interested in keeping me at arm's length." He sounded more curious than perturbed.

"That's the smart play, isn't it?"

"You mean because I never called you?"

She laughed. "No, of course not. If that were the only issue, it would be no big deal." *Liar.* "I mean, it seems smart to keep my distance while we're resolving this zoning problem."

As much as she'd love to knock him down a peg or two for leaving her hanging after that night, she didn't need Roberta's voice in her ear to remind her that it behooved her to play nice even as she played hard to get. She hated being beholden, but she forced herself to think long term about what building a friendly relationship with Jake could do for the future of the outreach annex. Stupid behooval. Behoovement? Whatever.

"Why would that matter?" he asked, interrupting her irregular verb nominalization. "That's business."

She refrained from a jaw drop. Barely. "It's not business for me," she said. "My heart would absolutely break if we lose the annex." She leaned forward conspiratorially until her cheek almost touched his. "As if that weren't bad enough," she whispered, "I think you're going to be crushed when you lose." And she made sure her lips brushed his ear before she stepped around him and made her second killer exit of the day.

Chapter 6

Jasmine shuffled into work the next morning, looking . . . frazzled. A hot roller clung to the back of her head.

"Uh, Jasmine," Sandy said, not sure she wanted to brave the dark cloud hovering over her friend's head.

She got a grunt in reply.

"You have a, uh . . ." she trailed off and simply pointed to the back of her head.

Jasmine's hand flew up and snagged the offending curler then tossed it on her desk with a growl.

"So," Sandy asked after a beat. "Good weekend, huh?"

Jasmine's head dropped down to join the curler with a thump. "I hate moving," she moaned. "I hate it, I hate it, I hate it."

"I feel you. But you've got a little time. What's the hurry?"

"You have clearly never had to fight with two kids over every toy and which ones to donate and which ones to pack. They need all the time they can get to deal with the emotional trauma of the toy sorting." She stabbed a finger at the play center in the corner. "Look for new inventory coming soon."

Sandy laughed while Jasmine dragged herself to the coffee maker and poured herself a cup. "Our toys are worn out," Sandy said. "They could use reinforcements."

It was probably the only area in the center not in top-notch condition. Roberta was adamant that most of their funds go to expenses that directly affected the women they served, but she also felt strongly that their office needed to look professional for the recruiters who came to hire their clients. The front of the center was a large, open workspace full of modern desk furniture, up-to-date equipment, and lots of plants to soften the sleek edges.

Sandy had once commented on the sparsely decorated walls to Jasmine, who had then explained that Roberta wouldn't authorize buying expensive original art and had also vetoed cheesy motivational posters and prints long ago. Sandy had to agree that soft yellow paint on the plain walls was a better alternative than lame slogans about hanging in there or soaring like eagles or whatever.

Sandy knew Jasmine's coffee had perked her up when she heaved a satisfied sigh and indulged in a full-body stretch in her office chair.

"I don't know how you make it through your day without java," Jasmine said. "It's my fuel."

"I get by fine on oatmeal."

"Tell me about your weekend, mama. You've always got some good stories about your dates." Jasmine settled back in her chair and waited.

Sandy shook her head. "Prepare to have your mind blown. Guess who showed up at my church yesterday."

"I don't know any Mormons besides you."

"You know at least one, and he found me before I could run away."

Jasmine looked perplexed. "Who?"

"I've heard lots of talk *about* the devil in church before, but yesterday, I got to talk *to* him."

"El Diablo?" Jasmine gasped.

"In the pointy-tailed flesh."

"Jake Manning goes to your church?"

"Bummer, huh?"

"Tell me about him," Jasmine demanded. "Wait, no. Let me guess. He's short, kind of a pipsqueak, right? Ooh, with a receding hairline. And I bet he wears stacked heels on his shoes because he's always overcompensating. Did I get it?"

Laughing, Sandy shook her head. "No. Unfortunately, he's—"

"Tall, dark, and handsome?" Jasmine interrupted as the door chimed.

Sandy glanced up to find Jake Manning standing on the threshold. Jasmine patted her hair down to make sure all the curlers were truly gone and then whispered, "I'll handle him."

"That's Jake Manning," Sandy murmured.

Jasmine's jaw dropped. "*That's* Jake Manning?"

Sandy nodded and stood to meet him. He crossed to her desk, and she held out her hand for a businesslike handshake. He took it and smiled.

"Nice place you have here."

She eyed him, on guard for any sarcasm or signs of disdain on his face now that he was in lawyer mode, but she found none. "Thank you," she said. "This is our flagship location."

Jasmine cleared her throat.

"Jake, allow me to introduce you to Jasmine Clemente."

He leaned over to shake her hand too and flashed her his half smile. "I understand you're moving on. Congratulations. I'll miss sparring with you."

"Right," Jasmine said, slightly dazed.

Sandy hid a grin; she knew the feeling. "What are you doing here?" she asked him.

"You invited me last week, remember? Is the invitation still open?"

"Of course. Would you like a tour?" she asked, giving Jasmine a chance to snap out of it.

"That would be good, thank you."

Sandy crossed to Jake's side of the desk, glad she'd worn her favorite black suit. The fitted skirt and feminine jacket flattered her figure, and her shiny red stilettos lent the whole outfit a dash of sass. With a gesture for him to follow, she led him to the center of the main room. About half the desks were empty since many of the center's employees spent their days out of the office recruiting new trainees or lobbying for funding, among other things. The rest of them were engaged in their usual low-level clamor of answering phones, talking with clients, and hustling to stay on top of their paperwork. "This is where the magic begins," she said. "When we have new recruits, we start the intake process here."

"Sounds like the armed forces."

"That's not a bad analogy," she said, smiling. "This is where these women sign up to secure their own personal freedom. They want the tools and skills to be competitive in a cutthroat workforce, and this is boot camp for that."

"Boot camp with toys?" he asked, indicating the play center.

"Until we can help them place their kids in subsidized daycare, sometimes their littlest ones tag along for the first meeting or two. We try to make it as pleasant here as possible for the kids while their mothers complete their paperwork or undergo skills assessments. It's a temporary measure. We're not running a daycare." She kept her voice even, but inwardly she bristled. She had no intention of giving him any grounds to block their zoning application.

She guided him through the rest of the front office, explaining their programs as they walked. She tried to ignore the surreptitious glances from her coworkers. She guessed it was normal for him in a room full of women.

It was *not* normal for her to suddenly feel the need to poke every last one of them in the eye. *You're an idiot,* she scolded herself, but she sped up that part of the tour anyway.

She paused before leading him to the back half of the center. "Any questions so far?"

He eyed several of the empty desks. "I'm not sure what I expected, but maybe more employees? Are there always so few people here?"

She wondered how big his law firm was if more than two dozen people scurrying around seemed sparse. "It depends on the day," she answered. "We have a lot of field liaisons who spend time building relationships with other organizations. They try to help stabilize sketchy home situations for some of these women so they can focus on job training. They visit our newly placed workers or seek new employers who are willing to offer these women jobs."

"What do you mean by 'stabilize'?" he asked.

If there was a minefield, this was it. She needed to explain this piece of their mission clearly so there could be no misinterpretation, even in the hands of a skilled lawyer.

"Most women come to us out of rough situations," she said, "but the exact nature of that situation is different case by case. Ultimately, all of them need a new skill set so they can earn their own financial independence. In some cases, they're not ready for career training. We have an established network of resources to help women who need to do everything from kick a drug habit to escape an abusive relationship before they can handle the rigor here. Some of them are in shelters and eating from soup kitchens. They're not in a position to tackle coursework or new careers. We refer them to the right organization, and when the women are ready, we're here waiting."

"Can you overview the type of clients you see here?" he asked. The reserve in his voice tipped her off that he had a concern he wasn't voicing.

"Why don't you ask me what you really want to know?" she prodded gently.

"Okay, you mentioned drug addiction. What percentage of your clients struggle with that or with alcoholism? And how many of the women who come here have criminal records?"

She knew this was a major point of contention for the River Oaks group because Jake kept mentioning that these mystery people didn't want to fear for their lives with the opening of the annex. "I can't give you an exact number off the top of my head, but I'd ballpark it around a quarter of clients or less for substance abuse. And anyone with a known history of drug use or alcoholism is required to enroll in a recovery program and submit to a drug test before employment."

"And criminal records?" he prompted.

"Many of them," she admitted. "But they're generally nonviolent crimes. I've had several moms who were busted for shoplifting things like baby formula or diapers. These are women who were caught in tough circumstances and made desperate choices."

"You said they're *generally* nonviolent."

She'd known he wouldn't overlook that.

"What about your violent offenders?"

"Let me show you something." She led him to a conference room in the rear of the building, where she stopped near a plaque reading "In Memory of Patrice R. Williams."

"Patrice had a criminal record when she came to us. On paper, it looked bad. Assault and battery. In reality, she came home from her night shift as a custodian to find a couple of local thugs terrorizing her kids after breaking in to steal stuff."

"That's awful," Jake said.

Sandy nodded. "She hit one of them with a baseball bat, and he fell down two flights of stairs. His friend took off. The guy she hit had a serious skull fracture and two broken bones. She was tried and convicted of assault because the guy who ran off testified as an eyewitness against her."

"She got a raw deal."

"Yeah." Sandy sighed. "But Patrice got the minimum sentence—credit for time served and four years of probation. She came here looking to make a change that would help her get her kids out of Anacostia, which is the worst part of town. Roberta took her in without looking back. Patrice is exactly why we do what we do."

"What happened to her?" he asked.

"Two weeks before Patrice was going to move her kids out to a safer neighborhood, her son came home from school and found her at the bottom of the stairs. Gunshot. No one had even called the police." She stopped. She had never known Patrice but had already met a dozen women like her in her short stint with the center. It pained her to think of anything similar ever happening to any of them.

She studied Jake, wondering what he thought. "Yes, she had a violent criminal record. But sometimes you have to look at the story behind the paperwork."

"I understand." He fell quiet, processing what he'd heard.

"Do you want me to show you the rest of the center?"

When he nodded, she led him back into the computer lab, where she explained the training they offered. Three women, including one old enough to be his mother, checked Jake out while Sandy showed him around. Sandy bit back a laugh when Jake caught the cougar at it and flushed. By the time she concluded the tour, Sandy hoped she had softened Jake's opposition. "What do you think?" she asked.

He took his time responding. "This is obviously a well-run program. Out of curiosity, why would one of your clients choose to come here and not a technical college?"

She grinned. "We do all of this for free."

"How do you fund it?"

"That's the director's job. Roberta has great connections. We receive significant corporate funding, and she can write a grant application like nobody's business. In fact, we received a huge federal grant to fund the new annex, but the clock is ticking. That's why we're hoping to resolve this zoning dispute quickly." She swept her arm across the room again. "Even political conservatives can get behind the ideology here."

He smiled, acknowledging her hint.

"My turn for a question," she said. "Last week, coming down here was out of the question. What changed your mind?"

"You," he said. "I honestly assumed this place was run by either liberal feminists or neo-hippies who value social justice above the rights of individuals. You're neither, and I thought maybe I better come see if I was wrong about anything else."

"You have a problem with do-gooders?" she asked.

"Only if they're funneling criminals into my client's neighborhood." He held up his hand to stop her protest. "I know that's not what you're doing."

She calmed down. "I hope you can tell we view ourselves as apolitical. Most of our funding comes from the private sector, and in exchange, they get first pick of our graduates."

"It's a smart approach. It's good that you believe in what you're doing."

His tone bugged her. She'd uprooted her whole life and moved across the country to be part of a cause she cared about, and he said it like he was congratulating her for working hard to sell Girl Scout cookies.

She clamped down on her temper. "Based on what you saw today, what concerns do you think your clients will still have?"

"River Oaks has worked hard to emerge from urban blight. They're attempting to attract new business and a slice of the capital's tourism traffic. They want to make sure new establishments entering the community are committed to the same goals. They would base any objections on disharmony with those goals." His tone was noncommittal.

"You didn't answer the question."

"It's the only answer I'm prepared to give."

Her eyelid twitched. "I'm sorry to have wasted your time."

"It wasn't a waste of time coming down here. At all."

It sounded like another line, a subtle bit of flirtation. Too bad. She wanted to rip into him, but she remembered the role she had adopted.

"It was nice to see you. I better get back to work," she said, knowing she sounded subdued. Maybe if he cared, it would have a positive effect on his report to his clients. "I'll see you Sunday."

"I'll be back in Boston," he replied. "I don't think I'll see you again until the next zoning meeting."

"Fine," she said, her voice polite. "I'll see you in two weeks."

"This is business, Sandy. It's just business."

She stared him full in the face. "Maybe to you, Jake. But for me, this is about changing lives, not increasing the property value for your comfortably middle-class clients."

"Can we agree to disagree?" he asked, smiling.

"Nope. Sorry. We're just going to disagree, and I'm not going to stop trying to change your mind."

"I look forward to it. Good-bye until round two," he said with another smile and slipped out before she could think of a retort.

Chapter 7

LARRY GLARED AT HER WHEN she walked through the door.

"Nice to see you too." She glared back, and Larry slunk off toward the kitchen to pout over her empty bowl. It pleased Sandy to have bested the cat for once.

She dragged herself into her bedroom, tripped over a pile of clean but rumpled towels, and managed to dig a pair of yoga pants out of her bottom drawer. She grabbed her "Go, Banana Slugs" T-shirt from another pile and headed for her living room and a yoga DVD.

Her cell phone rang during her cobra stretch. Deciding it was safe to answer since it wasn't "Crazy Train," she was surprised to hear Jake's voice on the other end.

"Hi. I couldn't get a flight out until morning," he said. "Want to grab some dinner?"

She wasn't in the mood for more of him, but maybe she could still salvage something from his tour that morning. She rallied her flirting skills. "Is this a dinner between colleagues, old friends, or two people who dig each other?"

"Which answer is going to get me dinner with you?"

"The truth," she said.

"The truth is I want to see you, and I'll use any excuse. I'm going with dinner between old friends because I bet you can't say no to that."

"Check you out," she said. "You're not just a pretty face. Pick me up in half an hour?"

"See you then."

When he knocked on her door exactly thirty minutes later, she was ready to go in a pair of jeans and a purple sweater. His black pullover and worn jeans fit him well. She itched to find out if his sweater was as soft as it looked. She clenched her fists in case they tried to sneak a feel.

"Where to?" he asked.

"I'm a vegetarian." She detected the tiniest of quivers around his eyes. "Did you just refrain from an eye roll?"

"Yes. I'd like credit for that. It was a major effort."

She had to laugh. That often happened with him. As annoyed as she was over his inability to see her vision for the annex, he somehow found a way to slip past her guard. She found annoyance infinitely more comfortable. She would keep up the flirting because she still wanted to teach him a lesson, but she would do it from a safe emotional distance. It helped that he was bound to do something to irritate her again sooner or later.

"I know a good deli that should work for both of us," she said.

"A deli, as in real meat and not spongy tofu?" he asked.

She sniffed, and he laughed and led her to his car, a sedan with a license plate frame from a rental company. She wondered what he normally drove and if it was fueled by sulfur and brimstone. Cracks about her diet choices offered a great reminder that he was still El Diablo, no matter how deliciously soft his sweater looked.

She had picked the deli because it stayed busy; she had no interest in a cozy, quiet dinner with Jake. She ordered a veggie sub, and he picked the owner's special, a huge sandwich piled with several kinds of Italian cold cuts. When she didn't say anything about his order, he looked surprised.

"Aren't you going to lecture me about eating meat?" he asked.

She shrugged. "Why would I do that?"

"I thought you were going to try to convert me."

"Tofu is a very personal choice," she said as she led the way to a small corner table that a middle-aged couple had just vacated.

"Most vegetarians I know are pretty militant about their antimeat stance."

"I'm more of a live-and-let-live kind of girl."

"I might believe that if you weren't trying to wear me down over the River Oaks thing," he said, but he smiled to show it was an observation, not a criticism.

"Maybe some things are too important to let go," she said.

"Definitely."

She knew by the glint in his eye that he was referring to her, and she was about to change the subject when her phone went off. "Sorry," she said and sent it to voice mail.

"Wow," he said. "Who earned 'Crazy Train'?"

"My mother."

He raised an eyebrow. She raised one back.

He changed the subject. "It's nice to take a break. I've been working like a dog."

"Your firm is pretty demanding?"

"I kind of choose to work that hard. I get caught up in my cases and forget to come up for air."

She couldn't help herself. She laughed.

"Are you laughing at me?" he asked, looking slightly offended.

She shook her head. "I'm laughing because so many people in my life are super committed to their work, like my best friend. And suddenly me, with this job. Or they're way into their lifestyles, like my mom. She's very into the New Age spiritualism and earth awareness and all that. I seem to attract intense people."

"Your mom isn't LDS?"

She shook her head. "No, I'm a convert. I joined the Church when I was sixteen."

"What did your mom think about you converting?"

She stared at him, amused.

"What?"

"I came out with you because I'm hungry. Swapping life stories sounds a little date-ish."

"I'm not trying to find out your life story, I promise. I was raised in the Church, so the conversion thing fascinates me. I like hearing people's stories, that's all."

"Me too." Sandy nodded at the counter boy who dropped off their orders. She snagged a bell pepper to crunch on then made a decision. "All right. My mother was really encouraging at first. She was all about me finding my own path. But she's decided over the years that Christianity is evil, and she's convinced that if she can connect me to the right guru or shaman or whatever that I'll find my *true* path." Magdalena's ringtone sounded again, and Sandy hit ignore once more. "Sorry," she said. "She can be kind of persistent about getting in touch with me."

"She sounds colorful," he said.

"That would be a good way to put it."

"What about your dad?"

She shrugged. "My parents split up when I was four. I don't remember him much."

"You haven't seen him since then?"

"No. Magdalena kept us on the move a lot when I was a kid. The checks always rolled in from him. After a few years, she started on a string of marriages, and then one day, I was old enough to be bitter that he never wanted visitation, and I haven't looked back."

Jake stared. "A *string* of marriages?"

She nodded. "Five, including my dad."

He let that process for a minute. "Would you ever want to see your dad?"

"This is life-story territory," she said. "Want to talk about the weather?"

He smiled to acknowledge her boundary enforcement. "Sore spot?"

"Why would it be? Their dysfunction had nothing to do with me."

He said nothing but looked doubtful. Before she could address it, her mother called again.

"Maybe it's important," he said.

"I've already talked to her four times today. This will be round five of an argument about why I'm not going on her next New Age retreat with her."

"I don't mind. I can eat my sandwich and not feel guilty about it."

"You shouldn't feel guilty about it, anyway. I'm not the PETA poster girl."

The phone stopped. She grabbed it to turn it off when "Crazy Train" blared again.

"Seriously, it's fine. Take it."

"You sure?" When he nodded, she answered. "Hello, Magdalena."

"Sweetie, where are you? Why haven't you picked up your calls?" Her mother sounded frantic. Nothing new there.

"I'm having dinner with a friend."

Her mother didn't take the hint. "Darling, the *worst* thing has happened! I just got back from a spirit walk and my stomach chakra is blocked."

"Does it hurt?" Sandy asked.

"Only metaphysically. But I need to have it balanced at that retreat this weekend."

"What a surprise," Sandy muttered.

"You stop that. These negative vibes won't help. Now I *need* to go on that retreat. Normally the top expert on this kind of thing would be in an ashram in India, but—"

"Let me guess," Sandy interrupted. "This one time only, he'll be at the retreat."

"Yes!" her mother said, ignoring Sandy's tone. "You'll love him, and—"

"And I'm not coming," Sandy said to preempt her mother's inevitable emotional blackmail. "I have to work."

"But this is a once-in-a-lifetime opportunity!"

"Then you should take it. Without me."

"Is it so wrong for me to want to share this experience with you?"

Sandy couldn't resist an eye roll. Jake's forehead furrowed. She shook her head and addressed her mother again. "That's the fourth once-in-a-lifetime opportunity you've told me about this year. I'm sorry you don't want to go by yourself, but you know I'm not into that stuff. I'm sure you'll make a friend if you go."

"Yes, but your chakras are awful," Magdalena said. "It's because you're so uptight."

Sandy gritted her teeth and took a deep breath, trying to ignore the criticism. "I appreciate you thinking of me, but I have to work."

"You work too much."

"I don't have a divorce settlement to live off of."

At that, Jake's eyes widened in surprise, which nicely punctuated her mother's wounded intake of breath. "You're not being very nice."

"And you're not listening, Magdalena. I'm not going to go to one of your guru sessions, and I don't know of any more ways to say that politely." She tried to keep her tone even and not let her irritation show, but seriously, she was soooo tired of having the same argument.

"I need to go lie down and calm my chi," her mother said, and Sandy imagined her fanning herself dramatically.

"You do that. Have some green tea or whatever it is you're using this month." She knew she didn't sound particularly gracious, but she was about a dozen phone calls past caring.

She stabbed the off button until the phone went dark and then smiled an apology at Jake. "Sorry. Conversations with her can wear me out at the end of a long day."

"No problem," he said. "You should eat. You'll feel better."

She smiled her thanks, and they ate in companionable silence. After a few minutes, he cleared his throat. "Can I ask why you call her Magdalena?"

She took another bite and considered whether she wanted to answer. She swallowed and shrugged. "She was on some kind of anti-authority trip after she and my dad divorced, and she believed that children should be encouraged to call their parents by their proper names to foster a sense of equality. I think that's what it was, anyway. She wanted to change back to 'Mom' when I was twelve, but by then, I was paying her back for my name."

He cocked his head at her. "I did sort of wonder how a redhead came to be called Sandy."

She rolled her eyes. Might as well get his punch lines out of the way now. "Magdalena named me Sand Dollar after some folktale she'd heard."

He struggled to smother a grin.

"Go ahead and laugh," she said. "It's funny. But that's also why I legally changed it when I was twenty."

"What was the folktale?" he asked.

"Something about how the five white marks on the sand dollar would release doves if they broke open. Then the doves supposedly spread peace and love throughout the land or something like that." She could sense that he was holding something back. "What?"

He hesitated. "You weren't exactly spreading peace on the phone just now."

"That's none of your business."

He leaned forward with the look of someone trying to puzzle something out. "I'm not judging. I just can't get you to add up. I'm trying to figure out what the problem is."

"*The problem*?" she enunciated carefully. "The *problem* is that you are stressing me out so much this week that I can't relax. That's a *big* problem." It was the end of a long workday, she hadn't finished her yoga workout, her mother had worn her down, and now Jake was criticizing her tone of voice. How much was a girl expected to take?

"I'm sorry I'm stressing you out," he said, "but I'm not going to apologize for doing my job."

She didn't bother to clarify that the stress he was causing went way beyond work. She glared and then dropped her head to her hand and rubbed her temples. "I'm sorry," she said. "It really is the extra stress."

"Believe me, I'm not doing it on purpose."

"I know. But episodes like this are exactly why hanging out outside of work is a bad idea. Maybe I'd better call it a night."

"I don't think this is that big of a deal," he contradicted her. "But sure, I'll take you home. I have an early start tomorrow, and I should probably get going anyway."

She mustered a tired smile and followed him to his car, unsure why she suddenly felt the need to kick its tires. It was a quiet ride back to her house. When he eased the car into the driveway, she stopped him from pulling his keys out of the ignition with a light touch on his arm.

"I'm not going to make you get out of the car," she said. "I can walk myself in."

He pretended to check over both shoulders and then faced her in consternation. "What if someone sees me breaking man code? Let me see you to your door. That way I can beat up any imaginary lurkers in the bushes. I promise to shove you inside and run away so you don't have to think of awkward reasons why you can't invite me in."

She smiled and nodded, realizing she owed him some graciousness after her earlier outburst. "How am I supposed to resist an offer like that?"

He was as good as his word, walking her to the top of her landing and standing with his hands in his pockets, a slight smile on his face while she slipped inside after a small wave.

Once she heard his car pull away, she dug a coconut sorbet out of her stainless-steel freezer and collapsed onto the sofa. Larry prowled over and settled on the sofa's arm, her tail twitching as she regarded her mistress with her usual inscrutable expression. "That could have gone better," Sandy grumbled.

Larry's slit eyes left no doubt about who the cat felt was responsible.

"I need something to scrub Jake Manning from my brain," she mused aloud when her treat was nearly gone. "What do you think, Larry? Time for more LDS Lookup?"

Larry twitched her tail and leaped down from her perch to head for the kitchen.

"Nice to know I'm second place to kitty kibble." She stared at the ceiling for another half hour, too tired to do anything. Deciding she was being pathetic, she dragged her laptop off the coffee table and onto her lap.

Logging into LDS Lookup, she felt better seeing that she had a message already waiting for her. "Someone appreciates me!" she called to Larry; then she opened her inbox, and her complacency evaporated. She didn't recognize the screen name, but she knew the face in the thumbnail photo.

Jake Manning.

Chapter 8

Fantastic. It wasn't enough for him to haunt the halls at church and stalk her at work; it seemed he needed to infiltrate her social network too.

The message was short and to the point. "Sorry to bother you on Lookup," it read. "Your cell phone is still off, and I didn't think you'd love the idea of me showing up at your door again. Since every single person our age I know is on this site, I thought I'd give it a shot and search for you. If you happen to get this message before tomorrow morning, would you please call me? I promise to keep it short. And not date-ish."

Strange. She wrinkled her nose. And businesslike. A glance at the clock showed it wasn't quite nine yet. Did she feel like calling? Yeah. Besides, it couldn't hurt to sweeten her earlier vinegar with some honey. She dialed his number.

"Hi," he said, after three rings. His voice was deep and clear.

"It's Sandy. I got your message."

"I know you're already stressed, so I wanted to give you a heads-up."

Foreboding tickled her spine. "Go ahead."

"It was getting tense toward the end of dinner, so I didn't want to make it worse, but I also don't want you to walk in tomorrow morning and feel like you got ambushed."

"You're freaking me out. What's going on?"

There was a long pause on his end. Then he sighed. "I liked what I saw at New Horizons this morning. I like the philosophy you guys have of the hand-up versus the hand-out approach. It's a well-run program, and the center is impressive."

"But you won't tell River Oaks to drop their challenge?" she guessed.

"I can't. I don't think an expansion is the right fit for River Oaks."

"But why not?" she burst out. "That site gives women near the area a chance to leave their bad streets for a place where they can aspire to live. It's a great step toward putting their dreams in reach."

"Yes, that's the problem," he said. "The risk of women with a criminal past or, worse, with abusive husbands or boyfriends from their past who would track them down at the center, is too big a risk. I mean, you can't guarantee that we're not going to see some of the more dangerous people from their pasts popping up in River Oaks."

"It doesn't matter if we can or not," she bit out. "We don't have to. I'm sure there are some antidiscrimination statutes that would support our right to lease a space in River Oaks Landing."

"You're right," he said. "But those aren't the official grounds for our objection anymore."

"What on earth would any right-minded people have against a bunch of women trying to turn their lives around? It doesn't make any sense."

"The River Oaks group has valid concerns," he countered. "They've had a previous negative experience with community activists and aren't eager to repeat the experience."

She pulled the phone back for a minute to stare at it. She forgot what a pompous snot Jake could sound like. As much as she wasn't thrilled with the overlap between their work and personal lives, she was even less excited about his return to Uptight Jerk Attorney.

"Jake? Why are you being so . . ." She stopped, sure that calling him names wasn't going to get her anywhere. "Why are you being so distant?" she asked.

"It seems appropriate when discussing business. I'm trying to respect the boundary you set."

"That's why you contacted me on a dating website to ask me to call you?"

He heaved a sigh, but when he spoke again, he sounded more like a normal human being instead of a lawyer addressing the court. "I can't win with you. You tell me we shouldn't socialize because it's going to interfere with work. I treat you the same as I did last week before we met, and you complain that I'm being distant. No disrespect, Sandy, but you need to pick a lane."

"Me?" she nearly yelped. "*I* need to pick a lane? I'm not the one trying to flirt with you today and bury you legally tomorrow." Okay, maybe she was flirting. Um, and trying to bury him legally. But he'd started it.

"I'm not trying to bury you. It's an issue my clients have with your center."

"So what's this motion?"

"We want River Oaks Landing to be given historical preservation status."

Her jaw dropped. "It's a flipping strip mall."

"Yes, it is. But that's your heads-up. Maybe we can talk about something else now," he suggested.

"Like what? I haven't wrapped my head around this historical preservation thing."

"Like . . . we can talk about what happens after the zoning hearing in a few weeks."

She took a deep breath, finding it nearly impossible to switch gears. "After the hearing, I start working on opening the annex because the commission is going to rule in our favor."

He laughed. "I'm going to let that go but only because I wasn't talking about work."

She struggled to get into her flirty role. "Then what are we talking about?"

"I was thinking more in terms of getting to know you better," he said. "That's not a problem, is it?"

"That depends. Are you always this friendly with your opposition?"

"Of course not. They're usually middle-aged and paunchy."

She forced a laugh. "Give me a cheese pizza, and I can be paunchy too."

"I doubt it. You couldn't look paunchy if you tried."

"Couldn't I construe this as sexual harassment?" she joked.

"But you didn't." She could hear a grin in his voice. "That's the advantage of having a good personal relationship beyond the work thing, right?"

She sighed. "Kidding aside, I've never tried to mix work and dating before, and I'm pretty sure it's because I can't."

"So don't. We let the hearing play out and then we see what happens."

"Sounds like you have this all figured out."

"Nah. If I did, I'd know how to convince you to date me now, not later."

"Who said I'll date you later?" she demanded, beginning to enjoy the sparring. "Maybe I don't want to. I think I need more convincing."

"I'm going to let you figure it out alone. And you will, Sandy. You will."

He wrung another laugh out of her. *Dang it.* "My mother used to read these stupid Harlequin romances when I was a teenager. I would sneak them and read them when she was off waving incense and cleansing her aura somewhere. You sound exactly like the alpha males in those books."

"Is there anything wrong with that?"

"If you have to ask, then you don't get it. I'm all for being friendly, but alpha males are not my thing."

"I'm not trying to be cocky."

"But it's your default setting?"

He ignored that and continued. "I'm sorry I didn't handle The Factory right. I was a jerk. But I'm going to make up for it."

"I really think you need to let The Factory thing go. I did," she lied. "Anyway, I should go now. I need to pace myself for when your motion shows up in the morning. Should I expect you to detonate that bomb in person?"

"Sorry to disappoint you. I have client meetings all morning, and then I fly out."

"Back to Boston?"

"For a while. I'll be around all the time before you know it."

"Is that a threat . . . or a promise?"

When Jake hung up laughing, Sandy headed for her laptop again. She needed more distance from him.

Hello, LDS Lookup. This time she'd be browsing through the Jake-free section.

Chapter 9

JASMINE'S PUERTO RICAN TEMPER HIT the roof when Sandy told her about the newest nail in the River Oaks coffin the next morning.

"What! It's a strip mall. What kind of historical value could it possibly have?"

"I don't know, but I guess I better do some checking around. I can't tell you how glad I am that I get to Google strip malls instead of help people. Awesome."

Jasmine eyed her sympathetically. "I'm sorry you're stuck dealing with him. If it's any consolation, you're handling him better than I did."

"Oh, that's because I've only been dealing with him for about a week. I can tell this is going to end badly. He said something about the River Oaks people having a negative experience with a group like ours in the past. Do you know what he was talking about?"

"Wait, you were talking to him last night? On your own personal cell phone?" Jasmine asked. "Don't be fooled by the devil's handsome face. He's still the devil."

Sandy laughed. "Believe me, I'm not getting sucked in. He wanted to tell me that he'll be sending over a copy of their new filing this morning."

"How did he get your number?" Jasmine asked.

Sandy knew it wouldn't exactly sound right if she mentioned dating sites and e-mails, so she skirted the issue. "You were going to tell me about their issue with some other group?" she prompted.

Jasmine stared her down before answering. "CHEP—Communities Helping End Poverty."

Sandy winced. She remembered all too well the national headlines the organization had made when a major cable news network filmed CHEP staffers encouraging people posing as pimps and prostitutes to lie about their background and income so they could get housing.

"I didn't realize that was the same area," Sandy admitted.

"It was close enough. But that was almost five years ago," Jasmine said. "With our reputation, we didn't think anyone would still be hung up on that."

"Not to mention we deal with two completely different issues."

"Yeah, but we fall under the 'social justice' umbrella, and that doesn't sit well with a lot of folks."

"It bugs me so much that I can't get to these River Oaks people. If I could appeal to them directly, I think I could make them feel a lot better."

"Jake Manning will never let that happen," Jasmine said grimly. "They're paying him to keep us out, and he's not going to risk the billable hours he gets from dragging on the fight."

"I better tackle this historical landmark garbage. I have no idea how he thinks he's going to pull this off, but if he found some remote possibility to hang their chances on, then I can find it too. Can you handle Kayla today?"

The young mother was due shortly for her first skills training session. Their lab tech, Geneva, a graduate of the New Horizons program, would handle the hands-on instruction, but Sandy liked to start each client's first session by reviewing the center's expectations and helping the women set progress goals. Today, Jake's latest move demanded her attention instead.

"No problem. I like that girl," Jasmine said. "She's quiet, but she's got a backbone. She'll do well."

Sandy thanked her and Googled historical sites in the Capitol area. With a sigh, she resigned herself to several long hours at her desk and the charming prospect of leftover yogurt for lunch while she slaved over her keyboard.

Squaring her shoulders, she investigated the first link. Eating leftover yogurt would be worth it if it meant Jake would eat crow when she was through.

Very worth it.

* * *

Three hours later, she picked a piece of a sticky fruit roll-up off of her polished cotton skirt. Tyson, the toddler who had grabbed her for balance, smiled up at her with all four of his front teeth. "Bah!"

"Yes, bah," she said. Stupid fruit roll-up. She'd gotten the skirt back from the dry cleaners on Saturday, and now a grubby handprint smudged the perfectly starched hem. Fabulous. She sat in her desk chair and tried not to pout.

"Sorry about that." His frazzled mother, Shenae, shooed him away. "My daycare lady called because they had a chickenpox outbreak, and we all had to come get our kids so she could disinfect everything. I wouldn't have brung him otherwise." A resounding crash sounded, and Sandy glanced up to see that Tyson had toppled a large bin of Legos off of a shelf that should have been too high for him to reach. Delight wreathed his face.

Sandy sighed. "Shenae, I admire you for keeping your class commitments, but I'm going to give you a penalty-free retake of your session so you can spend some time with Tyson today. He's not going to let you get anything done. Just reschedule with Geneva before you go."

Looking grateful, Shenae hurried to help Tyson clean up his debris field and then gathered him up along with his dirty coat, overstuffed diaper bag, and galoshes. "Sorry, ladies. I promise I'll be back tomorrow. He should be back in daycare by then." She hustled to the computer lab, and relative quiet crept in to replace the noise and chatter of her little boy. Sandy exhaled with relief.

"You don't like kids or something?" Jasmine asked.

"I like them," Sandy said. "I guess. I just forget how . . . *much* they can be." In truth, she had scant experience with kids. As an only child, she didn't have a ready supply of nieces and nephews. She'd never even experienced stepsiblings. Magdalena's modus operandi had been to marry much older men with deep pockets and no kids to disrupt her chi or her chakras or whatever it was children messed with.

"You're going to have some one day, and you'll feel differently," Jasmine said with a sage smile.

Sandy didn't say anything but wondered if that was true. Not even the kid part either but the marriage part. She wasn't against it by any means, but it was a totally foreign concept. She didn't remember much about her parents' marriage, and Magdalena's next four husbands had all occurred during a ten-year period starting when Sandy turned sixteen. After the first one, she hadn't even invested the energy in thinking of them as stepfathers since each marriage topped out at around two years.

She clicked back through her browser bookmarks to see what jumped out but found nothing promising. There were no battle sites or famous people's homes or anything else near River Oaks Landing that would qualify as historical.

Tired of looking, she closed the bookmarks and switched to a fresh project. Focusing on the annex, she reviewed the staffing levels and deadlines they would need to meet. This had been her strength in human resources at Macrosystems; she knew how to match the right person with the right job. She was poring over a schedule mock-up an hour later when Roberta came in.

"What are you working on?" she asked, peering over Sandy's shoulder.

Sandy smiled up at the older woman. "A staffing spreadsheet. I want to make sure we can hit our hiring targets for the annex."

"I'm all for initiative, but don't you have a zoning hearing to get through first?"

Sandy's lips thinned. "We'll get through it. Jake Manning is desperate now. Our client base is going to be too sympathetic for a liberal-leaning district council to ignore, and he's scrambling for a long shot. We're fine."

Roberta accepted this with a nod, and Sandy appreciated her boss's faith in her. She still felt so overwhelmed by the size of her learning curve that she had days she could only pray that Roberta's faith wasn't misplaced. "Roberta?"

Roberta's eyebrows drew together. "I've never heard anyone say my name so nervously. What's up?"

"Are you sure you don't want to handle the hearing yourself?"

"Of course I want to handle the hearing myself. And I would if I thought you couldn't handle it. But you can. And you'll have to. You know that."

Sandy did know that. The night of the zoning hearing conflicted with a state dinner at the White House, which Roberta had been invited to attend as the guest of an undersecretary in the Labor Department. It's not the kind of thing Roberta could send polite regrets for.

"I know," Sandy said, forcing a confident smile.

"*I* know. I know you'll be great. You want to tell me differently?"

"No. I've got this," Sandy said. "You don't have to worry about this. Sorry I made you doubt me."

"I didn't, I don't, and you shouldn't. Now, there's still a lot of time between the zoning hearing and opening our doors to new clients. You don't think it's too early to start on staffing it?" Roberta asked.

"I won't be doing much hiring until a couple of months before we're ready to go, but I need to look for quality candidates now. I have to know what kind of spots I need to fill. Ergo, my spreadsheet, the HR girl's best friend."

Roberta smiled. "You're more than an HR girl now, Sandy. Remember that. When Jasmine heads up to the Harlem office, the brunt of day-to-day management shifts to you as the sole deputy director."

"Someone has to answer the phone while you're shaking people's pockets loose," she joked. Her boss looked startled and then laughed.

"I guess that's the gist of it," she said. "As a matter of fact, I need to go finish up another grant now."

Sandy pointed at Roberta's door. "I'm not trying to tell you how to do your job, but seriously, go! Get us money."

Roberta laughed again and walked away, but not without a last prediction before disappearing into her office. "Jake Manning might be in trouble."

"Believe it!" Sandy called as the door shut behind her.

Turning back to her work, she got so caught up again that she didn't even notice her cell phone ringing until Jasmine, exasperated, begged her to pick it up.

Shannon's voice chirped through the phone.

"Hi, Sandy. I hope I'm not bugging you."

"It's fine," she reassured her downstairs neighbor.

"I know you get home late sometimes if you have Pilates or whatever—"

Yoga, Sandy silently corrected her.

"—but our home teachers wanted to drop by tonight. When will you be here?"

"Probably after six," she said, resigning herself to a date with her DVDs instead of the yoga studio. She wasn't a big fan of home teaching, but she'd learned early that much like flies, home teachers came back even if you swatted at them, so it was best to let them in and be done with it.

"Cool. See you downstairs," Shannon said.

They hung up, and Sandy had barely refocused on her staffing puzzle when "Crazy Train" sounded from the depths of her handbag. She pulled it out with a sigh. "Hello, Magdalena."

"Darling, I saw a vision!"

Sandy scowled. Her mother's visions were sporadic but inconvenient. A disconcerting number of them "foretold" what Sandy should or would be doing, whether those plans fit her life or not.

"Your last vision for me was that I should adopt a chinchilla," she said. "I have to say the cat's working out fine." She wondered if her mother could tell she was lying about the cat.

"Oh, Sand Dollar, this is serious. We're talking about auras now."

"Oh, then *very* serious," she said.

She sensed Jasmine craning over for a better eavesdropping position. Sandy glared. Jasmine grinned.

"I was meditating with a new mantra Guru Lalan taught me when I suddenly saw a whole scene unfold in my mind's eye," Magdalena said. "You were wandering through a dark forest and wearing a shimmery dress—"

"That's a perfume commercial."

"Sand Dollar! You were trying to get away from something, a dark presence. It got closer, and your aura dimmed until it was almost out. When I emerged from my trance, I knew immediately what I had seen."

Sandy sighed. "What, Magdalena?"

"It had a distinctly human feel. Except kind of devilish."

Sandy almost laughed at how apropos the imagery of a devil chasing her was. "I thought you didn't believe in the concept of devils and angels. Did you change your mind? That's awfully Christian of you."

"I don't mean one of those little red devils. I meant more of a blighted presence, something drawing away your light."

It would do no good to try to convince Magdalena that there was nothing to her "vision," so she simply said, "I'll keep an eye out."

"Better make it your inner eye," her mother warned her dramatically. "It sees all."

"Okay. I'll, um, wake it up or something?"

"You can!" Magdalena cried. "Start with some ginger tea infused with turmeric and then—"

"Wait!" Sandy said, quick to cut off a stream of diet and meditation advice. "I'll Google it, but I have to go now. My home teachers are coming over, and I need to leave work on time."

"What do they teach you?"

"They give us a spiritual message and check to see if we need anything."

"That sounds nice," her mother conceded. "Are they good girls?"

Sandy corrected her. "Home teachers are male."

She could practically feel her mother tense. "That's patriarchal. Why do the men have to do the teaching? Do the women get to go teach them?"

"Mm, interesting point. How many of your gurus and swamis are women?"

"But I'm not part of an organized religion," Magdalena argued. "I listen to all different kinds of teachers."

"How many of them have women leaders in their organizations?"

"Some do! Not yours though. It's all men, all the time. It's not healthy or progressive."

Sandy decided to break it down for her mother another time. "Regardless of your opinion, I still have a train to catch. I need to wrap up here."

"Fine, but beware, darling. Something is trying to dim your aura."

"Thanks for worrying," Sandy said. "I'll let you know if I need tea recommendations or something."

After they hung up, she turned to find Jasmine leaning all the way over her desk, looking expectant.

"What was that about?" she asked.

Sandy shook her head. "Trust me, you don't want to wade into that much crazy. I'm leaving right at five tonight. Do you need anything from me before I start packing up?"

"No, but you owe me some entertainment tomorrow. I want to hear all about the teachers coming over. Are they hot?"

Sandy shrugged. "I don't even know who it is. My roommate set it up. But we have a lot of hot guys at church, so the odds are good."

"Just as long as the goods aren't odd."

Sandy laughed. "Do you really have to go back to New York?" she asked. "Can't you stay here and crack jokes?"

"Sorry. It's too hard to get a good cannoli around here."

"You're not Italian."

"You're not Jewish, but you eat bagels."

"Fine. Move to New York."

"Fine. I will."

Sandy straightened the debris on her desk with a smile. Slinging her purse over her shoulder, she waved good-bye to the rest of the office and headed home for an exciting evening of home teaching. She really hoped the guys were cute.

* * *

"Cute. Real cute."

"What?"

Sandy eyed Jake, who was lounging on the girls' sofa when she came downstairs for the six o'clock appointment. He had his scriptures by his side, which led her to believe that due to some kind of cosmic joke, Jake was her home teacher.

"What are you doing here?" she asked. "Shouldn't you be in Boston somewhere, plotting against me?"

"I had to stay for a few more days," he said. "When Ty called me, I had no reason not to come."

He meant Ty Fenton, the elders quorum president who assigned the home teachers, but she didn't believe for a minute this assignment was a coincidence. It was kind of low to use a church calling to get to her.

She said nothing else and settled into a beanbag on the floor then studied her nails. A beat of silence passed while the other four girls in the room groped for something to say. Cami, who had no stomach for tension, attempted to break the ice.

"So, Jake. Where's your companion?" she asked.

"He should be here any minute."

"What's his name?" Shannon chimed in.

"Lee," he said. "I didn't get a last name."

Four heads whipped around to stare at Sandy, who resisted a groan. Of course it was Lee. The cosmic joke continued.

"Is there a problem?" Jake asked.

"Nope." Sandy didn't elaborate, and the other girls took their cues from her and kept quiet. A knock announced Lee, and Brooke leapt out of her armchair to answer it, most likely because her mischievous streak found the situation hilarious.

Lee followed her back into the living room, a smile on his face. Sandy shot a quick look at Jake, who had clearly recognized him as the guy she'd been speaking to on the porch Sunday. He rose to shake Lee's hand and make room for him on the sofa, but Sandy intervened.

"Hi, Lee," she said, smiling. "Come sit here." She patted the beanbag next to her, shifting to allow him some room. She snuck another quick glance at Jake to see if she had made her point. Instead of seeing disgruntlement, she caught the tail end of a knowing smile.

"Thanks for letting us come over tonight," Jake said, addressing the whole group. "Sorry this is a little thrown together. I got the assignment from Ty this afternoon."

"No problem," Shannon said, her smile cheerful.

"Yeah, don't worry if you don't have a lesson," Brooke said, sounding hopeful. "You can just read us a scripture or something."

"Oh, but I do have one," Jake countered, causing her face to fall. "I'm trying to rack up points for my promotion to elders quorum president."

That startled a laugh out of Sandy, who turned it into a cough. She saw his half smile flash, but he said nothing and leafed to the scripture he wanted. "This month the message is about charity," he began.

That was rich coming from a guy who was trying to block a really great charity from operating because of his clients' financial interests.

She listened to the short scripture he read and the familiar answers the other girls gave about how charity meant the pure love of Christ. She couldn't figure out how Jake sat there with his "message" of kindness and kept a straight face. She took a conspicuous glance down at her watch, an unsubtle hint that Jake should hurry up. The only pressing thing on her evening schedule was some yoga and a big salad, but that wasn't any of his business. Maybe he would think she had something exciting lined up for later.

Lee took the hint and suggested that it was time for them to go. With a nod and a couple of social niceties, she excused herself while Cami babbled about treats in the kitchen. Sandy had nearly made it to the base of the stairs when Jake caught her.

"What did I do wrong today?" he asked.

"Do you ever go away?" she snapped.

"Do you ever say anything nice?"

"All the time. To people who don't make me spend hours researching lame historical claims instead of doing more productive stuff." She placed her foot on the bottom stair.

"I didn't make you do anything."

"You might as well have." She almost felt bad, knowing her crankiness was coming out of left field for him, but she seriously needed a break from him. If he wasn't in her house, then he was in her head. "Good night, Jake." She headed up the stairs but paused in front of her door, unable to resist. "No, make that bad night. I hope you lose the next eight hours to some totally useless activity. Then we'll be even."

She thought she heard him laugh as she shoved her door closed behind her.

Chapter 10

"THAT WAS THE LONGEST SUNDAY in the history of ever," Sandy complained when she finally dragged Shannon and Brooke out to Shannon's car. "I should have known to drive myself to church today."

"Um, hi? Grouchy Pants? That's how long we always stay on Sunday," Brooke reminded her.

"What, a year? Because I think that's how long we were in the cultural hall picking at the Chips Ahoy."

"No, Brooke picked at the cookies, and you sulked. I visited."

"Visited?" Brooke echoed. "That's one way to say it. How many guys did you invite over for dinner, anyway?"

"I don't know. Four, maybe." Shannon said.

"Four!" Brooke yelped. "What are you going to do with four guys?"

"Relax," Shannon said. "It's not like I invited them over to make out. I invited them to *hang* out. Besides, that's still not enough for all of us in the house." She looked anxious. "Maybe I should have invited more."

"Not on my account, thanks," Sandy said. "I'm going into my she-cave for the night."

"Will Larry let you do that?" Brooke teased.

"Ha, ha. I'm being serious though. I need to decompress." After another rough week at work, she needed a night to be antisocial and possibly an hour of that to complain to Jessie.

"It's safe to come down," Shannon said. "Jake won't be there, I promise."

Sandy shrugged. "Like I care either way."

Her companions exchanged knowing glances, the animosity between Sandy and Jake earlier in the week already duly noted and analyzed.

"What?" she demanded.

"You don't feel any sparks flying when you guys are in a room?" Brooke asked.

"No, I don't. Not unless you mean the kind from two swords fighting and sparks fly off and then the good guy kills the bad guy. Because maybe there are those kinds of sparks."

Brooke leaned from the backseat to tap Sandy's shoulder. "That kind can still start a fire if you're not careful," she said.

"I'm not going to get into a whole bunch of weak fire-and-sparks analogies just so I can give you guys more reasons to tease me."

"Don't stop now," Shannon said. "It's fun!"

"I'm going up to my apartment, and I will chuck a shoe at any head that pokes through my door. You'd better warn your guests," Sandy said.

"She has a lot of shoes," Brooke said. "It could be a good show."

"I'm ignoring you until we get home," Sandy said. "Then I'm going to ignore you some more." She turned to smile at Brooke to show she was teasing. She liked all of the downstairs girls, but Cami, Leah, and Shannon were so young and, in Shannon's case, so relentlessly happy that Sandy didn't always relate to them. Brooke was almost her own age and pretty settled in her career. Sandy liked her. She was the only one who was comfortable enough to give Sandy a hard time. It made her miss Jessie.

When Shannon dropped her off at her outside entrance, she hurried up the stairs to find her phone. She seriously needed to unwind with a long conversation about why men were so lame. She kicked off her teal crocodile heels and loosened the tie of her cream wrap dress. Ah, better. In fact, her first order of business before calling Jessie would be to climb out of the Spanx that made the cream wrap dress possible.

She slipped into faded leggings and a T-shirt then curled into the sofa and dialed Jessie.

"Should I get the boring wedding stuff out of the way so we can gossip about your life?" Jessie answered in lieu of hello.

"Yes."

Jessie rattled off some details about the flowers in her bouquet and a menu addition that her normally mild-mannered father was insisting on. "In conclusion, Dad doesn't understand that fried catfish doesn't fit the Mediterranean theme we're going for. The fun never stops around here. What's new with you? And by new, I mean, tell me about the boys."

Sandy laughed. "There are lots of them here. I haven't exactly figured out the right ones to date yet, but I'll get there."

"Let's see . . . you've been out there, what, two months now?"

"Just about."

"And I've heard about dates with five different guys. Yeah, you're definitely behind the curve," she teased.

"It's practically a drought."

This time Jessie laughed. "I thought you were going to slow down on the dating thing for a while."

"I did in Seattle when I ran out of options. But out here, there are so many LDS guys and so much social stuff going on that I don't know how to fit it all in."

"It's a hard life you live," Jessie said.

"Hey, it's not all fun and guys. This story has some villains too."

"Ah, is this where I get my El Diablo update?"

Sandy made a rumbling noise. "I really, really don't like him."

"Oooh, sounds good. Do tell."

"I don't know why, but I swear he's going out of his way to make my life miserable right now. I can't turn around to sneeze without finding him standing right there."

"Sneeze on him, then. He'll go away."

"Gross."

"All right. Work less hours. Then you'll see him less."

"It's not only work stuff. I spent a couple of hours with him on Monday morning because he wanted to look at the center and get a feel for what we do—"

"Yeah, right, that's what he was checking out."

"*Anyway*," Sandy said, ignoring her friend's jibe, "then he shows up at the house Tuesday night because get this—he's my home teacher."

Jessie giggled.

"And if that weren't bad enough, his companion is Lee."

"Lee? Why do I know that name?"

"He's one of my LDS Lookup experiments. We've hung out a few times."

"How'd that go?"

"Not as well as it should have. Tons of potential but the chemistry is wrong."

"So, opposite of Jake, where there's no potential but the chemistry is excellent."

"Remember my plan?" Sandy asked. "It's pretend chemistry."

"How does the saying go?" Jessie mused. "Looks like, smells like, quacks like, is?"

"I didn't call you to be psychoanalyzed," Sandy said. "I called you so I could complain about my love life and get some sympathy."

"You're averaging a date a week. How does that deserve sympathy?"

"Oh, you know . . . I was hoping for super-hot guys with large bank accounts and flashy cars. I keep getting pretty-good-looking guys with Sizzler budgets and moderate tastes in vehicles."

Jessie laughed out loud. "The day a bank account trumps personality for you is the day you have officially turned into your mother."

"Shhhhh!" Sandy hissed. "You'll summon her if you mention her aloud."

"You're a saint, you know. I have no idea how you put up with her." Jessie had been subjected to a few visits from Magdalena when they were roommates and knew well her more colorful idiosyncrasies.

"This is why we're friends," Sandy said. "You appreciate my amazing patience. Anyway, I'm serious about my love life being lame. I've gone out on five dates, yeah. But they've gone nowhere. With nonmember guys, there was always the whole difference in standards. With the LDS guys, it's about not fitting into their mold of what a good Mormon girl should be. I don't think I can win."

"If I know you, this is a temporary funk, and you're not going to try to win on any of those terms. You'll set your own. You're Sandy 'Man-Eater' Burke. It's what you do. These guys don't stand a chance."

Sandy was quiet for a minute. "Why do I feel like I should stick my hand out and shout 'Go team!'?"

Jessie giggled. "That was cheesy. I'm an accountant, not a motivational speaker. You and Ben are the only people on the planet who find me as funny as I do. When you find someone who thinks you're as funny as you do, then that's who you marry."

"That's what I'm supposed to be looking for?" Sandy asked. "I thought I was supposed to be looking for a good guy, worthy priesthood holder, a paragon of virtue—or failing that, someone with a pulse and a job that pays his bills."

"Nah. It has to be someone you can laugh with. Has anyone made you laugh on these dates?"

Not on purpose, Sandy thought. Except Jake. And it wasn't a date.

"Or what about someone who laughs at your jokes? Have you found someone who does more than the courtesy chuckle?"

Jake, Sandy silently admitted again. "Not really," she hedged.

"Hold out for that."

"So, basically the bar's now set at laughing. That's what I should be looking for in Mr. Right?"

"Yeah. And until you find it, line yourself up a bunch of good-looking Mr. Right Nows and entertain yourself."

"I always do," Sandy said, but she acknowledged to herself that it was getting old again. "Maybe I should give that Lee guy another shot."

"Only one person you've mentioned has made even a blip on your radar."

She could hear a clear challenge in Jessie's voice. "Jake Manning?" Sandy snorted. "Forget it. I'm toying with him, not dating him."

"Yet," Jessie said. "But you will if you're smart."

"No way," Sandy said. "Every time he starts to seem pretty cool, he reminds me of what a jerk he is, and I remember that flirting in this case is a battle tactic."

"Fine," Jessie said. "But he got to you a year ago more than any guy I've ever heard about, and he did it in one night. It's even worse now, and when I say worse, I mean that's a really good thing."

"I love you, roomie, but you're making about as much sense as Magdalena."

"That hurts," Jessie said, not sounding hurt at all. "I'm going to hang up and go find Ben to comfort me."

"Great. I'm going to go drown myself in veggie soup and see if I can get my cat to talk to me."

"Maybe you should have her pick your next LDS Lookup victim. It could be a good sign if she takes to someone."

"Larry is an equal-opportunity misanthrope. She hates everyone."

"Why did you get her?"

"Because Magdalena said not to," Sandy admitted.

Jessie laughed, and they hung up, Sandy dropping her head back against the sofa to stare at the slightly cracked ceiling. She inhaled the sweet scent of the pomegranate candle burning on her wrought-iron end table. Maybe she could divine some sort of message in the spidery pattern above her. A moment passed before she realized how very Magdalena-esque that was, and she sat up to open her laptop. LDS Lookup had to be a better route to true love than hidden messages in her ceiling plaster.

Larry wandered over as soon as she opened the computer and sat watching from a haughty distance. Sandy typed in a search for guys in the DC metropolitan area again, set it to look for twenty-six- to thirty-two-year-olds, and excluded any profiles without a picture. Call her shallow, but she wasn't going out with anyone sight unseen.

When the results pulled up, they automatically sorted, starting with the newest faces in the area. Immediately, Jake's picture caught her eye.

Obviously, he'd edited his profile information to reflect Virginia as his place of residence instead of Boston. Larry took a sudden light leap down to Sandy's lap and stared at the screen. Then she darted her head forward and tapped Jake's photo with her nose before leaping down to the ground and wandering off toward Sandy's bedroom.

Sandy stared after the retreating cat and then at the slight smudge her nose had left on Jake's picture. "Unbelievable," she muttered. "Now I have proof that my cat hates me." She snapped the laptop closed and headed for the kitchen. "Veggie soup it is, then. At least I know it'll be 100 percent Jake Manning free."

Chapter 11

A PERSISTENT TAPPING NOISE INTRUDED on Sandy's nap. After attempting to muffle the sound with a throw pillow over her ear, she woke enough to realize someone was knocking at her door. She pulled herself upright, reluctant to leave the sofa. She glanced at the darkened window; there had still been some light out when she'd lain down with her half-finished copy of *Reading Lolita in Tehran*.

The knock sounded again, followed by a dull roar from downstairs. They must be playing a game down there. She pushed herself up with some effort and stumbled to answer it. Wishing she had brought a shoe to chuck like she had threatened to do, she yanked the door open midknock.

"Stop," she said.

"You have a sock in your hair," Jake said.

Her hand flew up to pluck at a brown woolen sock caught in one of her curls. She stared at it and then accusingly at Jake.

"I didn't put it there," he said drily.

"I'm sure if I think about it long enough, I'll figure out how it's your fault."

He smiled. "Can I come in?"

She glanced down at her worn pants and wrinkled long sleeved T-shirt, the gray cotton pilled and balling after multiple washings. Deciding it didn't matter what she looked like, she shrugged and stepped aside. "What are you doing here?"

"Doing here in Arlington or doing here at your house?"

She shrugged. "Both or either."

She walked to the sofa, not bothering to check whether he followed, and picked her way around a couple of Larry's discarded cat toys, her yoga mat, and a copy of *Marie Claire* magazine. When she turned to sit, she found Jake right behind her. She waved toward the opposite end of the short couch and curled up in her corner.

"I'm still in Arlington because my clients needed me, and I'm at your house because . . ."

She glanced up from the lint ball she was worrying and waited for him to finish his sentence.

"Because I wanted to be."

She plucked the offending ball from her shirt and flicked it to the carpet. "Why?"

He leaned back and smiled, as if amused that she asked. "I like your roommates."

"Neighbors," she corrected. "Sort of."

"I like your neighbors," he amended. "Sort of. They're sweet, and sometimes they make me laugh. But I sat down there for twenty minutes thinking that the whole evening would probably seem funnier to me if you were there too. Since you weren't, I came up here."

"I guess answering the door with a sock in my hair is a pretty good trick," she muttered.

"That *was* funny," he said. "But I figured I'd be in for some entertainment even if you opened the door dressed to kill." He thought for a minute. "Well, maybe dressed to kill someone besides me. I've been the target of your death-ray stare way too often lately."

"I do not have a death-ray stare," she said, glaring.

"And there it is."

She jumped up and crossed to the vintage mirror that hung over the small table in her tiny entryway. Her reflection showed that she did look pretty, um, formidable. The dark mascara smudges under her eyes right above the sleep creases in her left cheek from the couch didn't help either. She stifled the urge to shriek. Instead, she turned. "Would you excuse me? I need to powder my nose."

Jake smothered another smile and nodded. "Sure. Do you mind if I browse your bookshelves while you do that?"

"Fine," she said with a wave over her shoulder. "I'll be back in a minute."

The minute she clicked her bedroom door behind her, she flew into action, snatching up a pair of dark-wash jeans from the floor and a fitted red V-neck tee from the top of a bin in her closet. In the bathroom, she swiped a damp towel over the mascara smudges and whipped her wild hair into a subdued low ponytail. After a lightning-fast tooth brushing, she padded back out to the living room in her stockinged feet, proud that she had made herself presentable in four minutes flat, even if doing so proved that she did care what Jake thought. Well, it was only natural. She couldn't beguile him looking like a deranged yeti with a sock fetish.

He was standing near her bookshelf glancing over the titles. Nearly half of them were self-help New Age guru nonsense her mother sent her regularly. Sandy kept them on the shelf so she wouldn't forget to dig them out when her mother came to visit a few times a year. The remaining books were her true favorites, classics and modern classics in literature and fiction.

He fingered the spine of a book titled *Healing Your Inner Child through Crystals* then ran his finger across a dozen more similar titles. "Are these any good?"

"No idea," she said. "I use them for leveling out crooked tables or stack a few to make a stool when I can't reach a high shelf." No need to admit that she had read a couple of them that made a surprising amount of sense.

He laughed. "I knew you weren't the New Age type even before I overheard your conversation with your mom the other night."

"What gave me away?"

"You don't smell like patchouli."

She laughed. Her mom often trailed a wake of the cloying incense behind her. "What type do I seem like?"

Jake tilted his head and watched her. "I'm not sure you are a type. That's probably why I can't stay away." He sat on the sofa next to her. It was a small couch, chosen to fit her small space, and she could feel the warmth radiating from him.

"Oh, I forgot. You're the alpha male, and I'm the challenge," she said, her tone amused.

"That makes me sound pretty calculating, like I prowled up here to play some kind of game." He shook his head. "That's not what I'm doing."

"Hm. Then maybe you're trying to soften me up so I won't go after you at the zoning meeting next week."

"No offense, but I'm not that worried about it."

"You're that confident?"

"I'm confident I don't want to talk about work right now. I think we were analyzing you."

"Go on, then. I like it when it's all about me."

"Maybe," he said. "I don't think it bothers you to be the center of attention. But I also don't think the limelight matters to you one way or the other."

His perceptiveness surprised her. "Lucky guess," she said.

Jake waved his hand to encompass her apartment. "This is a perfect example of what I mean when I say you're hard to categorize." He pointed at an impressionist painting of a California poppy hanging on the wall above them. "I would have bet that I'd have found some crazy avant-garde sculptures and chrome and glass furniture. Not flowers on the wall."

"You said you expected me to be a hippie at first."

"I did. Then I thought you were on a career path toward corporate America via the obligatory stop at an NPO. I figured you for power suits and modern art. Turns out, you're neither."

"I own power suits. And an incense burner. Maybe I'm a hippie playing dress up."

He shook his head again. "I don't think you're playing at anything. Whatever you are, it's real."

Unease licked at her. She was playing a major game with him. Wasn't she? This was all about showing him that getting someone interested in you and then dropping them was bogus. She would play until they worked out an agreement for the annex, and then she would let the other shoe drop. It was his fault if he wasn't smart enough to be more guarded. Right?

She pushed the doubt down and cleared her throat. "My turn. You're on my couch. I get to play amateur shrink."

"Is that what we're doing? I thought I was just getting to know you." He relaxed into his corner, and his knee bumped hers as he shifted.

"Quiet," she said, suppressing the tiny tremor his touch threatened to send down her spine. She studied him like he had studied her, taking note of his entire look. "I'm at a disadvantage here since I don't get to snoop through your house."

"Give it your best shot."

She considered him for a minute. "Regulation corporate haircut, but no product in it. Button-down shirt, but the top is undone and the sleeves are rolled up. I'd have to ask you to get up to figure out what brand of jeans you're wearing, but I'll spare you the ogling. Half boots, toe neither too square nor too pointy." She sat back and pretended to think.

"What's the verdict?"

"This is a much better look for you than your suits."

"Not to sound like a jerk," he said, "but I have a couple of prime Hugo Bosses. How are those not a better look?"

"You don't sound like a jerk. A different, less kind word comes to mind," she said.

"Sorry," he grinned. "But I can't believe I spent all that money on those stupid suits when I should have been showing up to court in my jeans. Why didn't I know this sooner?"

"You should have asked a girl. We know everything."

He smiled, and then it slipped, and he pointed at her yoga mat rolled up and propped against her TV. "That's a shame, you know."

"My yoga mat?"

He sounded mournful. "It's in the perfect spot for an X-box. How can you live without the latest version of *Madden?*"

"I don't know." She sighed. "I wonder how you can live without weekly manicures and pedicures. It's amazing that men and women have anything to say to each other."

"You're right. There's too much talking." He bridged the small space between them and paused a whisper away from her, his dark eyes trained intently on her mouth.

She moved it with every intention of saying something like "Go away," but no words came out. Amusement caused his ridiculously sexy half smile to appear in the split second before he closed the gap and kissed her. Feeling like Larry when the passing headlights of cars sometimes mesmerized the cat through the window, the only clear thought swimming through her mind was, *Mmmmm.*

When she felt Jake's smile broaden against her lips, she realized she'd said it out loud, and the flush of anger that had budded in her cheeks blossomed into scarlet embarrassment. She couldn't even form a coherent objection. The heady pressure of his lips on hers again disrupted every synapse in her brain except for the ones that buzzed with that same lovely "Mmmmm" that had already slipped out of her once. She quit thinking.

Moments or minutes or maybe even a lifetime later, Jake broke off the kiss and sat back. What was that look on his face? Once she had accidentally knocked Larry on the head with her bedroom door, and Jake now wore the same expression her befuddled cat had worn.

Neither of them said anything. Uncomfortable with how fast her state of mind was unraveling, she pulled herself together. "That was a bad idea."

"No, it was a great idea, one of the best ideas I've had in a long time. If I were a smarter guy, I'd have done that a year ago at The Factory, and maybe things would be different now."

"We're too far apart for that to happen again," she insisted.

He glanced down at their knees, two inches from touching over the center cushion.

"I meant a metaphorical distance, and you know it," she said. "You don't get me. At all. You don't get what I do, and you have to get that to understand who I am."

He sat back, letting some of the supercharged ions between them dissipate. "I didn't come up here to do that."

She pushed herself up from the sofa. "I stayed up here tonight because I wanted some peace and quiet. Let me walk you out."

"Are we going to talk about what just happened?"

"No."

He followed her to the door. "I didn't mean to upset you."

"You didn't." She kept her voice calm. "It was a great kiss, but it was still a bad idea."

His half smile appeared. "I don't see it that way."

Steeling herself against the wistfulness in his tone, she leaned past him and opened the door. "Have a fun rest of your night." She winced as a loud cheer swelled from downstairs.

His half smile grew to a full grin. "Staying up here isn't going to buy you the peace and quiet you want." Another loud cheer confirmed his point. "I hate leaving like this, feeling like things are off between us. Let me make it right."

She rested her head against the doorframe, curious in spite of herself. "How? Are you going to beat everyone up until they agree to keep the noise down?"

"I was thinking more like whisking you away to somewhere quieter, somewhere I can sit and listen to you explain more about why you're so invested in your annex."

She studied him, the pull of the kiss they had shared eroding her good sense. She ought to stick to her guns and send him away, but another raucous yell floated up the stairs and sealed the deal.

"Jake," she murmured, leaning closer. "Are you using my love of the annex to lure me out of my house?"

"Yes."

"You play dirty."

His lips nearly touched hers again as he answered, "No. I play to win."

They stood frozen that way until she slowly drew back. She couldn't resist the challenge. "I could use some fresh air. I'll meet you on the porch in a second."

He headed for the stairs, and she shut the door behind him, wondering if her own game was working against her, but she didn't care. Sitting upstairs, trying to ignore the noise from below while picking the lint from her V-neck tee, somehow didn't sound nearly as appealing as matching wits with Jake again. And that's all she would match with him. There would be no more lip action.

She headed for her bathroom to touch up some more. A few minutes later, she was ready, subtly glossed and mascaraed, defining her best features with a light hand. She slipped on a pair of ballet flats and fired up her willpower, determined not to let Jake past her guard again. He might think he'd talked her into spending more time with him, but she knew the truth. She'd bought herself more time to plead the New Horizons case. She wasn't going to let his smooth talk—or his smooth lips—distract her anymore. No way.

Chapter 12

"Where are we going?" Sandy asked as they headed off the porch.

Jake shrugged. "We'll know when we get there."

"What's that?" She pointed at the paper bag he carried by the handles.

"You'll see."

They had reached the corner of her tree-lined street and its parallel rows of quaint houses, but instead of turning or crossing the intersection, Jake set the bag down and crossed his arms over his chest.

She leaned sideways for a peek inside the bag. He pushed it behind him with his foot and pinned her with a stare.

"What?" she asked.

"Ground rules, that's what," he said. "I'm trying to perform an act of service, so you need to humble yourself enough to be my charity case."

"I'm the most humble person you'll ever meet." That made him laugh. Man, she liked that sound.

"Then let's see how you do with my ground rules for this service project. First, no stressing for the next hour. No picking fights, no arguing, no jumping to conclusions."

"Are these rules for you too?" When he nodded, she lifted a skeptical eyebrow. "So you're not going to argue or jump to conclusions either?"

"I'm going to be so open-minded my brains might fall out."

"Really?" she drawled, moving closer and resting a hand on his folded arms. "Even if I talk about the annex all night and how awesome it is and why you should quit fighting it?"

He grinned. "If that's what it takes to keep you with me, then yes, I'll listen to you."

"That's big of you."

He didn't answer for a minute, his eyes fixed on her hand where it touched his. When he glanced up, his gaze made her feel . . . shivery. It was kind of delicious. Annoyed, she took a step back and then wished she hadn't when a smile flickered across his lips.

She cleared her throat. "We were talking about rules?"

"Yeah. Rules, like being open-minded. And no name calling or making fun of my job."

"I don't make fun of your job."

"Uh-huh. And if I had a dollar for every time you made a crack, I'd never have to bill any hours again."

Okay. She'd possibly made a few snide remarks. "Fine. But that's a one-night-only deal. Are there any more shady clauses and fine print in this verbal contract of yours?"

"Sandy," he asked, his voice silky. "Was that a crack about my job?"

"It was my last one."

"I haven't laid out all the terms of this contract. Any violation of the terms will result in drastic consequences."

"Like what?"

"Like if I hear any more job insults, I'll have to take extraordinary measures to silence you. With my mouth. On yours."

She coughed and took a step back. "Lawyers are great. We need more of them. Especially here in DC. Can't get enough of them."

"I thought so," he said. "Now can we get on with our evening? You're not a super-cooperative charity case." He reached over and snagged her elbow then slid his hand down her arm and closed his fingers around hers loosely enough that she could easily pull away. She didn't know what to think about that. She was way more comfortable kissing someone than holding his hand. But this felt . . . like she could handle it. Maybe.

"It's dark," he said, interpreting her hesitation. "Call it my protective Boy Scout instincts. I'm trying to make sure my charity case doesn't walk into traffic or fall into a ditch. You don't want me to slack in my duties, do you?"

One street light was out, the one they were passing beneath. The rest of them shone steadily as far down the road as she could see. But she didn't pull away. "Okay. In the name of charity, I'll hold your hand."

That made him laugh, and warmth spread through her chest, easing the frustration that had been lodged there for days. She considered their joined hands as they walked in easy silence. Only the occasional crackle of the paper bag he carried broke the quiet. It was too early in the spring for the low hum of insects or birdcalls. It was just . . . still.

How had she been irritated to see him one moment and kissed him the next and now walked down the street with her hand in his? It was strange alchemy, but it felt right, and she had enough of her mother's impulsiveness to go with it. She held her peace for several minutes until they reached a park.

"I didn't even know this was here," she said. "That's sad since it's only a couple of blocks from my house."

He led her to a picnic table and set the mystery bag on top. "You haven't been in DC that long. You've got plenty of time to explore."

"You've been here a fraction of the time I have, and you knew it was here."

"This isn't my first time in DC."

"You lived here before?" She hadn't considered that. She figured him for some kind of Boston blueblood or something.

He nodded. "I did some of my schooling here."

That was a vague statement, considering the twenty million colleges in the surrounding area. "Which school?" she asked. He'd already told her a great deal by not serving the information up right away, the way most people did around here. It meant he hadn't attended one of the top-tier schools. It didn't matter to her, but she found it interesting that he wanted to downplay it.

He didn't answer right away, instead digging some foil-wrapped food out of the bag and laying out paper towels and forks she recognized from the downstairs kitchen. She'd almost forgotten her question by the time he answered. "Georgetown Law."

Whoa. Not just top tier but very top of the tier. "Did you like it there?" she asked.

"Law school wasn't the most fun, but I had a good program, so it was at least worthwhile."

She nodded, but by now, the foils were peeled back to reveal their treasures. She zeroed in on the smuggled brownie and considered how much effort it had taken to get her jeans buttoned. Better to err on the side of one brownie. Or two. She darted her fingers past him and pinched a bit of the nearest square. Definitely the Ghirardelli mix . . . mmmmmm.

Jake picked up the piece she had snitched from and extended it toward her. "You can have the whole thing, you know."

"Believe me, I will. I'm savoring it, that's all."

He put the piece back in the foil. "It's there when you want it." He sat on the table instead of the bench and patted the spot next to him. And, not coincidentally, next to the brownies.

She was nobody's fool. She sat and pinched another piece.

"I think that's a girl thing," he observed.

"What is?"

"Eating dessert piece by piece. My sister told me once that it's because when you break off the pieces that way, it shakes a few calories loose before you can eat them."

"That's totally true," Sandy said. "I read an article about it once in my fitness magazine."

He laughed and leaned back, bracing himself with his hands on the table behind him. "Thanks for coming with me tonight."

She nodded, too busy with more brownie to answer out loud.

"Why did you?" he asked.

She paused in her chewing and then continued slowly, giving herself time to consider the answer. Why had she said yes to him? When the brownie was as chewed as it could possibly be, she swallowed and gave him a response that surprised her. "Because I wanted to."

He smiled slightly.

"That's funny?"

"Yes, but not ha ha funny. I was thinking about how much this feels like the first night I met you a year ago."

"How do you figure?"

He reached out to brush a crumb from the corner of her mouth. She flushed, hoping she didn't have chocolate gobs stuck in her teeth too.

"The vibe," he said. "The me-and-you vibe. Sitting with you right now feels like it did that night."

"How's that?" she asked, knowing that throwing out the question was inviting him even closer. She forgot about the brownies.

"I find myself in this space with you that feels different from anything going on around us. It doesn't matter if it's a noisy club or here in this park. I can't figure it out," he admitted.

Sandy could. The crazy electricity that snapped between them was a clue, sure. But for her, as much as she loathed that he represented River Oaks, she felt a pull for him at a deeper level too. Realness radiated from him, and it was obnoxiously hard to resist. *He* was hard to resist. A low thrum of awareness and tension pulsed between them.

"Do you know what I mean?" he asked, interrupting the unsettling drift of her thoughts. She hesitated and, not wanting to lie, offered a noncommittal shrug.

"It's just me, then, I guess." He smiled and didn't look bothered at all.

She changed the subject. "Weren't we going to talk about the annex? I can do it without stressing."

He smiled. "Confession time. I kind of hope you do stress out so I can enforce the penalty."

She blushed again. Man, she hated that. This was supposed to be *her* game. Besides, she had left those bright blushes behind in her childhood, learning to hide behind flippant comebacks or a facade of indifference against the embarrassment Magdalena routinely caused her. Jake kept sneaking past that defense. She was grateful that the dim park lighting hid her traitorous cheeks.

He bumped his shoulder against hers. "I promise to listen. Go ahead and lay it on me. What else do I need to know about the annex?"

Sandy searched his face, trying to decide if he was humoring her or if he was genuinely interested. Either way, this was the opportunity her flirting was supposed to have won her. She took it. "You saw what we do at the main center. The annex will be like that but on a smaller scale. If you surround these women with a solid middle-class environment, they begin to think about how doable it is for them to have the same kind of life. The philosophy is that if we help women in poor communities, their success can transform their neighborhoods into desirable places to live, but they have to see what's possible. It's a model we've followed with some success in other cities. DC is prime for something like this."

"How long does it take before these changes get any traction?"

"It's not overnight," Sandy admitted. "It takes a while for us to find the right candidates for job retraining, and then it takes time for them to complete the courses and begin earning the kind of income that can make a difference for their family. It can be up to three years before we begin to see a measurable difference in the community."

His brow furrowed, and she hurried to point out the positive. "The thing is, the communities *do* change, and the better news is that the change for these women begins almost immediately."

"Why is New Horizons so set on River Oaks? Did you look at other neighborhoods?"

"Of course we did," she said. "Most of that scouting happened before I started with the center, but my understanding is that this lease is our only viable option because of the cost and the proximity to Anacostia."

She let him think about it for a minute. She needed him to understand this work she had chosen for herself and to understand why they needed their River Oaks lease. It went past needing to win him over and into something deeper, something she didn't understand but could feel.

"We're going to lose our grant if we can't open the center on time." She took a deep breath. "So . . . how does that affect the advice you're going to give the River Oaks group?" A bubble of hope rose in her chest.

His long pause burst it. "I want to be careful here," he finally said. "And I want to be honest. I have to balance the obligation I have to my clients and what I believe to be right for them against my promise not to stress you out."

She tried for a joke. "All you have to do is tell me that you see it my way and that you'll call off the dogs. Anything besides that and I may smother my sorrows in more brownies."

He handed her another brownie. "I can't say what you want to hear."

"But why not?" she demanded in frustration. "If you understand what the annex is designed to do and why that location is so perfect, why can't you tell your clients to calm down?"

"There's more in play than you realize, Sandy. I can't openly discuss it without specific permission from my client, and that's where this gets tricky. All I can say is that I respect the River Oaks people. They're humble, they've worked hard to get what they have, and they're feeling threatened. Because of their bad experience with CHEP, most of them worry about a repeat where a do-gooding group comes in and funnels in pimps and prostitutes in the name of the Fair Housing Act and social justice. The River Oaks group deserves to have someone protect their quality of life too."

She gripped the table edge and willed her temper to settle. "You still have no idea what I do."

After a few moments, he spoke so low that she unconsciously leaned closer to catch it. "Yes, I do. I asked, and I listened to your answers, while you've never asked me to explain anything, only to defend myself like I'm automatically in the wrong. But you can't predict the future. You don't know that some of your clients' pasts won't come back to haunt them."

"I've got statistics from a dozen cities that say I can."

"That's the thing about statistics. It only takes something going wrong once to change things from a statistic to a tragedy."

That stung, and she didn't answer.

A long silence stretched between them, far less comfortable than the one that had enveloped them on their walk from the house. Her disappointment annoyed her. She knew her secret hope that Jake would have a major epiphany after seeing the women in the center and hearing Patrice's story was a pipe dream.

A laugh from Jake startled her. "We keep going in circles."

"It explains the dizziness."

"Shoot. I was hoping that was my nearness."

She laughed at his hangdog expression. His chiseled face wasn't built for such a dopey look. She regretted that the easiness between them had evaporated and that it was her fault. She wouldn't make any progress if she pushed the issue now, and honestly, she didn't want to. She offered him a slow, mysterious smile, determined to restore some lightness to the evening. "If it makes you feel better, being near you does cause me some serious issues."

He leaned closer and cocked his head, morphing in an instant from goofy to sexy. "Like what," he drawled.

She closed the gap between them until a mere breath separated them. "I have to tell the truth," she whispered. "Being this close to you is hard. I feel this overwhelming urge to . . ."

"What?" he whispered back.

"Kick you."

There was a moment of silence, and then he burst out laughing again. When he pulled himself together, he gave her hair a playful tug. "Leave it to me to find the perfect woman and have her hate me."

She froze for a minute. His perfect woman? He was teasing again. If she didn't believe that, she might not get her breath back. "Gosh, Jake," she said with an exaggerated bat of her lashes, "it's true I'm amazing, but perfect might be overstating the case."

"Not for me," he said, still grinning. He leaned back again and studied her. "I saw it a year ago in Seattle. I see it now. I just have to figure out how to make you see it."

She felt that weird tug that the moths flying into the light over the picnic table must have been feeling all night. "I can't be with someone who doesn't understand what I'm all about, Jake. If you got what I was telling you, you'd be on the phone first thing tomorrow with your clients telling them that their zoning objection isn't necessary."

He shook his head. "Understanding why this is important to you isn't the same as agreeing with you. I can respect your passion for what you're doing and still think there's a better way to make it happen."

Her answering shrug said more than words could have how much she disagreed with that assessment.

"I let you get away in Seattle, Sandy. I was an idiot because I was freaked out that in a few hours flat I was ready to fall for someone who wasn't Mormon and lived across the country. But it's so obvious to me that our paths crossing wasn't a coincidence then any more than it is now. I learn from my mistakes."

The intensity in his voice called forth that old Sandy, the one from a year ago that lived life more carpe diem style. She reached up and returned the kiss he'd given her earlier, shutting down thought, freeing herself from all defenses for the quickest of minutes, pouring her confusion and longing into that connection before pulling away.

He looked stunned.

"I learn from my mistakes too," she said quietly. "I should have kissed you that night. Now that's fixed. I know everything I need to know. Maybe you being here isn't a coincidence, but this is a temporary intersection. Our paths aren't parallel, Jake. We're each going to do what we have to do, and that takes us in totally different directions again."

He looked like he wanted to argue, but she shook her head to forestall him.

"You didn't make a mistake in Seattle. I wasn't ready for you then." She got up and gathered the containers, determined to pack them and leave. "I'm pretty sure I'm not ready for you now." If there was anything she'd learned from watching her mother's parade of divorces, it was that when two people were so different, sometimes the only thing that made sense was to walk away. She was done with her game.

Jake would figure out soon enough that the smart move was just to let her go.

Chapter 13

Jasmine rolled in a few minutes late to work the next morning, her eyes wide with anticipation.

"No," Sandy said.

"No, what?"

"No, I don't have a good story."

Jasmine eyed her, speculation glinting behind her contacts. "Look me in the eye when you say that."

Sandy stood instead. "I'm going to get yogurt."

"Ah-hah," her workmate crowed. "What was it? Super-hot church boys or what?"

"El Diablo."

Jasmine gasped. "No! Again?"

"Yep. I need to find a spray repellent that works on him."

"Girl, it's going to take more than some kind of spray to keep him away from you."

It appeased Sandy to find someone who wasn't eager to serve Jake up to her on a silver platter, unlike Jessie, who was convinced there was some unresolved romantic business between them. Sandy had pretty much resolved *that* issue permanently last night.

"He won't be coming round," she said aloud.

Jasmine brightened. "Is he dropping the lawsuit?"

"No, unfortunately."

"You didn't rattle his cage, did you? The last thing we need is for him to come after us even harder."

"No, I didn't do anything like that." But she felt guilty saying so because she wasn't sure that she hadn't provoked Jake.

"Then what happened? What do you mean he's not coming around again?"

"I meant he won't be coming around me."

"Sand Dollar."

Sandy shot her a dirty look. "Only my mother calls me that."

"Sand Dollar," Jasmine continued, unperturbed, "are you telling me that Jake Manning really did try to come after you somewhere besides in a legal brief?"

"Whatever inappropriate joke you're about to make, don't," Sandy cautioned. "And he didn't come after me." Then deciding that was awfully close to a bare-faced lie, she amended it. "Or he did, but I made the lines clear. He won't cross them again."

"Unless you stock up on pepper spray, how can you be sure?" Jasmine asked.

"Because I kicked him in the pride, and he's nothing without it. I'm safe, and the center is safe. Our involvement starts and ends in the city council chambers now."

Jasmine let it drop. It didn't come up again until late morning when Sandy discovered that she had underestimated Jake's stubbornness.

The morning played out normally. Sandy dove into her futile search for River Oaks Landing's "history," and after two more frustrating hours, she pushed away from her desk and headed back toward the computer lab. "I'm going to check on Kayla. I'll be back."

She made her way to Geneva's desk and winked before snitching a piece of milk chocolate from her top drawer. The tech smiled and waved her on. Sandy nibbled at it while she watched over Kayla's shoulder as the young woman clicked through a series of tasks.

"How's it going?" she asked when Kayla reached a stopping point.

Kayla smiled, but her shoulders slumped. "It's okay. They say the brain is a sponge, but mine seems to wring out the last thing I learned before it lets in anything new."

"I know a cure for that." Sandy darted over to grab another piece of chocolate from Geneva and brought it back to Kayla. "This improves memory function."

"Is that true?"

"No, but it'll make you feel better."

Sandy admired Kayla for sticking it out. The younger woman had opened up a little more each day she'd come to the center, and Sandy grew more impressed with her each time. Kayla's fierce determination stemmed from a desire to raise her daughter without any support from her parents, who had disowned her when Kayla refused to get an abortion. Heartbreak lurked in Kayla's eyes when she talked about it, but she used it to fuel her efforts at the center.

Sandy placed a hand over Kayla's and waited until she had her full attention. "You're amazing."

Kayla blinked and then nodded. "Keep telling me that."

"As often as I need to," Sandy promised. She patted her hand once more and headed back to her desk. When she emerged from the hallway, the sight of Jake Manning sitting in her desk chair caused the slightest hitch in her walk, but she willed her black stilettos to keep moving forward and thanked heaven she had wrangled the reams of paperwork that usually covered her desk into trays earlier in the day. When she neared him, he smiled and set down a framed picture of her with Jessie on Pismo Beach before he stood and leaned forward as if he intended to greet her with a kiss on the cheek.

So much for making herself clear the night before. She preempted him by sticking out her hand for a shake instead. He took it without comment, although he looked like he wanted to laugh at her formality. When she gestured for him to take the visitor chair, he rounded her desk with a grin and complied.

"What brings you here?" she asked, trying to sound warm but professional.

"I'm staying in town to finish prepping for the hearing. You available for lunch?"

Jasmine coughed conspicuously. Sandy ignored her.

"Thanks for the invitation, but I usually take a working lunch."

"Great. That's what I'm proposing."

"What would we work on?" Sandy said. "Are you going to spill all the details of your case to me?"

He smiled. "I have a couple of compromises from River Oaks. But I'm also hungry, so I thought I'd take a chance that you were too. Are you up for it?"

He had no idea how loaded that question was. She'd spent most of the morning wading through research, determined to compile more evidence supporting the annex. She had also spent way more time than she wanted to in fighting off unwanted flashes of memory, all of them replaying their kisses. Part of her felt drawn to the shiny newness he represented. It was the same part that had led her to buy a pair of yellow patent leather heels she didn't need a couple of weeks ago. *Not every impulse should be followed,* she reminded herself. So yes, part of her was very much "up for it." But that was the dumb part.

"I have so much work. Can you call me after lunch?" she asked.

His face grew serious. "This is only a little about the hearing, Sandy. I wanted to talk to you"—he dropped his voice with a sidelong glance toward Jasmine, who was leaning so far toward them it was a miracle she didn't fall—"about some other stuff."

She wouldn't put it past Jake to bring it up on the spot if she didn't get him out of there. She grabbed her trench coat off the back of her desk chair and shrugged into it. "Let's hear what the good folks at River Oaks have to offer. I'll be back in an hour," she said to Jasmine, who looked like she didn't believe it. Sandy slipped her purse over her shoulder and followed Jake out to the street.

"I thought we'd hit Mahi. Is seafood okay?" he asked, naming a popular steak and seafood restaurant a couple of blocks over.

"Sure." She turned and headed the right direction.

Easily pacing her, he broke the short silence with a compliment. "I like that color on you."

Since she wore black, white, and gray, she knew he meant her deep violet coat.

"Thanks," she said. She liked his suit, a subtle navy pinstripe over a pale blue shirt and a boldly patterned tie. There was something to be said for classics. Not that she was going to say it.

He engaged her in small talk for the next few minutes as they closed in on the restaurant. She forced herself to relax and keep up her end of the conversation. He was a trained litigator, skilled at reading people, she reminded herself. She didn't want him interpreting anything from her except what she chose to let him see, and that was a calm and *indifferent* lunch companion. One that wasn't suppressing a quiver the two times their hands accidentally brushed as they walked. She shoved hers into her coat pockets to keep them safe.

At the hostess desk inside the restaurant, Jake requested a table for two. The hostess looked doubtful, but Jake merely said, "I'm with Booker-Hughes."

She smiled and grabbed two leather-bound menus from her neat stack. "Of course. Something just opened up."

"Membership has its privileges," Sandy murmured and fought the urge to dance away from the hand he placed at the small of her back to guide her through the maze of linen-covered tables.

Once seated, she studied the dining room. They'd gone for boring elegance, full of crystal, framed oil paintings, and heavy drapes. "Nice place," she said truthfully, even if it wasn't to her taste.

He followed her glance. "It'll do."

That took her aback. "Do you need something fancier?"

He shook his head. "More dialed down."

"Where would you go if you had your choice?"

He shrugged. "I'm good with a sushi bar, to tell you the truth."

"Then let's go there next time."

He grinned. "Next time? Sure."

"Wait, I didn't mean next time like that."

"Is there another definition of next time that I don't know?"

"I meant it as a figure of speech."

He smiled at her and glanced down at his menu. When their server arrived, they each stuck with water and gave him their lunch orders.

"You mentioned compromises?" she prompted him.

He took a long draw from his water goblet and studied her. "I told you that's not the only reason I invited you to lunch."

"It's the reason I'm here," she replied, her tone even.

"We left on interesting terms yesterday," he said. "I thought we could talk about it."

"We did talk about it. I explained that we couldn't date, and you walked me home."

"I wasn't referring to that part of the night."

She watched him, careful to maintain a faint smile designed to keep him guessing. He didn't need to know how unsettled she still felt.

When she said nothing, he pressed the issue. "I was referring to the kissing. Are we going to talk about it?"

"We're going to talk about why it isn't going to happen again. It doesn't make sense," she said. "I think you know that."

"You're right," he conceded, surprising her. "It doesn't make sense that remembering that kiss interrupts my train of thought ten times a day, but it does. Is that only me?"

She heard a quiet challenge in his voice, but she avoided the question. "I'm sorry that's happening, but I meant that kissing in the first place didn't make any sense. That hasn't changed."

"It's supposed to make sense? I thought it's the kind of thing that happens when the right two people are sitting on a small sofa and one has a sock in her hair."

She smiled. "Maybe, if you were someone different. Someone who didn't stand for the opposite of everything that I do."

"Opposites attract."

"Opposites drive each other crazy because they swing between 'Hey, great kiss' and 'Hey, I hate that you're undermining the cause I believe in.'"

"So . . . you thought it was a great kiss, then?"

"Stop lawyering me," she said, fighting the flush threatening to stain her cheeks. "We're talking about why being opposites is not a good thing."

"We're only opposites on this zoning issue," he argued. "But you don't seem to think there's a chance to explore this . . . thing . . . between us once that's all done."

"Do you really think you could lose in the zoning hearing and it wouldn't affect your feelings for me? I wouldn't want to date you if you won the hearing."

"Why?"

She rolled her eyes. "Oh, I don't know. Because your win would ruin people's lives?"

"Have you considered that it could potentially ruin my clients' lives? They have legitimate concerns." He sounded frustrated.

"No, they don't," she said. "And I can't understand how you can represent them."

He stared down at the tablecloth, and she tried hard not to fidget. Maybe she sounded combative, but she had already crossed some invisible emotional line with him that made his failure to see her side feel personal. So much for keeping a professional distance.

"You think this is all about you being the good guy and me being the bad guy." He held up his hands when she opened her mouth to interrupt. "I understand why you feel so passionate about your work. I absolutely believe it's important. I think expanding your program makes perfect sense."

"Then why have a hearing?"

"There you go again," he said, frustrated. "I would love to explain to you just once, without being bulldozed, why River Oaks can't let this drop."

"Sorry," she said, surprised at his heat.

"These are good people who have a real fear of history repeating itself. The economy is in such bad shape right now that they're scared of anything driving their property values down any more. For a lot of them, their homes represent investments toward their kids' college educations or their own retirements. They've already seen some serious erosion in those investments, and they're holding on as tightly as they can to what's left."

For the first time, she caught a glimpse of Jake separate from his flirtatiousness or his smooth lawyer persona. It rattled her.

He sighed. "As much as I respect what New Horizons does, River Oaks isn't the right neighborhood for it."

Her stomach dropped. The discouraging realization that she wouldn't be able to argue him out of his position by sheer force of will sank in. She could fight ignorance, but someone who had all the facts and viewed them differently was a far tougher battle. She struggled to find the emotional distance he had erased over the last few days, circling the rim of her glass with the tip of her finger while she collected her thoughts.

He misinterpreted her silence. "Maybe lunch was a bad idea," he said. "I guess I was wrong about you. I thought I'd met a different person in Seattle last year. But you're not . . . you aren't her. I'm sorry. It's never been my deal to go where I'm not wanted and definitely where I'm not respected." He jammed his fingers through his hair, and it forced the neat strands up into disarray. It was the first time she had seen him less than calm, cool, and collected. She wanted to rush into the short silence and demand that he explain himself, to insist that she was the same girl from a year ago. But she didn't, because she wasn't.

She had grown into a better person, she hoped. Someone who would fight tooth and nail for the people life tried to pass by. In some ways, she was the same Sandy that had found an instant connection with a stranger in a bar last January. But in the really important ways, she wasn't. She kept silent.

"I should have listened to you before. I let my memories outweigh the here and now. I was way, way off. I'll e-mail you an outline of our proposed compromises. I think you'll find them reasonable." He stood and pulled his suit jacket on. "At a personal level, you don't have to worry. I'm done. I apologize for pushing this." He nodded at the waiter returning with their plates. "Don't feel like you need to rush. I'll tell the maitre d' to bill it to the firm. Enjoy anything else that looks good. I'll be in touch about negotiations."

He walked out, leaving her mouth half formed in a protest, but there was nothing to say. He'd finally done what she'd asked and left her alone. And she kind of hated the feeling.

Chapter 14

SANDY JUMPED AT THE SOUND of more pounding on her door Friday night. What was up with people this week? Brooke poked her head around. "I'm having a shoe crisis. Be my shoe fairy," she begged.

Sandy waved her in. "What's the problem?"

"What are you wearing to The Mansion tonight?" Brooke was referring to a house full of guys from the ward who regularly threw parties on the weekend. In a former life, it might have counted as a minimansion, but time and the regular rotation of guys who lived there made the title more ironic than anything.

"I haven't thought about it yet," Sandy answered.

"That's because you have the greatest wardrobe in the history of ever, and you don't have to stress about an outfit for three days beforehand. I've solved the outfit problem only to have shoe issues. Help me."

"Is that what you're wearing?" Sandy asked. "It's cute."

Brooke wore a pair of light gray corduroy pants with a pink blouse in a vintage floral print. The cropped maroon swing coat she layered over it added a funky feel. "It's what I'm wearing if I want to go barefoot. I love this jacket, but I never know what to wear with it. What goes with maroon? Black? Brown?"

Sandy laughed. "You do realize that shoes come in other colors, right? Hang on." She zipped back to her bedroom and dug through the jumbled pile of shoes in the corner, emerging with a burgundy pair. The three-inch stacked heels and leather appliqué flowers on the rounded toes complemented the vintage vibe of Brooke's outfit.

"Perfect!" Brooke snatched them out of Sandy's hands in delight. "Can I? Huh? Can I, can I, can I borrow them?"

"Yeah, but no puddle jumping. I got them on sale, but it was an Anthro sale."

"I swear I'll give you my firstborn if I mess these up in any way."

"Oh no. That's not nearly enough. If anything happens to those shoes, you're keeping Larry for a month."

"Wow, way to guarantee them coming back in perfect condition."

"I thought so," Sandy said, grinning. "When are you leaving?"

"The Mansion boys said eight o'clock, so I figure we'll leave closer to nine."

"I'll meet you down there."

Once Brooke left, Sandy returned to the closet to contemplate her own outfit for the evening. Digging out a favorite mohair sweater, she had to smile. Wearing the odd shade of mustard yellow was one of the perks of being a redhead. Very few people could get away with a color like that, but when she added a chunky necklace in bronze with amber beads and a pair of killer boots, well . . . she could. She ran down the stairs to meet the other girls and figure out carpooling. Twenty minutes later, all of her roommates squished into her sporty Mazda, and they jetted for The Mansion. The radio blared a Lady Gaga classic, and they sang themselves giddy, Sandy grinning as the tension from her week dissolved. Friday night, a bunch of single girls headed toward a house full of single guys? The game was afoot.

The revolving list of roommates at The Mansion ranged from six to eight, depending on who shared rooms and whether someone bunked on the couch. Even though they had a reputation as a party house, The Mansion boys were a good bunch of guys. Two went to law school at Georgetown, a couple of them worked in different government offices, one had an affiliation with the CIA that no one asked about, and the sixth one worked in sales at a major utility company. The weekdays stayed quiet as they all went about their schooling and business, but the weekends often saw the house bursting to accommodate the crowds of clean-cut young people who descended to party.

LDS partying was a whole different thing, one Sandy hadn't adjusted to yet. On the upside, the only "buzz" came from the hum of animated conversations and bursts of laughter, not the liquid courage of vodka.

The downside was the school snobs, the ones who found a way to drop in the name of their impressive university alma mater and tried ferreting out hers to determine whether she was one of "them." She used to answer honestly: she had a master's in public administration from Stanford, thanks to her emotionally delinquent but financially generous father. She soon tired of being judged by the value of her college degree and offered some vague answer about a state school she'd never finished instead. This always won her a plastic smile, which amused her. She'd considered claiming a junior college for the entertainment value.

She stopped at the living room threshold to get her bearings. She recognized many of the faces from the ward or other activities. Even a large LDS young adult scene like the one in DC was a pretty small pond when it came right down to it. Still, she glimpsed enough new faces to promise an interesting night. People often dropped in from Baltimore or even Boston and New York to socialize for the weekend. It was a bit like restocking the deli case, she thought idly as she watched a herd of girls converge on one new, very cute guy. Fresh meat, poor boy. Too bad he looked too young for her.

She wandered into the den, where several people watched a Wizards basketball game, and she paused, deciding where to go next. Should she brave the rickety deck out back, which was both chilly and possibly life threatening?

Shannon bounded up before she could decide. "Come with me," she ordered, tugging at Sandy's wrist.

The people huddled outside looked cold anyway, so Sandy followed without objection. They wound through the kitchen and into the converted garage now serving as the game room. Board games crammed one shelf, and several boxes of cards littered the top. A battered foosball table crouched in one corner, and beanbags squatted in homely but comfortable lumps all over the room. The real attraction, though, dominated an entertainment center on the main wall. A huge plasma TV occupied the place of honor, and multiple video-game systems with hopelessly tangled cords and controllers crowded every other surface of the shelving. What didn't fit spilled out onto the floor.

Sandy checked out the game screen and gave a succinct, "No."

"Yes!" Shannon said. "You have to."

"No, I don't."

"We're down one round, and you can catch us up."

Sandy eyed the screen once more. "You dragged me in here to play *Dance Battle*?"

"Yes. We're losing. You have to help us."

When Sandy shook her head again, Shannon's voice took on a wheedling tone.

"I'll clean Larry's litter box for a week if you do."

"Done," Sandy said and pulled off her boots.

"You just suckered me."

"You need to drive a harder bargain," Sandy teased. "Did you really think I could hold out against *Dance Battle* for long?"

"Dang. You're up. Go make litter box duty worth my time."

Sandy took her spot against a girl she didn't recognize. "I'm Sandy."

"Amelia," the girl replied with a nervous smile. "So you're pretty good at this game?"

"Yes," Sandy said without any false modesty. She'd discovered a latent talent for the complicated dance game by accident at her first Mansion party. Brooke had deemed her a borderline savant.

"I am too," Amelia said. "I guess? I mean, yes. I am."

"Let's go, then."

Amelia selected the song. Sandy stayed loose and kept her weight on the balls of her feet. The opening bars of a techno song played through, and then the steps flashed on the screen, indicating a split second before the next beat where their feet should hit. Confident, even with the quick tempo, Sandy focused on the music and the arrows telling her what to do, nailing each piece of the rhythm. A minute and a half later, she stepped off the mat and waited for her score to flash. Amelia had scored "Expert" but so had she, only Sandy had hit two more steps right.

Sandy flashed her a congratulatory smile. "You're really good," she said.

"Not good enough, I guess," Amelia said with a return smile. "Do you practice at home or something?"

"Nah," Shannon chimed in. "My other roommate thinks it's a *Rain Man* kind of thing. We're tied!" she called to both teams. She turned back to Sandy. "One more and we win. Can you do it again?"

Sandy grinned.

"All right! We're putting Sandy up again," she called to the other team. The other team conferred in murmurs for a minute, and then Amelia turned around. "I guess I'm up again too. Your turn to pick the song."

One of the guys who'd been dragged to the *Dance Battle* tournament by his girlfriend broke into the song debate. "You have to add something to this besides skill for the win," he said. "You need to keep it interesting. Like have a panel of impartial experts who judge on style and not just points."

Shannon eyed him. "Uh-huh. And where will we get this panel of esteemed experts?"

He smirked. "Give me five minutes. I'll be back with some judges."

She turned to the girls on deck. "You okay with that?"

Sandy and Amelia traded a look.

"Sure," Amelia answered for the both of them. "Anything to be interesting."

Sandy's lips twitched, and she let out her smile. "Funny."

"I'm not precious about my art."

Sandy offered her a high five.

The guy loped off in search of his panel, and the girls retired to beanbags to regroup. Shannon crouched down by Sandy. "I feel like I should bring you a towel and a spit bucket," she said. "You up for this?"

Sandy shrugged. "Why wouldn't I be? It's just a game."

"No, it isn't. Didn't you notice who's on the other team?"

Sandy glanced over again to scan the faces. "They're all from the ward, right?"

Shannon rolled her eyes. "Specifically, they're all from the Daisy House. They can't win."

Sandy laughed. "What's up with the rivalry?"

The younger girl narrowed her eyes. "Everyone who moves into our house inherits this rivalry. It will continue long after we move out. This is about bragging rights, Sandy. And I don't want to listen to them brag."

Sandy smothered another smile at Shannon's intensity and nodded instead. "Okay, then. For the glory of Somerset!" Their house was known simply by the name of the street it occupied.

Shannon's eyebrow quirked, and Sandy knew she was trying to decide if Sandy was taking this all seriously enough; then Shannon said, "Think about song selection. You need something you can really get into." She wandered off to the rest of the team and left Sandy to mull over her music choice.

She found the whole situation silly but enjoyed the challenge. If *Dance Battle* happened to be one of her talents, then she'd do her part and magnify it with—

"Booty shakes."

"Excuse me?" she said, glancing up at Brooke, who now stood over her.

"Booty shakes. That's how you're going to win. Channel Beyoncé." She dropped down beside her. "Heather's boyfriend is going to bring back a bunch of guys as the panel. If you want to win on style points, you're going to have to do some booty shaking."

"Uh, no."

"Then you'll lose, and Shannon will whine for the rest of the weekend."

"Don't care." Sandy shrugged. "I'm not going all Beyoncé. I'll think of something else."

"Okay." Her friend shrugged back. "But I just handed you the key to the imaginary trophy that no one except Shannon cares about."

"I'll remember that," Sandy said. "Grab the controller for me, would you?"

Brooke obliged, retrieving it for her and then drifting off again. Sandy scrolled through the song options, trying to figure out which one was her best bet when a selection caught her eye.

"Perfect." With no sign of their self-appointed judge recruiter, she put a sudden stroke of genius into action. Grabbing Brooke on the way out of the room, she didn't slow down or answer any of her neighbor's questions until they'd reached the bathroom door.

"What are we doing?" Brooke demanded.

"You ever play that dumb bridal shower game where you have to make a wedding dress out of toilet paper?"

"Yeah."

"Well, we're going to kick it up a notch, and I'm going to win."

Looking intrigued, Brooke followed her into the bathroom. Several minutes later, they re-entered the game room with two heaping armfuls of bath tissue. The Daisy House girls all stared, but no one asked what was going on.

Five guys squished in shoulder-to-shoulder on the lone sofa in the room, and Shannon raced up to Sandy. "The judges are here," she said, pointing to the packed couch. "Are you ready?"

"Ready," Sandy said.

"Do I even want to know why it looks like you mugged a mummy?" Shannon asked.

"You really don't."

Shannon shrugged and called to the Daisy House. "We're ready! Hey, judge, you want to lay out the criteria here?"

Heather's Boyfriend, who didn't have another name that Sandy had been able to catch, stood up. "We're adding another possible ten points to each score based on the value of the player's performance. A creative interpretation of the song could lead to a win even if the other person hits more beats. We're looking for originality here. Our scores will be displayed using a high-tech point-keeping system." One of the guys on the sofa waved a napkin and a ballpoint pen. "May the best house win."

Sandy waved to Brooke, who hurried over with her heaps of tissue. Within a minute, Sandy was dressed in a goth-style toilet paper wedding dress from midthigh all the way up to her tattered veil. Shannon handed her the controller, and Sandy pulled up the eighties menu to make her choice. When the title flashed, Amelia grinned.

"Very good," she said, and left it at that.

By now, the room had grown uncomfortably crowded due to word spreading about a *Dance Battle* death match. The growling notes of Billy Idol's classic "White Wedding" thumped from the speakers, and the girls went to work. The footwork was much easier than for Amelia's pick, which meant Sandy could easily hit the beat while mopping up the judges' votes. Amelia would have to perform if she wanted to compete, and Sandy knew from experience that out of fear of embarrassment, few people would go to the lengths she would. Being unburdened by little things like caring about her social standing left her free to rock her Billy Idol–loving heart out in a toilet paper dress.

She watched Amelia moving through the steps, nailing the footwork and throwing in self-conscious fist pumps for variety, and Sandy grinned. She'd figured out years before that not caring what other people thought always had the ironic effect of elevating their opinion of her anyway. Tearing into the last part of the song with relish, she shredded a few measures of serious air guitar, dramatically ripped her tissue couture into even more punk rock shreds, and finished with a fall to her knees and a classic death throe. The crowd went wild.

She straightened when Amelia walked over to offer a hand up. "We don't even need the judges on this one." The younger woman waved her hand to encompass the hooting onlookers, and Sandy took it all in with another grin—until her gaze fell on Jake. Who was laughing. She froze for a split second and then ignored him and calmly picked wisps of toilet paper from her hair while the judges conferred.

Another cheer went up when the screen score showed that Amelia had managed only a few more correct beats than she had. Everything would fall to the judges, and there was little doubt how that would turn out. Amelia's napkin score went up first, and she averaged a 6.0. Heather's Boyfriend shushed the crowd and instructed the judges to reveal their scores for Sandy. After another whispered conference, the guys on the sofa sat back and then simultaneously thrust their napkins aloft.

"Perfect ten!" Shannon shrieked as she swooped in for a celebratory hug. The rest of Sandy's neighbors danced around each other, slapping fives and bumping hips. The Daisy House girls exchanged glances of good-natured defeat. Amelia approached Sandy again with more toilet paper in her hand. She'd twisted some of Sandy's dress scraps into a tiara topped with a bedraggled tissue flower.

"You've earned it," she said, a mischievous glint in her eyes. She stood on tiptoe and rested it on Sandy's curls. "Just right." She moved out of the way to make room for well-wishers. Soon Sandy found herself engulfed in a cloud of "Awesome!" and "You rock!" It parted after a few minutes to admit Jake, who stood watching her with his irritating half smile.

"Who knew the difference was toilet paper," he said.

She plucked the tissue tiara from her head and shook it at him. "You should take this as a lesson, Jake. I'll do what it takes to win."

He nodded. "I see that."

He fell silent, and Sandy wondered what he wanted since he'd made it clear that socially, they were done.

"I didn't expect to see you here," she said to break the awkward pause.

"I didn't expect to see you either. The real you, anyway. This is who I remember from The Factory." The soft smile he wore unnerved her, and she struggled to find a buffer.

"I figured you'd be slaving over your speech for the zoning board or something."

"Don't need to. It's under control."

She smiled. "Glad you feel good about it."

He hesitated and then took a small step, his hand reaching toward her. "Sandy—"

An ecstatic Cami swooped in for a big hug. "Honey, you were amazing!" she said, her Georgia accent making the declaration sound even sweeter. "Come on in the kitchen. I have some victory snickerdoodles."

Ignoring Jake, Sandy grinned at her neighbor. "Do you carry baked goods around in your purse or something?"

Cami smiled. "My mama taught me never to show up at a party empty handed."

As Sandy turned to follow Cami out, Jake caught her elbow in a light grip. "We're not done here," he said softly.

"Aren't we?" She stepped away from him and went to join the rest of her housemates in their celebration.

She and Jake were back on her terms now.

Chapter 15

THE BEST THING ABOUT CHURCH starting after lunch was the chance to sleep in, so when "Crazy Train" blared early Sunday morning, it irritated Sandy more than usual. With a grunt, she groped through the pile of paper scraps and magazines hiding her nightstand to grab her cell phone. She tightened her grip on it, wishing for a split second that her fingers were wrapping around Magdalena's neck instead.

"Yes?" she grumbled.

"Good morning, Sand Dollar. I hope I didn't wake you."

"No, this is my wide-awake morning voice," she retorted, the frogginess in it underscoring her sarcasm.

"It's a beautiful day. You should probably thank me for waking you in time to enjoy it."

She cracked an eyelid open far enough to see weak and watery light coming through her window, definitely not a harbinger of a "beautiful" day. "I don't know what health spa you're calling me from, but I guarantee you it's not in the same weather pattern as my apartment."

"Oh," her mother said, sounding nonplussed for a moment. "I'm in Sedona, and it's gorgeous here. You should really—"

"I'm not going to visit, and I'm not awake enough to find a polite way to say that. Move on."

"I just thought—"

"Magdalena, is this why you called me first thing in the morning? Because if it isn't, could we get to the point?"

Her mother was quiet, and Sandy felt a twinge of guilt for her abruptness. Magdalena cleared her throat and complied. "Since you don't seem to want to come to me, I thought I'd come to you," she said brightly. Too brightly.

Lingering guilt and sleep deprivation overrode her survival instincts, and Sandy conceded ground she knew she would regret. "Sure. I'll check my schedule and see when it looks clear."

"Oh, don't worry about that," her mother trilled. *Trilled!* "You're too tied to that Blueberry of yours." *It's an iPhone,* Sandy corrected silently. "Anyway, I already got a ticket."

That jerked her awake. "When are you coming?"

"Tonight! Isn't it wonderful?" More trilling.

Sandy wasn't taking the bait. "Magdalena, this is the worst possible week. I have a huge hearing on Wednesday, and I have to focus on that. I can't take any time off. In fact, I'll be working more than ever."

"Don't worry, darling. If I had to wait for you to not be busy, we'd never get to visit. I'll stay in the background, quiet as can be. I can practice spirit stillness. I learned about it in our focus and centering workshop yesterday."

Feeling a flood of New Ageism coming on, Sandy scrambled to stem the tide. "I promise to find time next month, maybe during the cherry blossom festival out here. This will be my first one, and I hear it's gorgeous. But if ever there was a week where I will literally not have enough hours in the day, it's this one. Just get a ticket voucher. I'll pay the cancellation fee."

"I don't know where all this negative energy you have comes from," her mother said, sounding wounded. "I want to see my only baby girl. It's been months, and you haven't accepted one invitation to come visit. I'm not willing to be a stranger, so I'm actualizing my dream of a healed relationship between us by coming to see you. Am I so terrible that I can't even make myself part of your backdrop for a few days?" Her mother's voice sounded small and sad, and somewhere inside, Sandy's conscience throbbed in a way that wouldn't quit until she gave in.

"All right," she said, sighing. "But I'm warning you, I'm up against one of the craziest weeks of my life."

"Sounds like I'm coming at the right time to help, then," her mother said, sounding all smiles once more. Magdalena clearly wasn't getting it. No surprise there. Sandy smothered another sigh. "Give me your flight information. I'll be there."

When she ended the call, she could already feel the first pulses of a headache behind her eyes. Not the start to the week she'd been hoping for. At all.

* * *

When they pulled into her driveway that night, Sandy drove around back to her parking spot. Like most big cities, finding parking anywhere in the DC area could be brutal, which made paying extra rent for her guaranteed spot totally worth it. She hefted her mother's suitcase from the trunk, directed her to the stairs that led to the outside entrance, and then followed her up, enveloped by the signature patchouli scent that always clung to Magdalena.

"Cute house. Will I be meeting your roommates?" Magdalena asked.

Sandy shrugged. "Probably at some point this week. They're more like neighbors than roommates. We don't share a kitchen or bathroom, and I can come and go all day long without ever seeing them."

"Don't you like them?"

"Yeah. I like them a lot. But I also like having my own space. It's the best of both worlds."

"I don't know if I like the idea of you living alone."

"Magdalena, you're the one always preaching to me about how solitude is good for the soul. And they're one slightly raised voice away if I ever need something. And there's Larry."

"Your cat?"

"Yes." Sandy turned to unlock the door and then gathered up her mother's bag again and lugged it across the threshold.

"Is a cat much good as a guard animal?" her mother asked skeptically.

"I'm sure it has to be better than a chinchilla. Besides, she may not bark, but she could probably freeze an intruder in his tracks with a look."

Larry reinforced this point by prowling over to them, staring down her nose at Magdalena, and then sauntering away. Sandy found the staring thing particularly impressive given the height discrepancy.

"Charming," her mother murmured. She turned her attention to the rest of Sandy's place. "I hope it isn't too much of an inconvenience to put me up."

Sandy stifled a snort. Of course it was a huge inconvenience to have less than a day's notice of an out-of-town guest—especially a guest who would expect to see the many books and odd knickknacks and "power" objects she'd sent over the years on prominent display when she walked in. Sandy had spent every minute she wasn't at church digging out the odd crystals and sculptures she normally stashed in whatever nook or cranny they fit. At least the books had already been sitting on her shelf. Maybe if she was lucky, her mother wouldn't notice how few of their spines had been cracked. Or that some of them bore watermarks from serving coaster duty. Sandy waited for the inevitable criticism couched as a helpful suggestion. No matter how many bases she'd tried to cover, she knew she'd missed something.

Magdalena strode to the center of the room and stared straight up at the ceiling. The red curls Sandy had inherited should have looked ridiculous springing from her mother's head in long, wild tresses at her age, but they didn't. Her perfect skin showed only the slightest hint of age at the corners of her mouth and bright-blue eyes. As Magdalena stared, Sandy wondered if she'd developed the same fascination with the ceiling fan that Larry had. Her mother cocked her head to the side and said, "I thought you used feng shui in here."

Sandy sighed. "I did."

"You missed a spot."

"I did?" Feng shui was an old Chinese practice of situating the furniture and accessories in a home to maximize *chi*, or life energy. Sandy didn't really buy into the concept of *chi* but did enjoy the order it imposed on what would otherwise be her chaotic living space, a testament that a few of Magdalena's habits had crept into Sandy's life. Even though she'd never admit it to her mother, she probably owed vegetarianism, yoga, and, yes, feng shui to her influence. In fact, the minimal effort she exerted to maintain the feng shui might be the only thing that stood between her and a starring spot on *Hoarders*.

Her mother pointed at the ceiling. "You need to have money pinned to the center of the ceiling to encourage prosperity."

"As long as I'm prosperous enough to pay the rent, I'm fine. I don't need the money on the ceiling." She tried not to show her exasperation. This was one of those key differences between her and her mother. Sandy was willing to consider other philosophies and practices as long as they made sense; organizing her furniture in a logical way worked for her, so she adopted that part of feng shui. Her mother had no concept of moderation. To her, it all had to be fully embraced, even if common sense told a person that something was little more than a superstition.

"There's no reason to limit the universe," her mother said, the trace of a lecture in her voice. "I'm going to fix this." She darted over to the small café table in the corner where Sandy ate her meals. As Magdalena dragged the chair back toward the center of the living room, Sandy winced and hoped it wasn't disturbing the girls below.

After digging through her hand-woven purse, her mother produced a dollar, kicked off her embellished Chinese slippers, and climbed atop the chair. She reached up to pin it in place and then stopped. "Sand Dollar? Can you get me a tack?"

Ah, yes. Classic Magdalena. Her plans were always well intentioned but poorly executed. Sandy scrounged through her kitchen catch-all drawer until she finally located a thumbtack. She brought it back to her mother, who looked pleased.

"Red. A fortuitous color. You *do* listen."

Sandy didn't mention it was the only tack she could find. Her mother secured the money and hopped down from the chair. Sandy hoped the thump of her landing didn't alarm the downstairs girls. She foresaw a long week of reminding her mother to keep down the noise at night. Then again, Magdalena was all about early to bed and early to rise. Sandy decided to take the glass-half-full approach and believe that meant there would be a peaceful coexistence among all of them for the next seven days.

She believed that all the way until a knock sounded at her door. "Sandy?" It was Brooke's voice. "Sandy? Are you okay?"

Opening the door to the inevitable, she stood back and waved Brooke in. "I'm fine," she said.

"I heard a big thump. I thought I better make sure."

"The big thump was her," Sandy said, indicating her petite mother. They were physically similar, except for the four inches of height she had on her mother. "She jumped off of a chair. Sorry about that."

"Oh, no problem. Hi," she said, inching in farther and extending a hand to Magdalena. "I'm Brooke."

"One of the darling neighbor girls!" Magdalena exclaimed, waving the handshake away and embracing Brooke in one of her patchouli hugs. It looked funny since Brooke was even taller than Sandy.

"Yes, that's me: darling," Brooke said, smiling at Sandy over her mother's head.

"It's nice to meet one of Sand Dollar's friends. Normally, she keeps them hidden from me, like I'm going to brainwash them or something."

Sand Dollar? Brooke mouthed.

Sandy shrugged. "Now you know why I don't bring her around that much."

Brooke, not knowing what to do with the small woman still clinging to her, wiggled an arm free and offered Magdalena's head a pat. "Um, nice to meet you too. But we have company downstairs, so I should go."

"Company?" Magdalena stepped back, her expression brightening. "Lovely! Are they my daughter's friends too?"

Sandy shook her head frantically behind her mother.

"Not really," Brooke hedged, taking the cue. "A bunch of guys from another house stopped by to hijack our TV so they can watch the ball game."

"A bunch of young men down there sent a girl up to check on my daughter's safety? That hardly seems right," she said, turning to Sandy with an expression of dissatisfaction.

"You have to pick a lane," Sandy said. "Either we're all going to be liberated females or we're not. You can't pick for me to be liberated only when it's convenient. Congratulations to your generation on winning the fight for equality."

Magdalena sniffed. "How come you get to lecture me, but it's not okay for me to share a little life experience with you?"

Sandy opened her mouth to retort, but Brooke jumped in. "That's my cue to exit," she said before escaping back downstairs, probably to scrub off the patchouli cloud clinging to her. Sandy found herself alone with her mother once again. They stared at each other in silence, her mother's face strained and hopeful. Sandy guessed that her own face bore slight traces of annoyance.

Magdalena stepped back to run a more critical eye over her daughter, the faintest frown creasing her forehead. "Looking at you, it's clearer than on the phone that you haven't been taking care of your chakras. Never mind," she said with an airy wave. "I brought some green tea that'll fix you right up."

Sandy was in no mood to explain the Word of Wisdom to her mother—again. She grabbed her mother's huge tapestry-upholstered suitcase. "Follow me, and I'll show you to your bed."

The bulk of her cleaning time today had been spent wrangling the prolific piles of clothes on her bedroom floor into some sort of order. A few things had made it back into the closet or dresser, a furnishing she thought of as a large repository for socks but that now housed a dozen or so pairs of yoga pants and as many T-shirts. The rest of her laundry nested in a line of baskets borrowed from the downstairs girls. Rome wasn't built in a day, and it would take longer than that to clean her room given the size of her wardrobe. Creating even this amount of order out of chaos was a victory.

"It's very . . . nice," her mother said, after a survey of the room.

"Define nice," Sandy said, knowing she would regret it. Clearly, Magdalena found something lacking. It couldn't be the feng shui. All two pieces of her furniture were set in the right place with the right proximity to the door and window. Then again, considering the mess it had been for weeks, it was possible the feng shui wasn't actually doing anything.

"It's a little bare, that's all."

"Uh-uh. No fair complaining about bareness when you're the one always going on about eschewing belongings"—here she tapped the massive suitcase—"and the virtues of asceticism."

Magdalena didn't say anything, studying Sandy with knowing eyes.

Feeling the urge to fidget, Sandy busied herself instead by giving her mother directions. "The bathroom is right across the hall. There's a shower, no tub. Towels and extra blankets are in the linen closet by the bathroom."

Her mother responded by padding over on bare feet, tugging her toward the bed, and pressing her to sit. Once she had Sandy down near eye level, Magdalena stood in front of her and reached up to place her hands lightly on Sandy's temples. "Close your eyes, Sand Dollar."

"Stop—"

"Now would be a good time to practice your Christian virtue of honoring your mother," she interrupted with uncharacteristic firmness. "Be quiet and close your eyes."

Sandy complied with a distinct lack of graciousness. Magdalena pressed firmly for a minute then let go and stepped back.

"I thought you were having problems with your chakras," she said. "It goes much deeper than that. I think we'll have to spend some time this week working on your wounded inner child."

Sandy stifled her twentieth snort of the night. "Sorry, but not this week. Maybe some other time." She tried to get up, but Magdalena pressed her back down.

"This is not the kind of thing that can be put off," she said. "I've seen some amazing rebirth therapies, and I think we need to try it. We can wait until your hearing is over, but this is too important to skip."

"Rebirth therapy?" Sandy bounced off the bed, ignoring her mother's disapproving cluck. "Isn't that where you re-enact my birth by smothering me with pillows and all kinds of other craziness?"

"It's not crazy," Magdalena said, looking offended. "You're always so quick to dismiss my ideas, and you have no information about them. Rebirth therapy has produced some outstanding results in—"

"No," Sandy said. "Drop it, or I'm dropping you off at the local Marriott."

"Fine. For now."

Sandy pretended not to hear the last part. She'd take her temporary victory and call it good.

"Where's your room?" her mother asked.

"This is my room."

Magdalena looked confused. "Then where are you sleeping?"

"On the sofa. Don't worry about it," she said, seeing her mother's appalled expression. "It's not inconvenient *at all*."

Magdalena waved at the bed. "You should really sleep here," she said. "I'll be fine on a yoga mat in the living room."

Sandy scoffed.

"I mean it," her mother said, her tone serene. "It will help me prepare for the more primitive conditions on the Inca trail when I take my spirit walk."

"You're sleeping in the bed." Sandy left to raid the linen closet for bedding she could use on the sofa.

"No, I'm not," her mother said, floating out behind her. She drifted over to the TV and pulled out Sandy's yoga mat. "You can sleep on the sofa if you want to, but that means the bed will be totally unused. Do what you like though."

Sandy's jaw throbbed, and she realized she was grinding her teeth. She retreated back to her bedroom. "I'll have some Advil for you in the morning," she said. "You can have the bed tomorrow night after you change your mind about the floor."

"I won't," her mother said, her Zen calm still in effect. "And ibuprofen is toxic and unnatural. Not that I'll need anything, but willow bark tea would work far better and more holistically."

Sandy shut her door, proud that it closed with a quiet click and not a resounding slam. As she collapsed onto the bed, her last bit of energy drained away. She stared at the ceiling and wondered who would ultimately be responsible for her mental breakdown: Magdalena or Jake. So far, it was too close to call.

Chapter 16

MONDAY MORNING, SANDY DRAGGED HERSELF out of bed around six thirty, which meant she'd hit the snooze button at least three times. She braced herself to wake Magdalena and listen to a long and winding list of passive-aggressive complaints about sleeping on the floor. Instead, she opened the bedroom door to find her mother in a flowing white top and pants, facing the window and doing some sort of bowing and stretching thing in the direction of the anemic sunlight. It looked sort of like yoga but not quite.

"Good morning," Sandy said, testing the waters.

Magdalena gave a slight nod to show that she'd heard her, but she didn't disrupt her bowing and stretching. Sandy headed for the kitchen to scrounge up a breakfast. She considered her barely stocked cabinets before settling on an English muffin spread with peanut butter. Peanut butter had protein. Yeah, that was the ticket.

She settled at her small table and spread out the latest issue of *Lucky* to check out the deals she might have missed on her last mall run, tuning her mother out completely. This had the satisfying effect of making her morning feel like every other morning until Magdalena glided in and began rummaging through the cupboards.

After the fourth door closed and her mother seemed dissatisfied with her search, Sandy decided to play dutiful daughter.

"Can I help you find something?" she asked.

"Didn't I send you a box of Indian teas for Christmas?"

"Yes, but I don't drink tea."

Her mother turned to shoot her a wounded look. "But I do. Couldn't you have kept them around for my visits, or is this another way of telling me you don't want me here?"

"I do want you here," Sandy said, wondering if her mother could sense the lie. "Next week or any of the fifty other weeks this year might have been better. The missing tea is not a message. It must have gotten lost when I moved."

"I don't see how you can start your day without it," Magdalena said. "It really does perk up the soul."

"So does a shower and a deep-conditioning rinse."

"Tea isn't bad for you," Magdalena insisted. "That's superstitious nonsense your church feeds you with your health code."

Sandy struggled for patience. "Herbal teas are fine in moderation. Your chai and green tea can create dependencies. That's a researched fact, not religious mumbo jumbo."

"Science can twist anything to be healthy or not," her mother said. "I rely more on how I feel to tell me if something is good for me."

"Wow. That's your same argument for legalizing pot."

"Marijuana is overly demonized."

Sandy stared at her blankly and then blinked. "I'm going to go get ready for work."

"What should I wear?" Magdalena asked.

"Whatever you want, I guess."

"Doesn't your office have some sort of dress code?"

That stopped Sandy cold, and she counted to ten before turning to face Magdalena again. "You can't come with me," she said. "I'm sorry, but I told you what kind of week this would be."

"You're shutting me out again. I wish you would let me do that rebirth therapy. It would do so much to heal the sad little girl inside of you."

Sandy gritted her teeth. "This has nothing to do with inner children. My office does not sponsor a bring-your-mother-to-work day. It's not a place to hang out, and it's not a good day for guided tours."

"I don't need a guided tour. I'm happy to observe quietly. Besides, you work for a non-profit. Don't you rely on volunteers? I'm sure there's something I could do to make myself useful all day."

Sandy almost laughed at the idea of her mother trying to help their clients with the complex computer tutorials or trailing after Roberta on one of her grant-seeking missions. "It's a lot of technical and vocational training. I don't think that's your thing." When Magdalena looked like she wanted to argue, Sandy drove home another point. "There's also a ton of paperwork that only Jasmine and I can do. Sorry."

"Paperwork? That means filing. I can do that, can't I?"

Sandy grudgingly conceded that there was filing that needed doing. "Dress conservatively," she begged before retreating to her own closet in search of an outfit.

When she emerged half an hour later in a black sheath dress and gold wedges, she found Magdalena on the sofa in lotus position. "I said to dress conservatively."

"I did." Her mother stood and gestured to her outfit to make a point. She wore a billowy tunic that looked like it was woven from unrefined cotton and a broomstick skirt dyed an adamant shade of turquoise.

"You look like a hippie. We're going to a business office."

"This is the most conservative thing I own," her mother said, and Sandy knew that was probably true. Her mother's clothes often boasted embellishments from bright feathers to chunks of artistic wood and stone. She wasn't a bad dresser, Sandy had to concede. She had flair; it was just flamboyant. A simple cotton tunic did sort of represent a concession. Sandy ducked back into her room and re-emerged with a wide leather belt and flat-soled, equestrian-style boots in soft suede. Her mother would never go for heels.

"Try these," she said. "It'll tip more toward hip than hippie."

This time Magdalena heaved a sigh, but she accepted the accessories and waited for Sandy's inspection. "Hm. One more thing," Sandy decided. She grabbed an elastic from the bathroom and secured her mother's hair in a low ponytail. It didn't do anything to tame the curl, but it reduced the volume. "It'll do," she said.

"Thanks. I find that endorsement overwhelming."

"What happened to sarcasm killing the soul by degrees?"

Her mother sniffed. "It was irony. Can we go now?" She opened the door and flounced down the stairs, leaving Sandy to follow.

Sandy caught up to her and then set a brisk pace toward the Metro station, her mother trotting along beside her and pointing out every single flower and blooming shrub with delight, as if she hadn't pointed out an identical blossom three seconds before. One of the things that had drawn Sandy to the Somerset house when she moved was the neighborhood. She had recognized its quaint charm with the old, custom-built homes and tree-lined streets. That said, she'd never felt the need to sniff *every* flower on the half-mile walk to the train stop. She refused to slow her pace. The seven forty-five train got her to work at exactly the right time, and she wasn't about to let Magdalena derail her.

They squeezed through the train doors right before they swished closed. Sandy found them a pair of open seats, snagged an abandoned copy of *The Washington Post* from the seat across from them, and handed it to her mother, anxious to manage Magdalena's oddness. "Why don't you read this?"

Magdalena brushed it away. "It's all propaganda. I'd rather watch the people."

Sandy couldn't blame her. "Fine. But no pointing, and if you *have* to ask a question about someone, ask it in a whisper."

"Okay," Magdalena said then leaned over. "What's going on with *that* lady?"

Sandy sighed and settled in for a long ride.

* * *

When she strode through the door at New Horizons, her speed had less to do with her resolve to work and more with the vague wish that she could shake Magdalena. Sadly, her mother stayed right on her heels. She had a flashback to her first day of kindergarten when Magdalena had mortified her by trying to burn cleansing herbs in her new classroom. She had wafted around a bundle of some kind of stinky weed while Sandy's kindergarten teacher stared on, aghast. The smoke had set off the fire alarm, and Sandy had started her first day of school with an emergency fire drill five minutes after the morning bell while the fire captain chewed out her mother. The other kids had called her Fire Head for the next two years until Magdalena moved them. Again.

Sandy stowed her Coach bag in her desk and then turned to face the day's headaches. Jake's promised e-mail with compromises for the center hadn't materialized, and she grew more anxious every day that now it wouldn't; she still felt like she was floundering in this new job; and then, of course, she had her biggest headache of all to consider. "Are you serious about helping out today?" she asked Magdalena.

"Of course, Sand Dollar."

"Then the first thing you can do is not call me that."

"But it's a beautiful reminder of your spirit. I can't call you 'Sandy.'"

"Then you can't stay." She crossed her arms and stared until Magdalena blinked.

"All right," she said. "Sandy." It sounded as if she were speaking around a mouthful of mud to get the name out.

"Good. Secondly, there are only certain things I can have you work on without training or supervision, so when I give you those jobs, no complaining."

"I don't complain," her mother said serenely.

Sandy let that pass and led her to the children's center.

"What's this?" Magdalena asked.

"It's where our mothers let their children play when the kids have a hard time sitting still."

"I see. So small children are allowed to run around, but I'm somehow an inconvenience?"

Sandy narrowed her eyes in warning.

"I'm not complaining," Magdalena said. "What would you like me to do here?"

"We're at the tail end of cold and flu season," Sandy said. "We need you to disinfect this area to prevent the little ones from trading viruses with each other. Plus, the stuff gets jumbled."

"I'm going to be cleaning today?" her mother asked, her tone suggesting her distaste. Cleaning in Magdalena's home over the last ten years had been handled by a Romanian woman who needed extra income to offset the slow months in her palm-reading business.

"Yes, you're going to be cleaning." Sandy dug a tub of disinfecting wipes out of a nearby cabinet and plunked it down next to her mother with some satisfaction. "Is that a problem?"

"No," her mother said, her serene mask in place again. She plucked a wipe from the tub, fished out a grimy wooden block, and stared at the two with a furrowed brow. Certain she had freed herself from her mother for at least two hours, Sandy retreated to her desk.

When Jasmine came in right on time a few minutes later, Sandy returned her smile and then grinned as confusion crossed her face at the sight of a turquoise bottom poking out from a cabinet.

"Who the heck is that?" Jasmine asked.

This set the bottom to wiggling as Magdalena attempted to reverse.

"That's Magdalena," Sandy said.

"As in your *mother*?"

Sandy nodded.

"Why is she crawling around on the play mat and hiding in cupboards?" Jasmine asked.

Sandy shrugged. "I told you she was odd."

"That's not funny, Sand—er, Sandy," her mother said, finally free of the cabinet and heading toward them. A tendril of hair had escaped its elastic and had curled around her face. "I'm cleaning because I wanted to come to work with my daughter, and she said it would be inappropriate for me to just sit and watch all day."

"She did?" Jasmine said. "We've never had someone's mom come with them, but I don't think I'd say it was inappropriate, exactly."

"I'm still new here," Sandy reminded her. "I don't want to give anyone the idea that I think I can drag any of my relatives or friends in here on a whim. I work when I'm here. I can't work if I'm playing tour guide all day."

"So you told your mom she had to be our custodian?" Jasmine asked, her expression leaving no doubt that she found that even more inappropriate than having Magdalena hang out.

"No, I told her she could volunteer. The play area needs some disinfecting and organizing in a bad way, and she's willing to do it."

"Oh," Jasmine said, her tone doubtful. "I guess if she wants to."

"If this is what it takes to see my daughter." Magdalena shrugged. Sandy squished down her guilt. Her warning had been very clear on the phone, and *she* wasn't the one who had hatched this spur-of-the-moment visit.

"Are you ready to dive into the schedule this week?" Sandy asked Jasmine. "It's tight."

Jasmine needed no further prodding. She stowed her purse in her desk, fired up her computer, and pulled up the schedule. Sandy would miss her efficiency when she left. She'd get her own assistant, but she hated to sacrifice the easy rapport she and Jasmine had.

The biggest headache was how to compile all the crime statistics Jasmine had unearthed into concise bullet points. Sandy deleted her yoga classes from her schedule with regret, knowing yoga and almost everything else would have to wait until the next week when the hearing was done.

As she listened to her mother chanting soft "ohms" while she swabbed the Legos piece by piece, Sandy tried to convince herself that this week would work. In fact, she adopted it as her own morning mantra. *You can get through the next three days. New Horizons will win. You can get through the next three days. New Horizons will win.*

She believed that all the way up until the door chimed right before noon and she looked up expecting to smile at Malia, a city hall contact she was expecting for lunch, only to find Jake, whom she wasn't expecting at all.

"We need a different sound effect when he comes in," Jasmine grumbled. "What sound does the devil make when he appears? It should be like one of those big old drums they have at the symphony."

Even knowing Jake could hear Jasmine, Sandy didn't shush her coworker. After days of wading through strategy plans and reams of research because of his clients' stupid injunction, she wasn't in the mood to be polite.

"What can I do for you, Jake?" she asked coolly.

"I promised you some compromises. You want to hear them?"

"Of course. What do you have to put on the table?" she asked.

He settled into the office chair opposite her. "I know New Horizons already paid the deposit and first month's rent up front. The River Oaks homeowner's association would like to offer to buy you out of that lease so you have the money to invest in opening somewhere else." When Sandy looked skeptical he added, "It's a fair offer."

"It is," she said. "Except that even if we had the funds to go looking elsewhere, we don't have the time. We have to be ready for business by our grant deadline. We can't afford to do that."

He processed that. "What this comes down to is the grant, then?"

"That and the location," she said. "I can't guarantee that Roberta would go for a change of location even if we had time. A big part of her philosophy is that element of aspiration."

"Let's tackle one problem at a time," he said. "How big is this grant?"

Sandy hesitated, unsure whether it was something she should or could disclose. Reading her correctly, Jake smiled and said, "I can't do anything to hurt the center with the information; it can only help. Depending on the number, River Oaks may want to match it so that even if you lose the grant, you'll have the money you need when you find a new location."

"Great solution, except that it's a really big number," Sandy said. "I think it's probably a lot bigger than their discretionary funds can accommodate."

"Try me," Jake said.

"It's just over a million dollars," she said.

His eyes widened for a fraction of a second. "That's more than I'm authorized to offer," he said, and Sandy thought she heard a trace of frustration in his tone.

"I appreciate you coming here, Jake." She meant it. "I wish we could work something out, but I don't see it happening. We need that space. We're going to have to fight River Oaks' complaint at the hearing."

He sighed. "Do you want to brainstorm some more over lunch?"

She weighed the likelihood of them reaching a compromise against the need to meet with Malia and prepare for the hearing. If she didn't sit down with Malia today, they'd be at a serious loss on Wednesday night. Her pragmatic side won out. "I'm sorry. We're too far apart on the details to find a middle ground. I'm expecting company, so I can't do lunch, but if your clients have any other offers, please call me. We're willing to listen."

Magdalena wandered over, a tattered teddy bear in tow.

Jake did a slight double take when she appeared, interrupting her when she started to introduce herself.

"I'm—"

"You're Sandy's mom. I'd bet money on it."

Sandy bowed to the inevitable in the hopes she could get him out of the office faster. The less time he had with her mom, the better. "Jake, this is Magdalena. Magdalena, this is Jake Manning. He represents the other side in our zoning hearing on Wednesday."

"Nice to meet you," Magdalena said with an airy nod.

"You're holding a teddy bear," Sandy said.

Her mother glanced down at the tattered toy in surprise. "How did that get there?"

"Maybe when you were cleaning the toy area? You should probably go put it back."

Magdalena considered that for a minute. "I like it," she said and stayed right where she was. "Are we going out to eat?"

"No," Sandy said. "I have an associate coming, and we need to work through lunch."

"What about me?" Magdalena asked. "You're going to have yogurt, aren't you? I don't want yogurt."

"My lunch plans just fell through," Jake said, smiling. "And yet, I have a reservation for two. Since Sandy's busy—"

"No thanks to you."

He ignored her and focused on Magdalena. "Since Sandy's busy, I'm sure she won't mind if we go grab a meal together. Are you up for it?"

"No way," Sandy said.

Magdalena ignored her too. "That sounds lovely. I don't partake of animal flesh," she warned.

Sandy snorted at her mother's dramatic proclamation, but Jake smiled. "I was prepared for that contingency," he said. "I know a great place."

"Magdalena, may I speak with you in private?" Sandy asked, but her voice held a warning.

"I'm not okay with you going to lunch with Jake," Sandy whispered when Jake moved out of earshot. "He may try to pump you for information about me or my personal life. I'm keeping him at a distance for a reason."

"Have a little faith in me," Magdalena said. "I wouldn't break your trust."

"Not on purpose. But he's a lawyer. He specializes in cross-examining people. I really don't want you to go."

Magdalena looked surprised by her vehemence. After a long moment, she laid her hand on Sandy's. "I'm sure I need to go to lunch with him. Mother instinct is powerful. I trust it, and you should too."

Sandy badly wanted to comment on the distinct lack of maternal instinct Magdalena had demonstrated throughout Sandy's entire life, but she could see her mother's stubbornness about this lunch invitation written all over her face. "I can't do anything short of throw a tantrum to stop you, can I?"

"A tantrum wouldn't work either. I would still go to prove to your inner child that it needs mothering."

Sandy clenched her jaw and headed back toward Jake. When they rejoined him, he did his best to look innocent. "Everything fine?"

"It's fantastic," Sandy lied through gritted teeth. "Have a nice lunch."

"Let me get my things," Magdalena said and wandered off toward the play area to scrounge up the embroidered shawl she'd used in lieu of a spring jacket that morning.

"What are you up to?" she asked Jake, trying to sound unconcerned.

"Nothing. Your mom seems fascinating."

"I am," Magdalena said, rejoining them. "You'll like me. Everybody does."

Sandy let that pass, mainly because it was unaccountably true. Magdalena looped her arm through Jake's and headed out the door, her silver laugh tinkling behind her.

Jasmine emerged from the computer lab. "Where's your mom?"

Sandy tossed a pen down and whirled around in her chair. "She went to lunch with Jake Manning."

Jasmine laughed. "Seriously, where did she go? The restroom?"

"I'm serious. She left with him a couple of minutes ago."

Jasmine stared at her. "Nothing good can come of that. Why did you let her go?"

"Because there's no stopping her when she decides to do something, and she decided to go to lunch with Jake Manning. She's the most stubborn woman on the planet."

Jasmine shook her head. "She seems so . . . fluffy in person. No disrespect," she hastened to add.

"Fluffy? That's about the nicest way I can think to put it. And don't be fooled. The fluff hides a one-track mind that's always charging in the wrong direction."

A slow smile tugged at one corner of Jasmine's mouth.

"What?" Sandy demanded.

"I'm picturing El Diablo and Magdalena, Earth Goddess, sitting down to break bread. I kind of wish I could be a fly on the wall."

"I wish I could be a fly in the soup." Sandy scowled. "Jake's soup. He's up to something."

"It can't hurt the center though. She doesn't know anything that he can finagle out of her. Take some comfort in that."

The door chimed, and Roberta strode in. "Ladies, good afternoon. How is the hearing prep going?"

"Good," Sandy answered. "Malia should be here any minute to go through the last of the details with me."

"Keep me posted," Roberta said, already en route to her office.

"Roberta? My mother is going to be here all day. She's been sanitizing and reordering the toy area for us."

"How nice! Where is she?"

"She's at lunch," Sandy said, carefully omitting with whom.

"I see no problem with her staying if you can still focus on work," Roberta said. "We can always use an extra pair of hands around here."

"Thanks," Sandy murmured to Roberta's retreating back. She had hoped Roberta would order her to send Magdalena home.

Another door chime alerted her that her city hall contact had arrived. For the next forty-five minutes, Sandy and Jasmine absorbed Malia's information as she profiled each of the zoning commissioners and predicted their votes. After Malia left, Sandy leaned back, deep in thought.

Jasmine heaved a big sigh, breaking the silence. "It's not great news, but it isn't a disaster. It all rides on how you present it to the council on Wednesday. If you can put together a great argument, I think they'll uphold the permit. No pressure or anything." She studied Sandy. "Are you nervous?"

Sandy smiled. "Not about speaking. But I have to admit, I wish I weren't going up against Jake. His confidence worries me."

"Yeah, he's cocky."

"That's the thing. He isn't. If he were, I wouldn't be worried at all. That's pretty easy to defuse. But real confidence? That's earned, and I have a bad feeling that Jake has won enough cases that he has every reason to feel confident."

"Stop right there, girl," Jasmine ordered. "You'll psych yourself out. It's not a jury trial. He can't use the same tricks he does to fool a bunch of jurors."

"I don't know. Maybe he can. It's still a panel of people who need to be convinced." Sandy picked up a pen and tapped it against her desk, the rhythm quick and staccato. "I wish he would have spent the same amount of energy trying to understand the need for this annex as he has in trying to undermine it."

Jasmine blew out an annoyed curse.

"Well, that was to the point," Sandy said, smiling.

"I don't want to talk about El Diablo anymore. I'm going back to criminal research. It gives me more warm fuzzies."

Sandy laughed and turned to her own paperwork.

Several minutes later, Jasmine cackled. "Hope you're not busy tomorrow night." She whipped her laptop toward Sandy with a flourish.

Sandy leaned forward to check it out. "How did you find this?" she finally asked.

"My friend Google." Jasmine grinned.

"I can't believe we didn't think of this before." Sandy pulled the laptop even closer. "The River Oaks Concerned Citizens Forum meets tomorrow night to discuss the hearing."

Jasmine's smile stretched wider. "Let me guess. You're going to drop in for a little tea and convo?"

"I'm definitely dropping by. I asked Jake for this a million times over the last three weeks, and he said it couldn't happen, but I think we're going to make our own break here." Sandy eased back in her chair, no less stressed but significantly more hopeful. Things were looking up. Jake Manning needed to worry, but he was too secure in his position to know it.

She stretched her legs. After a long morning in her chair, plotting and stressing, it felt good to work out the kinks. Wandering to the toy center, she inspected her mother's handiwork. The blocks looked grime-free, and she'd already gone through all the dolls and stuffed animals too. Sandy could tell because Magdalena had twisted them into yoga poses when she'd finished. Shaking her head, she leaned over and liberated a slightly mangy zebra from a downward dog stance and stifled a laugh. She didn't want the "cosmic echo" of her amusement to encourage her mother when she got back.

Walking to the cabinets Magdalena had been rummaging through earlier, Sandy peered in at the interior makeover. A dull glint in the far corner of one cupboard caught her eye. Kicking off her heels, she crouched down and stuck her head in farther to investigate, but the shiny object was too far back to discern. She inched in until the cabinet swallowed her nearly to the waist and she remembered Magdalena's earlier pose, and then she stretched until she could touch it.

"I don't believe it," she muttered. She grabbed a corner of the piece and tugged it toward her, wincing as she backed out and something snagged her hair. She tried to pull away from it, but the yank on her curl smarted, and she froze, thinking about how to extricate herself. She heard the front door chime, the sound causing her stomach to plummet because with Jasmine and Roberta accounted for, she knew who had just walked in.

Ten seconds later, Magdalena's voice, sounding strangely hollow to her inside the cabinet, asked, "Why is *your* bottom sticking out of the cabinet, Sand Dollar?"

Please let her be alone, Sandy begged silently.

A choking noise that masked a laugh told her that her Ridiculous Situation guardian angel was currently off duty.

"Yes, Sand Dollar," Jake said from above her. "Why? And how can we help?"

A burn crept up her neck and face. "I'm dusting. I'll be awhile. You should probably go back to work, Jake."

"And leave you here? You know me and my Boy Scout training. Sorry," Jake said, not sounding at all sorry.

Next she heard Jasmine's voice. "You crazy girl. You're stuck? Why didn't you tell me you were stuck?"

"Because I'm not. Why does everyone think I need help?"

Thick silence met her question, and she tugged at her tangled curl.

"Is there some other reason you look like you got swallowed by a cupboard?" Jasmine asked.

"I guess you don't believe I'm dusting."

Silence.

"I have a piece of hair caught on something," she admitted.

"Don't worry," Magdalena chirped. "I'll get some scissors."

"*No!*" Sandy hollered. "I need a little time, not scissors."

"I think I can probably help without scissors," Jake said.

"No."

"Sand Dollar, be nice."

"Don't call me that, Magdalena. It's not my name."

"I forgot," her mother said in the vague tone that suggested she really had. "But you should let Jake help. He's very capable."

"Thank you," he said politely.

"Did you get a merit badge in hair untangling?" Sandy asked, fed up with the new heights of absurdity the situation was achieving by the minute.

"I'm good with knots. I have fourteen nephews, and I haven't been defeated by a single one of their shoelaces yet."

Fourteen? Good grief.

"I've got this," Sandy said.

"All right," Jake said.

But she didn't hear the sound of his footsteps moving away. After another minute of tugging that only snarled her hair more, she heard the unmistakable snick of scissors outside the cabinet.

"I found these in your desk," Magdalena said. "I think I can reach far enough in to get at that hair."

Sandy froze.

"Before we do that, maybe I should give the untangling a shot. I'm the only one with arms long enough to reach," Jake said. "Why don't you set those scissors down while I try?" He sounded like he was talking an armed loony into handing over a gun.

Magdalena sighed. "All right. But if it doesn't work, either I cut her out with the scissors or we call the fire department."

Since there was no way Sandy was getting rescued from a hair snag by firefighters who had a million other things to do like their *jobs*, she decided to go with the least of three evils.

"Okay, Jake." That's all she said.

He knelt next to her and slid a hand along the bottom of the shelf above her. Her stomach flipped to have him so close to her. Even without touching him, she could feel his body heat. The farther in he reached, the closer he leaned, until the light touch of his other hand on her back made her jump.

"Sorry," he said. "I need to brace myself, or I'm going to fall over."

She thought she heard a muffled, "Yeah right," from Jasmine but said nothing since the sooner he was done, the sooner he was gone.

His hand brushed the tangle. It sent a tingle all the way down her roots to her scalp, and she jerked.

"Sorry! Did I hurt you?" he asked.

"No. I, uh. . . no. It's fine."

"All right, your hair is caught on a screw. I'm going to need some leverage. Promise not to take this the wrong way."

"Take what the wrong way?"

Instead of answering, he leaned forward and braced the full length of his arm on her back. "This should only take a minute, I swear."

"I think I should be the one swearing."

"Go ahead if it makes you feel better. I'll pretend not to notice."

She found his nearness so distracting that she couldn't remember any really good curses.

"Shoot."

"Shoot?" He laughed as he tugged gently on her curl. Goosebumps broke out on her arms. "That's the best one you've got?"

"No. It's the best one I can say out loud since I gave up cursing for Lent."

"Hang on, I have to give this an extra hard pull."

She stiffened then hissed as he yanked.

"Sorry! I'm almost done, but these last few strands are the most stubborn."

"It's okay," she said through gritted teeth.

"What in the world is going on here?" It was Roberta.

Jake stayed where he was, leaning as far into the cabinet as possible with his hand still planted on Sandy's back.

"I'm stuck!" she called, wincing at how ridiculous her hollow voice sounded.

"Why are you stuck?" Roberta asked.

"I was trying to get something out, and my hair snagged."

"I see," Roberta, who clearly didn't see, said. "What were you trying to get?"

Jake gave one hard last tug, and as she yelped, Sandy felt her hair come free from the screw. She tightened her grasp on whatever it was in the corner and crawled backward.

Jake stuck a hand out to help her stand when she emerged from the cabinet.

She accepted it and turned to face her boss.

"I was trying to get this." She extended her arm so everyone could see the crystal, roughly the size of a nectarine, lying in her palm.

Everyone stared. Jake looked amused, Jasmine looked confused, Roberta looked annoyed, and Magdalena looked plain guilty.

"Why was this in there?" Sandy ground out with a hard stare at her mother.

"I put it in there."

Sandy said nothing, knowing that spitting out the "duh" she was fighting would crack a dam stopping up a slew of other things best left unsaid.

"I think Sandy's asking *why* you put it there," Jake said before she could explode.

Magdalena's smile was beatific. "I thought I'd invite some Zen energy to the children's section."

"Crystals aren't Zen," Sandy snapped.

Her mother was mixing her religions as usual. She knew the differences, of course, but practiced shopping-cart religion, where she took a sample of everything that sounded good and made her own Magdalena mishmash.

"They bring good energy, and I thought it would be nice for the children to have something extra in their corner. You know . . . literally."

"It's a nice thought, but I would worry about the crystal enticing the little ones into the cabinet," Roberta said. "Perhaps it could serve a better purpose somewhere else."

Sandy set the crystal down on the counter behind her. "I'll handle it, Roberta. I'm sure we'll find a place for it at home."

Roberta nodded and continued toward her office after she offered a "Nice to meet you" to Magdalena.

Once Roberta's office door clicked closed, Sandy turned on her mother.

Jasmine murmured something about needing to make a phone call, and Jake cleared his throat.

"Magdalena, thanks for keeping me company at lunch today."

"My pleasure," she said, reaching over to grip Jake's hand in hers. "You have a wonderful energy."

He smiled, and Magdalena turned to Sandy. "His chakras are vigorous," she said. "Do you know what that means? He's incredibly virile—"

Jake choked, and Sandy could have kissed her mother for wrong-footing him so easily, but she knew better than to let her continue about Jake's virile chakras.

"Thank you for taking Magdalena to lunch and for helping me get unstuck."

"Yes, thank you," Magdalena chimed in. "I don't like the archaic notion of damsels in distress, but there's something to be said for Jungian archetypes when someone like you makes the rescue."

Sandy smothered a grin when she saw the dull red flush staining Jake's face. Maybe Magdalena deserved a reprieve.

"Um, well. I better go," he mumbled. He backed away, did a quick about-face, and nearly ran for the door.

As soon as it closed behind him, Jasmine burst out laughing, and Sandy glared at her mother. She couldn't encourage that kind of behavior, even if it was funny. "You embarrassed him."

"Yes."

"Of course you did and—" Sandy stopped. "Wait, did you just agree with me?"

"Yes."

She stared for a minute. "You did it on *purpose?*"

"Yes," Magdalena said quite calmly.

"Why?"

Generally, Magdalena's hippie meanderings embarrassed people on accident because she was clueless.

"You wanted him gone, and he's gone now, isn't he?"

"Well, yes." Sandy had to think for a minute to find an explanation for why Magdalena was in the wrong on this one. "I could have asked him to leave though. Running him off was a little extreme."

"You could have asked him to leave, sure. But then you would have seemed ungrateful after he helped you. Doing it this way saved face for you." Magdalena twitched her skirt back into place. "My way was more fun."

Sandy gaped, and Jasmine laughed again. "Good point, Magdalena. I'm glad you're here today."

Not willing to go that far, Sandy settled on a noncommittal, "Mmm . . ."

"What am I working on this afternoon?" Magdalena asked.

"Staying out of trouble. You need to find a quiet corner and a book to read," Sandy said. "I don't want any other crystals turning up."

"Oh, come now, Sand Dollar. Sandy," her mother corrected herself when Sandy's face darkened. "I'm not done with the play area, and I have no more crystals. I'll just work in the children's center some more. I'm finding cleaning to be cleansing."

"Okay, but seriously, no crystals. No weird chalk symbols, no burning herbs, none of that. Just disinfect."

"Yes, daughter," Magdalena said and turned before Sandy could be sure that in fact her mother *had* just rolled her eyes.

With a sigh, Sandy returned to her desk and offered a silent prayer that nothing else interesting would happen for the rest of the afternoon.

Chapter 17

By the time she and Magdalena got home, it was well after six. Larry growled a demand for dinner. Sandy emptied a can of insanely expensive cat food into the dish for the ungrateful pet. Or maybe "pet."

She tugged off her wedges and collapsed onto the sofa, happy to sink into the cushions and let her mind go blank for a while. "A while" turned out to be a minute before some delicate throat clearing demanded her attention. She cracked an eye open. Magdalena stared back with an expectant look on her face.

"Yes, Magdalena?"

"Are we going to have dinner?"

"I'm too tired to cook. Think of skipping it as part of a purification ritual or something."

"I'll make dinner."

"Great. Pretend I'm not here, and knock yourself out."

By the time Magdalena's soft "Sand Dollar?" broke her tired daze, Sandy felt almost relaxed. Magdalena held out a salad.

"This looks good. When did you get all kitcheny?" It certainly hadn't been in her mother's repertoire of skills when Sandy was growing up. Most days, she liked to hold it against Magdalena, especially when Sandy was muddling around on the stovetop, trying to fix something for herself.

"I still don't cook," Magdalena admitted. "But I can throw together a few salads that do the trick."

"This is great," Sandy said after a bite. Her fork held a combination of raw greens, zesty black beans, and some chopped vegetables and spices. "I didn't think I even had all this in there."

"I had to look for a while. The beans were the jackpot."

"Thanks for making it," Sandy said.

Magdalena nodded and ate in silence. By the time Sandy had chased the last stray green leaf around her bowl, she felt much better. "I wish I had caught this second wind earlier," she said. "We could have gone to my yoga class."

Magdalena smiled. "We don't need a class. You have a perfectly nice space in here. Why don't you change while I clean these dishes, and then we'll do some stretching?"

Sandy realized that sometime during her stupor, Magdalena had slipped into clothes more suitable for yoga. She handed her mother her plate and headed back to her room. It felt odd to have her mother behaving so maternally. It was a first in their relationship.

She returned to the living room a few minutes later in her favorite Lululemon outfit, a purple tank trimmed in black with matching pants. Jessie made fun of her for spending four times as much on the outfit than similar pieces cost at Target, but she considered it a fair price for clothes so comfortable she felt like she could live in them forever. Her mother had decided on a hatha session for the night, which suited Sandy's mood with its slower pace and introductory stretches. A loud knock on the door interrupted the silence at the peak of a camel stretch. Sandy climbed to her feet to answer it and found Shannon standing there, bouncing in place.

"Are you coming to FHE?" she asked.

"No. I'm hanging out with my mother," Sandy said. She hardly ever went to family home evening activities, but it never stopped one of the downstairs girls from asking her about it every week.

"But it's at our place this time," Shannon said. "You can pop down easy-peasy and bring your mom. We can all borrow her for the night."

"Horrifying as that sounds, I think I'll pass," Sandy answered.

"What's FHE again?" Magdalena asked. She was kneeling on the mat, her head cocked to follow the conversation.

"It's that thing we do on Monday nights where we have a lesson with our fake family and then play some game and eat stale Oreos," Sandy said.

"Oh, come on, it's not that bad," Shannon protested.

"Oh really? Then what's the plan for tonight?"

Shannon flushed and avoided an answer. "I'm not in charge. Leah and Brett Langston are, but I'm sure it will be fun. You should come, Mrs. Burke," she called over Sandy's shoulder.

"She's not Mrs. Burke," Sandy corrected her. "She's Magdalena Holland-Burke-Filipepi-Taylor . . . wait, who am I missing?"

"I'm back to Holland," her mother said, not taking the bait.

"For now," Sandy mumbled under her breath.

Shannon looked uncertain. "Oh. Okay. Well, Mrs. Holland, you guys should come downstairs. It'll be fun."

Sandy recognized the earnest expression on her neighbor's face. She wasn't going to let up, so Sandy offered a compromise. "We'll come down for the lesson, but that's it. When are you starting?"

"In five minutes." A pleased Shannon grew nearly Tigger-esque with delight.

Sandy waved her away before she could hurt herself. "You don't have to perp walk us down. We'll be there in a few."

Shannon left, and Sandy turned to face Magdalena. "I know you don't like the organized religion thing. You can stay up here, and I'll be back in about twenty minutes so we can finish, if that's okay."

Magdalena smiled. "I'd like to come with you. *I'm* open minded."

Sandy bit her lip to keep in the snippy comeback threatening to tumble out. "Let me grab a sweatshirt, and we'll go." She emerged from her bedroom a moment later with a black hoodie on and led the way downstairs. In the living room, about a dozen people sat or sprawled on the floor and furniture while the cochairs of the group, Brett and her neighbor Leah, conferred with their heads together.

A young guy jumped out of his spot on the sofa and offered it to them. *Cute*, she mused, but he was clearly fresh off of his mission. She preferred her guys with more seasoning. She expected that the lesson would start any moment, but a few more minutes passed while the hum of conversation grew to a dull roar and Brett and Leah looked as if their conference with each other had escalated to a fight.

When Leah finally stood, she made her way to the sofa instead of calling everyone to order. "Hi," she said, stopping in front of Sandy and Magdalena.

"Hello," Magdalena replied.

"Sandy, we wondered if you could help us out with something tonight."

"Depends on what it is."

"We were supposed to do this game of scripture Twister but *someone*," she said with an evil glare at her FHE husband, "forgot to bring the game. So we need to do something different."

Even the mental picture of scripture Twister couldn't distract Sandy enough to dull a tickle of foreboding. "Bummer," she said.

"Yeah. So we thought since everyone's already dressed to be active tonight that maybe you could teach us some yoga stuff."

Sandy's stomach sank at the same time her mother's face lit up.

"How wonderful! I'll help you, and it will be so fun!" Magdalena gushed.

"I love that idea! Say you'll do it," the girl next to them on the sofa said.

"No yoga," called a guy who'd overheard her enthusiastic exclamation. "Yoga is for sissies."

His buddy elbowed him, and Sandy heard him mutter, "There's lots of bending and stretching, dude. *Chicks* bending and stretching. They love this stuff."

The first guy called out, "Never mind. Yoga sounds good."

"Say yes," Magdalena urged her. "I'll do it without you, but I'd much rather teach them with you."

That clinched the deal. No way would Sandy turn her mother loose, unsupervised, to spout a bunch of her New Age garbage while teaching a hostage class the warrior pose.

"Give me a minute," she said to Leah. She found Brooke and Cami organizing refreshments in the kitchen. "Any chance Jake Manning will show up tonight?"

Brooke glanced up from a tray of brownies she was trying to display artfully. "No. I've never seen him at an FHE before. The regulars are here already. You want me to call him?"

"Heck no," Sandy said. "I wanted to make sure before Leah ropes me into teaching yoga tonight. He makes a bad habit of turning up right when my behind is in the air. I don't want to tempt him too often, because one of these days he's going to kick it."

Brooke grinned. "I'd say you're safe."

"All right, girls. If you want a crash course in 'Crazy Magdalena's Personal Views on Yoga,' put the brownies down and join us in the living room."

She left the kitchen and informed a relieved Leah that they would teach. Leah hushed everyone enough for a lesson to begin, and after a rousing rendition of "The Wise Man and the Foolish Man" and an opening prayer, Brett gave a short but well-considered lesson on Ether's sermon about strengths and weaknesses. The thoughtful expression on Magdalena's face pleased Sandy.

When Brett finished, Sandy reluctantly took center stage. "All right, guys. We're going to teach you some yoga stuff, but the two things you're going to need are space and something to pass for a mat. I'll give you five minutes to figure yourselves out."

Several of the guys jumped up to rearrange furniture while the downstairs girls all hustled to find extra towels and blankets that could serve as mats. Soon a roomful of expectant faces turned to her, and Sandy waved toward her mom.

"This is Magdalena," she said. "She'll be teaching you. I'll demonstrate the poses, and then she'll check you to make sure you get them right."

Magdalena stepped up with one of her hazy smiles. "You're all so lovely," she said. "I know Sandy doesn't like it when I talk about chakras, but this room—"

"—is full of people waiting for a yoga lesson. Let's get to it, okay?" Sandy kept her voice neutral, but she was determined to curb any of Magdalena's wilder philosophies.

Magdalena began with a corpse pose, and seventeen people learned that it wasn't as simple to lie corpse-like as they might have assumed. She moved them into another pose and then some neck exercises, which Sandy demonstrated, easily sinking into each stretch. It offset the tension of her mother rambling about asanas and inner peace. She didn't stray far enough for Sandy to intervene, but Sandy kept a watchful eye on her, wary of the dreamy glaze that would cloud Magdalena's eyes if she was about to launch a New Age verbal crusade.

By the time they were helping with bow pose, Sandy unwound enough to realize that Magdalena was going to respect the boundaries for the evening. She moved from person to person, making adjustments and gently shushing some of the sniggering guys, but Sandy didn't hear a word about chakras, virile or otherwise.

After a half hour of good-natured groans and several choruses of "Is this how you do it? Is this right?" she signaled Magdalena to bring the session to a close. In less than a minute, the room cleared as their students went in search of brownie-fueled enlightenment.

Sandy surveyed the abandoned blankets and towels with a sense of relief. They had survived, and everyone had seemed to enjoy themselves, especially the guys, who had appreciated the view. She sighed. Boys will be boys.

"Thanks, Mom," she said.

Magdalena looked surprised.

"What? I know how to say thank you."

"You called me mom."

"Oh." Sandy decided not to think about it too much. "Let's get some brownies."

But as she led Magdalena toward the kitchen, she saw the slight smile on her mother's face and wondered if being a "mom" had somehow become important to her. Finally.

Chapter 18

EVEN THOUGH SANDY WOKE WITH her alarm Tuesday morning, she still found Magdalena already dressed in her yoga clothes and facing the dark window like she could sense some sunlight streaming through that no one else was privy to.

Sandy said nothing and went about her routine. Larry's bowl was already full, and the cat greeted her with indifference instead of malice, which meant that a good part of the food had already made it to the beast's belly. Sandy fished out a box of whole-grain cereal and settled into her chair to enjoy it. Or at least eat it. She figured she should probably learn the art of cooking an egg so breakfast was more exciting than cold cereal, but the remembered whiff of past burnt efforts had her chewing her cold flakes with a new appreciation. Eggs were hard to cook. Easy to break, easy to burn, but not so easy to make into something edible.

Magdalena joined her a few minutes later. "Protein is better for you," she said. "Maybe bean paste on bagels or organic peanut butter on whole wheat."

"This has a hundred percent," Sandy said, not looking up from her bowl as she chased a dehydrated strawberry around it with her spoon.

"A hundred percent what?"

Sandy shrugged. "I don't know. A hundred percent of stuff that only tastes okay and therefore must be good for me."

Magdalena shook her head. "Breakfast shouldn't be a punishment. I'm in charge of it tomorrow."

"I can't believe you learned to cook," Sandy said, finally dragging her eyes up.

"I told you, I didn't. But there's lots I can make that doesn't need cooking, and that's what you're getting tomorrow morning."

"Okay." She rose and took her bowl to the sink for a quick rinse before heading to her room to get ready.

"What am I doing today?" Magdalena asked.

"Whatever you want," Sandy said. "I've got cable, and the remote is pretty easy to figure out. I'll leave you a key in case you want to go for a walk or something."

Magdalena looked wounded. "Didn't I do a good job in the kids' center yesterday?"

"Yes."

"Then why can't I come help some more today?"

Sandy sighed. "Because the only cleaning left to do is in the computer center, and letting you near keyboards is about as smart as me trying to cook eggs."

"That's not fair."

"No? How many hard drives have you crashed because you've accidentally downloaded a virus that no one could clean off?"

"Three. Is that a lot?"

Sandy nearly snorted before she caught the gleam in Magdalena's eye. "Have you really destroyed three computers?"

"Yes," Magdalena admitted. "But I do realize those are bad odds."

"You're definitely not getting near the computers."

"There have to be other things I can do. Didn't you say something about some filing?"

In fact, she had, but Sandy didn't want to impose on Roberta's patience by bringing her mother to work two days in a row.

"Magdalena, today and tomorrow are especially bad days for me. I have meetings both nights, and I need to spend the next two days preparing for them. Please, find something here to do, and I promise I'll spend some time with you on Thursday."

"So you're going to be gone all day and night for *two* days?" Her mother's pitiful expression was designed to make Sandy feel guilty. It worked.

"I'm sorry," she said, the guilt making her tone irritated. "But I warned you about this when you called on Sunday."

"Was it so terrible having me at your office yesterday? I didn't get underfoot at all."

"And yet, I ended up stuck in a cabinet."

"I didn't make you go in there," her mother reminded her.

"No, but you did put the crystal in there that I had to fish out."

"I won't bring any crystals or anything else with me. I don't want to stay here all day."

The guilt won out. "Let me make a phone call."

Three minutes later, Sandy returned from her bedroom in defeat, Roberta having undermined her last remaining out. "Sure, have her come in," she'd said. "If you guarantee she won't be a distraction this time, we're not in a position to turn down free labor with all these budget cuts we're dealing with."

"All right, Magdalena. You can come in today but absolutely *not* tomorrow. And you have to do exactly what I tell you and not try any of your special improvements."

"I promise," Magdalena said with a happy flutter of her hands. "I'll go get dressed."

"Nothing too hippie!" she called as Magdalena disappeared into the bedroom to plunder her suitcase.

She sighed again and followed after her, ready to raid her own closet for something to offset whatever Earth Mother getup Magdalena produced. Her already long day was stretching longer, and the sun wasn't even up. *Please don't let this be an omen*, she begged silently. She'd be tapping her reserves to get through the day as it was.

* * *

By noon, it seemed someone had been listening to her plea. Her mother had spent a quiet morning reorganizing the file cabinets that lined the conference room, leaving Sandy free to prepare for her presentation. It was nearly done; every last piece of research she could find, statistic she could quote, and any emotional appeal she could make was neatly outlined and organized for maximum impact. There was still one last chance she wouldn't need any of it though. Not if her meeting tonight went as planned.

She found Magdalena in the conference room, surrounded by a few tidy piles of files.

"How's it going in here?" She noted that it looked as if Magdalena had things under control, and there were no signs of crystals or whiffs of strange incense.

"All is well, Sand Dollar." Her mother shuffled through a couple more files, and Sandy realized Magdalena had probably lost track of time.

"It's lunchtime," Sandy said. "I thought we'd go to a good Vietnamese place up the street and grab some pho."

"Mmm." Magdalena looked pleased with the suggestion. "I love pho. Where should I put these while we're gone?"

Sandy helped her move the files to the table, and then after checking to make sure Jasmine and Roberta didn't need anything, she headed to lunch with her mother.

Much like on the train, Magdalena was absorbed in people watching. She didn't keep with the flow of foot traffic, and Sandy had to grab her arm a few times to keep her from bumping into someone while she stared in distraction at someone else. Sandy breathed a sigh of relief when they made it to the restaurant safely. Magdalena regarded the building with a quizzical tilt to her head.

Correctly interpreting her expression, Sandy reassured her. "I know it looks like a total dive, but trust me; you'll be amazed at what they can do with tofu."

She sent Magdalena to secure them a small table in the corner then placed an order at the counter for her favorite variation of their noodle soup, rich with flavor and a kick of spice. Pho was new to her but fast becoming one of her favorites.

She rejoined her mother, and they sat in silence. Sandy twirled a soy sauce bottle and then progressed to fiddling with the sugar packets near their napkin dispenser.

Magdalena stayed still, her eyes slightly glazed.

"Um, are you in there?" Sandy asked.

She got a faint nod. Okay . . .

"So it looks like the filing is going well." Was it this hard for other people to make conversation with their own mother?

Magdalena smiled, and her eyes focused again. "Don't feel like you have to think of things for us to talk about," she said. "You told me it would be a rough couple of days, and I promised to stay out of your way. I told you I could practice spirit stillness, so I am." She returned to her zoned-out expression.

"What is spirit still—never mind," Sandy interrupted herself. Satisfying her curiosity was not worth the price tag of the long ramble her question would likely send Magdalena on. It was best to let her float in mental outer space.

Sandy found her own mind wandering to the River Oaks Concerned Citizens Group meeting later that night. She wavered between hope and anxiety that she would get through to them. Jake would be furious that she was crashing their monthly meeting, but he wasn't her boss. He had no say over who she could or couldn't talk to, she reasoned. She'd have to change tactics if he showed up tonight, but she was willing to gamble for the chance to plead her case.

The slim waitress bearing their steaming bowls of pho approached so quietly that Sandy jumped at the sound of her bowl meeting the table. The waitress smiled apologetically.

"You're tense," Magdalena said.

That might have been obvious to anyone else, but Sandy had to give her credit for noticing. Until this week, she hadn't seen much pierce Magdalena's perpetual fog.

"Yes," Sandy said. "I'll be fine after tomorrow."

"You should practice spirit stillness too," her mother said. "It quiets your inner voices so you have clarity."

An old TV mounted in the other corner suddenly blared, and Sandy saw a cook cringe and lower the volume on the game he had switched on.

"It's not so much my inner voices that are the problem right now." She tossed her head in the television's direction.

"Outside distractions hold no sway if your inner eye is focused," Magdalena intoned.

"And she's back," Sandy muttered.

"What, darling?"

"Nothing," Sandy said. "I don't want to rush you, but I need to get back to the office sooner than later. I have to get ready for tonight."

"What's tonight?"

Sandy suppressed the urge to shake her mother. "Remember how I've been telling you that I would be tied up tonight and tomorrow?"

"You won't feel tied up if your spirit is free," her mother said.

Swallowing soup to keep herself from choking out any snarky retorts, she gathered her patience. "I'll be at a meeting tonight. I'll show you how to order a movie on cable, and you'll be fine."

"Why can't I come with you?"

Sandy pictured her mother trailing after her in a caftan mumbling about auras while Sandy emphasized the ingrained professionalism of the New Horizons operations. Oy.

"I'm not even sure I should be there tonight, and one uninvited guest will be enough, I think." Any other mother would probably lecture her on not dropping in on people unannounced, but Magdalena, realizing she had no room to talk, held her peace. For once.

"All right," Magdalena said. "Do you have the nature channel? Sometimes I like to watch that if it isn't showing one of those ridiculous specials about pet tricks. Or animals eating each other. Those are terrible."

"Which is worse?" Sandy asked.

"The pet tricks," Magdalena answered without hesitation.

Sandy grinned, and her mother smiled back. "I'd rather watch a lion take down a wildebeest than a dog that can sing." Magdalena shuddered.

"Me too. We'll find something with lots of nature and no singing dogs."

"And you thought we had nothing in common."

Chapter 19

SANDY KEPT ONE EYE ON her GPS and the other eye on the row of buildings passing outside the car window to her right. Her nerves stretched tighter as another building slipped by without the right address. She felt anxiety over this meeting like she hadn't felt in a long time.

She wished she had a wingman. Or woman. This was the last meeting the River Oaks Concerned Citizens Group would hold before the zoning hearing the next night, and she had no idea how many people would attend in an effort to rally the troops. It seemed almost madness to walk into their territory.

She finally spotted the community center and pulled into the lot, the pit in her stomach throbbing. Cars jammed the parking lot, and the nearby basketball courts teemed with guys taking advantage of the nighttime lighting. She killed her engine and sat focusing on one of the basketballs and its rhythmic, soothing bounce. She took a deep breath, then another, until her heart rate felt normal.

Speaking in front of people rarely bothered her, but no one had asked her to be here. The crowd wouldn't exactly be predisposed toward hearing her message. And she dreaded running into Jake on his turf.

But she was right.

She believed in the annex enough to be here to fight for women who had almost given up on themselves before New Horizons came along. Fortifying herself with one last deep breath, she eyed the dashboard clock that told her she had three minutes to go and then headed into the lions' den.

The bored teenager at the information desk mumbled a room number when she asked about the meeting, and she followed a surprisingly quiet hallway until she reached the right door. Before she opened it, she plastered her most disarming smile on her face, ready to hit everyone she could find with a blast of Sandy Burke charm.

Whatever she had expected, it hadn't been the handful of people who all turned from their table to look when the door opened. Where were the angry hordes? The fired-up homeowners?

Where were the rest of them?

An aging gentleman smiled over his glasses at her. "Hello. Are you lost?"

"Maybe," she said. "I'm looking for the River Oaks group."

"That's us," he said, still smiling.

"Oh." Her plan to blend in and speak during the open-forum part of the program effectively disintegrated. Now what?

"Can we help you?" he asked.

"I'm sorry," she said, approaching the scratched table where they sat. "I expected a huge meeting."

One of the women tittered. "Just getting all of our committee members here tonight is an accomplishment."

A couple of other people smiled in acknowledgment.

"Why would you expect a big meeting?" the older gentleman said. "Come to think of it, why would you come looking for us at all? Have you recently purchased a home in the neighborhood? I don't recall seeing you before."

"Well, Mr. . . ."

"Stanich."

"Well, Mr. Stanich," she said, scrambling for the best way to explain her presence. "In a manner of speaking, I've recently purchased property in your neighborhood. Sort of."

Confused looks met her.

"How does one 'sort of' purchase something?" Mr. Stanich asked.

She took a deep breath. "I'm the incoming director at New Horizons, and I hoped to talk to you all tonight about the property we want to lease here." She figured that would set off a bomb in their tiny circle, but no one said anything. After an awkward pause, she held her hand out to the nearest circle member and introduced herself. "I'm Sandy Burke. Thanks for not throwing me out."

"You're welcome," the woman said. "I'm Nora Peasely." The other three women introduced themselves as well.

"Forgive me, but I'm not clear on why you thought it would help you to come here tonight," Nora said.

"I thought that a lot of people would be here to discuss the hearing tomorrow," Sandy explained. "I wanted to make a final effort to explain New Horizons and our goals to see if we could avoid a hearing altogether."

Mr. Stanich chuckled. "It's a nice thought, but I don't know that it would do you any good."

She had prepared for them to try to stonewall her, so she flashed a bright smile. "I realize your community has some serious reservations about this project, but—"

"It's not that, dear," Nora interrupted. "It's that we're not really a decision-making body. We get together once a month to compile a neighborhood newsletter, and that's about it."

Although she schooled her expression not to reflect her utter confusion over their passive attitude, something must have flickered across her face because Mr. Stanich chuckled again.

"Who you'll want to talk to is our attorney, Jake Manning," he said. "Nice fellow. He's the one who knows everything that's going on."

The whole situation struck her as very odd. Jake had led her to believe he was following the wishes of a group of irate homeowners who were practically ready to chain themselves to the front doors of the annex if it tried to open. Reality looked more like a few older people who worked on their newsletter as a hobby with no concern about the annex one way or the other. It didn't add up.

"Do you mind if I sit down?" she asked. A tiny woman who had introduced herself as Bertie waved her into a chair. Sandy set down her oversized bag full of handouts she would no longer need and thought about where to begin.

"Do you know what New Horizons is?" she asked.

Nora nodded. "It's kind of a halfway house where troubled women can go to get help."

"Not exactly," Sandy said, wondering what Jake *had* bothered to explain to these people. "We're a career training center for women who are trying to improve their families' lives."

"That sounds like what Jake told us," Mr. Stanich said. "It was that first bunch that told us about the halfway house."

Nora tittered again. "Oh, you're right, of course. There's been so much talk about this over the last month that I'm getting my facts mixed up."

Bertie gave her an understanding pat on the shoulder.

"What do you mean by 'first bunch,' Mr. Stanich?" Sandy asked.

"About a month or so ago, some young fellows came to the door to tell us about a zoning request your group filed. They said we should sign a petition to stop it from going through because it would have a negative impact on our neighborhood."

"They had lots of information about crime statistics and all kinds of things," Nora added. "It made me a bit dizzy, frankly."

"I'm confused," Sandy confessed. "Were these young men from the neighborhood?"

"I don't think so," Bertie said. "But they said they represented neighborhood interests, and they certainly seemed full of facts."

"Full of something," Sandy grumbled before she filtered.

Mr. Stanich barked out a little laugh. "You're saucy. I like that. Just like my Dorothy, bless her."

Sandy reined in her growing irritation at these mysterious young men and their "facts," not wanting to lose track of the real facts herself. "Did these men identify themselves with a particular group or state a specific agenda?"

"No group," Mr. Stanich said. "They just mentioned neighborhood interests and urged us to protect ourselves and our property investments by blocking the zoning request for the center."

"In what way did they suggest the center would threaten the neighborhood?"

"Well, they gave us all kinds of information about how many women drug abusers with criminal pasts become repeat offenders. It's a lot," Nora said sadly.

"How did they describe the center?" Sandy asked. "You said they mentioned a halfway house. Did anyone ever mention that it's not a halfway house at all?"

"That nice Jake said that it was for women who had been drug free for at least a year and hadn't had any criminal incidents during that time."

"Did he suggest that all of our clients are recovering drug addicts?" Sandy asked.

"No, he said some are not. But a lot are."

"A lot?" Sandy felt a twitch in her left eye and a viselike pressure squeezing her brain and her patience. "Two-thirds of our clients have no criminal record at all, and we have never had a crime committed on or near our center by any of our enrollees. Did he pass any of that along?"

Her vehemence provoked a few wary glances, and she reminded herself that these nice people were not her enemies. It looked more and more as if their decisions had been based on bad information, and the real culprit was whoever had put it out there. Sandy wondered how involved Jake was with that shadowy group and their "neighborhood interests."

"I'm sorry if I seem upset," Sandy said. "But I've been trying to get your organization some accurate information about who we are and what we do for over a month now. I was under the impression that you were all extremely opposed to New Horizons. Would you be willing to tell me if there's ever been a community-wide meeting addressing the presence of the center?"

"Sure was," Mr. Stanich said. "It was the young guys that put it on. I think the one that did most of the talking was named Mike, and I forget the other one's name. They told us all about how that strip mall was prime real estate and moving the center in would put criminal interests close to our homes and drive down our property values."

The vise in Sandy's head tightened, but she said nothing and waited for him to continue.

"You seem like a nice gal, but I must tell you, I've been here in this neighborhood for fifty years and I've seen it go from good to bad to worse and slowly creep back toward good again. I like the good stage, and after that whole mess with CHEP, I don't know if I'm comfortable having a liberal group like yours in here."

Sandy nodded. "If we were liberal or anything like CHEP, I'd understand. We're actually quite conservative. We do represent neighborhood activism but nothing like what CHEP did." She went on to explain that New Horizons developed different ties in the communities it served but that they weren't political. "In fact," she concluded, "we have nothing to do with housing or voter registration or anything even close. The majority of our connections are with major corporations who line up to hire our graduates because of their maturity and stability." She surveyed the small group. "Does knowing that change your opinions at all?"

A couple of them looked uncomfortable. One woman who hadn't said anything the whole time looked downright uninterested.

But Nora nodded. "I wish we would have heard all of this at that meeting with those men. They gave us so much scary information that I was just relieved when they introduced Jake to us so we could get some help."

"Wait," Sandy said slowly. "Jake came with these guys? Your board didn't go out and hire him on your own?"

"Oh, no," Bertie said. "Our homeowner's association fees could never afford someone so expensive. We use the money strictly to pour back into the neighborhood for things like maintaining landscaping in common areas or paying for the newsletter and such. That's why we were so relieved when he offered to represent us free of charge."

Fascinating, Sandy thought. *Something very, very rotten is stinking up the east side of the District tonight.*

She gathered up her bag and pushed back from the table. "Thank you for letting me sit and talk to you. I realize you challenged the annex based on incomplete information. Given what you had, I understand your choice. I wish I could talk to each person in your neighborhood to give you all the whole picture, but there's no way to do that before tomorrow night."

She stared Mr. Stanich straight in the eyes. "I believe with all my heart that what we do for women and their families through New Horizons is a good and right thing. I hope you go to the zoning meeting tomorrow night and invite all of your other neighbors to come too so you have a chance to hear what we're really about. It will help you feel good about us being a part of your community. Thank you for all the information you shared with me." She left each of them with another handshake and bright smile.

As soon as she crossed the exit, the smile disappeared. The River Oaks Concerned Citizens Group had very little to do with this challenge to their zoning permit. Now she knew the long, elegant fingers of El Diablo had stirred the pot.

She spent the drive home processing that particular bombshell. She was angry enough when she'd thought he was representing the group at their request and on their dime. That he had been less than up-front about his role infuriated her, but worse, she couldn't put together the new pieces the board members had handed her well enough to figure out which part of the puzzle she was still missing. Something definitely wasn't right.

She climbed the back stairs to her apartment while fighting a splitting headache, desperate to avoid the raucous good time pouring out of the downstairs windows. All she wanted was a mug of hot cocoa to wash down an aspirin and an extra hour of sleep tonight.

The second she opened her front door, more laughter drifted out, this time from Magdalena in that high, silvery tone she used that told Sandy whoever had provoked the laugh was of the male persuasion. She stepped inside, hung her coat up, and prepared her game face.

Once again, as if summoned, Jake sat there. Why would he not go away even after he said he would go away? Then again, why should it surprise her that he wasn't good at keeping his word? Hadn't this whole evening proven to her that what he said and what he did were two different things?

She refrained from stomping over, but when she parked herself in front of him, she planted her hands on her hips and gave him a hard stare.

"Good evening, Sandy. How was your meeting?" her mother asked.

"It was downright enlightening."

"Glad to hear you had a good night," Jake said lightly.

"I didn't say it was a good night. But it was eye opening." She stood over him a bit longer until he shifted uneasily, and then she took her seat in the nearby armchair.

"I went to the monthly meeting for the River Oaks Concerned Citizens Group," she said.

Jake stared at her. "You did what?"

"You heard me."

Magdalena, oblivious to the sudden tension that had frozen Jake, smiled again. "Do you know them too?"

"Oh, he knows them. As a matter of fact, he pulls their strings like a twisted puppet master." Sandy eased one of her stilettos off of her heel and let it dangle from her toe, where she bounced it nonchalantly as if she weren't seething.

"I don't know what you're talking about."

"Sure you do. I always pegged you as smart. Arrogant, but smart. I didn't realize it was of the evil-genius variety."

"Sandy!" Magdalena's shock was clear. "Why would you say something like that?"

"Ask Jake. He knows."

"No, I don't." Sandy could hear the edge in his voice. "I wasn't there."

"No, you weren't. Interesting choice on the night before the hearing where they're desperate for your representation."

He flushed. "You don't know the specifics of this case."

"I'm starting to figure them out. Three hours ago I would have said you made me mad. Now you make me sick."

"What is going on here?" Magdalena asked, sounding bewildered. "I thought after he helped you get untangled the other day that you guys were getting along. Why are you so angry?"

"Because Jake Manning is a liar. I *hate* being lied to," Sandy spat out.

He flinched as if she had reached over and slapped him. "I haven't lied to you about one single thing."

"How about who your real clients are? Did you tell the truth about that?"

His face hardened. "I represent the neighbors in River—"

"Oh, stop it. You do not. Who is paying your incredibly high rate for the hours you've put in? A bunch of nice middle-class people who have only the information you choose to give them?" She gave her head a hard shake. "No. Who is it?"

"My clients are the River Oaks group." His voice held no emotion.

"On paper they are. But they're not signing any checks for you, and I'm going to find out who is. I should have known," she said, sliding her shoe back on and standing. "It never made sense that a junior partner at a major firm like yours would fly all over the country hand-holding on major cases and then wind up representing an HOA in a piddly zone hearing. I should have asked more questions."

She stalked past them on the way to her room. "I walked in with a headache, and now I feel sick to my stomach. Maybe you guys should take your tea party downstairs, Magdalena. I'm so done."

She had barely kicked off her second shoe when her bedroom door flew open. She whirled to find Jake standing there looking furious.

"Get out!"

He laughed without any warmth. "No. You called me evil and a liar and then stormed out like a bratty teenager. It's your turn to listen, and then I'll leave."

She crossed her arms but said nothing. Maybe it would make him leave faster if he said his piece.

"Whatever you guess or think you know, I guarantee you it's not right. I can't believe instead of asking me about any of this, you start throwing around accusations like that. Every time I've tried to talk to you about *anything*, even this, you've shut me down. I figured I had a certain penance to do for being such an idiot in Seattle, but that's done. I don't owe you any more apologies, and now that you're flat-out calling me a liar, I don't owe you an explanation about River Oaks."

"This has nothing to do with them."

"What exactly do you think you know?" he demanded. "Stop with the vague hints, and say it."

"I know that this isn't about some random historical preservation garbage. I know that someone hired a couple of shady guys to go in and scare people with a bunch of misinformation to manipulate them into hiring you. How am I doing so far?"

He didn't answer.

"That's what I thought," she said, exhaustion washing over her. "Why don't you tell me who's signing the check for all this?"

"I can't disclose that," he said. "But you're wrong about one thing. My number-one priority is representing River Oaks."

"On someone else's dime." She rubbed her temples. "I'll figure it out, Jake. Not before tomorrow night, but I'll figure out who is so bent on sinking us and why. I promise you that when I do, I'll expose them *and* you and the way you've stood in the way of real and positive change."

He narrowed his eyes and prowled toward her slowly. She could see him working hard to control his temper in the tight clench of his jaw. When he stood less than a foot away from her, she straightened, feeling at a distinct disadvantage now that her shoes were off and she had to face him flat-footed. He loomed over her. It made her mad. How dare he charge into her room uninvited and *loom*? Refusing to give an inch, she glared up at him. "I told you to get out."

"And I told you that I don't owe you anything now that you've decided to rip my integrity to shreds, least of all the courtesy of doing a single thing you ask." He leaned forward to bring his face within inches of hers. "Does it upset you to have me in your personal space?"

She didn't flinch. "Right now, you upset me, period."

A muscle in his jaw twitched, and then a glint in his eye distracted her. "Do I?" he asked. "I think it's you who's telling a lie right now, even if it's to yourself."

Before she could challenge him, before a warning could even shoot from her brain to the rest of her body to instruct it to step back to safety, he closed the slight gap between them and . . .

And he kissed her.

In the full three seconds it took for her to process what was happening, her eyes had closed and her head tilted oh so slightly. The tiny part of her brain still capable of reason blared an alarm. She stiffened and tried to pull away. Jake buried his hand in her hair and cupped her neck, managing to hold her in place with the barest of pressure, never breaking the kiss.

The kiss.

Holy cow.

Given how angry he was when he stole it, he was surprisingly gentle. The curls captive under his hand tickled her and sent a shiver down her back. She really needed him to not touch her hair. Ever. It had a bad effect on her. Even with that small part of her brain telling her to escape, a languid paralysis kept her still, unable and maybe even unwilling to move.

And then he broke away and stepped back, his face dark. "Don't talk to me about honesty when you can't even be real with yourself about this thing between us." He took another step back and shoved a hand through his hair, the same hand that had held her still with only a whisper of effort. "You said before that you trust your instincts. Since it's those instincts that made you kiss me back, maybe you need to ask yourself if there's something you're missing in this whole conspiracy theory you're spinning. Maybe your instincts know something you don't."

She found her voice and kept it as level as possible. "This is where I'd make some kind of grand exit, but this is my house, so I can't leave. That means you have to. Let me repeat: get out." She didn't let her tone color the command in case it revealed how much havoc he had managed to wreak inside of a minute.

He spared her one last searching glance before turning on his heel and striding out. A long breath escaped her, one she hadn't realized she'd been holding until she had room to breathe again.

"Good night, Magdalena," she heard him say to her mother in the living room. "Sorry I can't stay to visit."

Sandy closed her door on Magdalena's reply and fished out a pair of favorite pajamas. A few minutes later, a soft knock sounded, and her mother peeked in. By then, Sandy had moved to her bed, where she whipped a brush through her hair as hard as she could without ripping any out.

Magdalena said nothing but made her way to the dresser, where she set three candles. She set three more on the nightstand near the bed's headrest. Sandy kept silent until Magdalena produced matches and lit the cream-colored pillars. "This better not have anything to do with my inner child."

"Aromatherapy," Magdalena said. "Lemon scent. I made these myself with essential oils, so they'll really work. Do you remember what lemon does?"

Sandy scanned her memory banks. Their house had always been full of scents when she was growing up, and Magdalena was convinced that each one had a measurable effect on mood or illness. "Can I just guess that it's an aphrodisiac?" Sandy asked. "That's what most of the essential oils do, right?"

"Only a few, darling. But I would think that's the last thing you'd need in here."

Sandy glanced at her sharply, wondering how much her mother had inferred from the argument she'd heard spill into the living room. Magdalena smiled. "Isn't it part of your religion to deny all of your normal physical impulses? I'm certainly not going to go waving ylang-ylang about and causing problems."

Deciding that she didn't have the energy to argue with another of her mother's misconceptions about Mormons, much less one on the scale of chastity, Sandy said nothing and flopped back on her bed to stare at the ceiling. She could already detect the faint citrus scent wafting from the bedside candles.

"Lemon helps with stress. I know you don't like the smell of lavender, so I brought lemon because of its soothing properties. Some experts suggest that lemon has a more calming effect than lavender anyway."

"Hm. I think the smell of fresh-baked chocolate chip cookies is downright curative," Sandy mused. "Too bad we don't have any of that."

Magdalena tensed. "I'm sorry I wasn't a more conventional mother," she said, her voice tight. "I suppose it's my fault you have psychic wounds, because I didn't master the art of baking when you were a child."

Sandy grabbed her mother's wrist and held her in place when she tried to move. "It wasn't a criticism, Mom. I wasn't even thinking about that when I said it. Thanks for bringing the candles." She let go and propped herself up on her elbows, gesturing toward the dresser. "That's domestic in its own way."

Magdalena looked mollified. "If you like the candles, you should see what happens when you add the right music. I have the loveliest Andean pipes CD. I'll get it and—"

Sandy caught her once more before she could hop up. "One thing at a time. I'm sure the candles will do the trick. Don't worry about the music."

Magdalena sat back down, and Sandy closed her eyes. Her mother's unnatural stillness got to her. She cracked an eye open to see what she was doing and yelped when she found her mother staring right back.

"Magdalena, you don't have to sit there. I'll be fine. Why don't you go find something to do besides watch me be exhausted? There has to be something better on cable."

Magdalena sniffed. "There's some ridiculous marathon of shows on about some man who thinks he can talk to dogs. Where do people get these ridiculous ideas?"

"Yeah," Sandy murmured, her tone heavy with irony. "Ridiculous. It's crazy what some people believe."

She let the silence settle between them, gradually lulled by Magdalena's deep, even breaths into a lemon-scented state of relaxation.

"Are you going to be okay tomorrow?" Magdalena asked quietly enough not to startle her.

She studied the back of her eyelids to see if the answer was written there. "Yes."

"Do you want to talk about it?"

She sighed. "I haven't talked about anything else for weeks. I need to go to sleep and get tomorrow over with."

Magdalena stood and headed for the door with a soft swish of her skirt. "Everything you need is in you, Sand Dollar. It will all work out as it should."

She closed the door behind her, and Sandy tried not to think too hard about why she heard wind chimes sounding from the living room a few minutes later. She tried not to think about how everything could go wrong at the hearing tomorrow night. And most of all, she tried hard not to think about why she could still feel the imprint of Jake's lips on hers.

Chapter 20

SANDY HEADED FOR THE OFFICE the next morning with a change of clothes slung over her shoulder, while Magdalena called out good wishes from her upside-down plow-pose position. Sandy appreciated that her mother hadn't attempted to tag along again today. The idea of walking out of her front door with tentative but positive energy between them felt pretty good. No need to risk an argument by hanging out together.

She caught the train that got her to work twenty minutes earlier than everyone else, stowed her suit for the hearing in the computer lab closet, and settled in to review the game plan for the day. She closed her eyes and ran through everything twice in her head, imagining how each piece would unfold.

She glanced up when the bell chimed to announce Jasmine's arrival. Her coworker smiled. "Girl, I don't know whether you were praying or you finally buckled to your mom's New Age visualization craziness, but I hope you picked whichever one is going to help us the most tonight."

"Tonight?" Sandy's tone was confused. "Is there something going on tonight?"

Jasmine laughed. Sandy returned to her files, carefully rereading every copy of the early correspondence with Jake about the zoning permit that she could find. She knew her presentation for the hearing inside and out; the best thing she could do now was see if she could ferret out who was funding River Oaks in this legal battle.

The few minutes she spent skimming through the old e-mails before Roberta's arrival were enough to tell her that the answer wasn't there. Her soft growl stopped her boss midstride, and Roberta changed course from her office to Sandy's desk.

"What's going on?" she asked. "Are you ready for tonight?"

"Yes, in every way I can be."

"But . . . ?"

"Can I see you in your office?" She glanced over at Jasmine. "Sorry to be so secretive. I promise I'm not gossiping about you, and if I hear any good gossip from Roberta, I'll report it to you immediately before I tell Geneva."

Jasmine waved her off, and she followed Roberta down the hallway. While her boss stowed her briefcase and settled into her chair, Sandy studied the walls. Awards of merit and pictures of Roberta with various bigwigs, primarily the political kind, hung on every surface. True to Roberta's efficient get-it-done nature, the pictures showed her shaking hands with hotshots from both sides of the Congressional aisle. Roberta played politics because she had to, but she was in no way partisan. It was one of the things Sandy respected most about her. Roberta sat back and waited for Sandy to speak.

"I went to a River Oaks group meeting last night," she began.

Roberta's eyebrows rose. "How did you manage that?"

"Jasmine found a meeting agenda posted for them on the Internet. I decided to drop in for a visit."

A small smile crossed Roberta's face. "That's the reason I hounded you to take this job, you know. You're an out-of-the-box thinker."

Sandy shook her head. "Thanks, but right now, I feel completely boxed in. I stumbled over some information, and I can't make sense of it. I'm not even sure where to tug to unravel it."

"Let's hear it."

She talked about the mysterious men who had riled up the neighborhood and her suspicion of The Man (or Evil Corporate Interest) Behind the Curtain. Roberta's expression grew serious as Sandy outlined the situation. By the time she had finished, all the Botox in the world couldn't have smoothed her boss's distressed brow.

"I can't believe this," Roberta said.

"It's all true."

"No, I mean I can't believe that I didn't sniff this out before now. I have a finely tuned radar for institutional misconduct after years of dealing with the most expert smoke-blowers on the planet." She inclined her head toward the photos of politicians.

"I don't have any idea who's behind this, but I'm guessing it has to be some big developer," Sandy said, relieved that Roberta didn't think she was crazy. "It's the only thing that makes sense. The River Oaks group is sincere in their concerns, but they've been used and don't even know it."

Roberta nodded. "I think you're right."

"What do we do?" Sandy asked. "I'd love to walk into that hearing tonight and expose whoever is bankrolling this zoning fight." She slumped against the chair, discouraged. "I just didn't find out about this soon enough."

"Maybe, maybe not," Roberta answered, totally unruffled. "I know where you can start looking."

Sandy straightened. "Tell me. I'm so ready to take Jake Manning down."

"Jake Manning?" Roberta asked. "Isn't he just the face of the problem?"

"That's what I meant," she answered, managing not to squirm. "He's a symbol of corporate arrogance, upper-class entitlement, bossiness—"

Roberta's laugh interrupted her. "Bossiness? Sounds to me like things have gotten personal." Her smiled faded, and she studied Sandy closely. "Are you going to be able handle this?"

"Yes." She wouldn't embarrass herself by revealing how far beneath her skin Jake had gotten, and she said nothing else.

"Okay." Roberta gave a single, sharp nod. She liked that Roberta trusted her enough professionally to accept her answer without grilling her any more. "Find out if there were any prior eminent domain claims for that property. Maybe whoever is behind this tried that route before they took this one. It could be your smoking gun."

"And I thought you had nothing left to teach me," Sandy teased.

"Stick around, young lady. You'd be surprised at what's in my brain for downloading."

She believed it. She'd developed a great deal of respect for Roberta and her ability to navigate the intricate capital politics that snared so many less-capable people in pitfalls and moral compromises. "Thanks," she said before heading out to spend quality time with Google. "I won't let you down."

"I know," Roberta said. "Go rattle some cages."

She returned to her desk, fired up and ready to find the culprit behind the River Oaks mess, but an hour later, her keystrokes and mouse clicking were subdued.

"It's not here," she told Jasmine. "I thought I'd find it, an eminent domain claim with a flashing red arrow pointing to the name of some company I could call and threaten with a PR nightmare. But there's nothing."

"Why don't I randomly choose a company from the phone book, and you can call and threaten them until you feel better?"

"That might cheer me up," Sandy said. "Except that I don't hate corporate America generally. I'm really, really ticked at the company behind this situation specifically."

"So now you need a plan B." Jasmine sat back and folded her arms expectantly. "What is it?"

Sandy rolled her eyes. "I don't know. Let me check my purse and see if I can find my copy of *The Master Plan of What to Do When Everything Starts Falling Apart*." She pretended to unfold and study an imaginary piece of paper. "Number One, beat up Jake Manning."

"If only," Jasmine said. "But I'll help you if you ever need me. Maybe I can hold him, and you can punch him."

Sandy grinned at her. "I changed my mind. I'm not okay with you moving. I demand that you stay here."

"Right. I have you, the yogurt yogi, on one side and my Puerto Rican mother who will kill me if I don't move her grandbabies closer on the other. Whatever will I do?"

"Um, move to Brooklyn and live to fight another day?"

"You must know some Puerto Rican mamas."

"Yeah," Sandy smiled. "You."

"Me times ten equals my mom, so I'm going to move back rather than reckon with a force of nature."

"Fair enough. But now we've wasted ten minutes on solutions for finding Evil Shadow Corp, and I don't think any of them will work." Sandy rubbed her right temple, trying to diffuse the tension gathering behind it.

"Evil Shadow Corp?"

"Doesn't that sound like the kind of company that would hire El Diablo to represent them?" She sat bolt upright. "Maybe that's it! Maybe I can get a copy of the client list for Booker, Hughes, Pennington, and Washe and narrow it down to who would most likely have an interest in that property."

Jasmine shook her head before Sandy even finished. "They're not required to disclose who their clients are."

"Okay, but let's think about this. If this is a development company big enough to keep Jake's firm on retainer, and if this is a sample of their business tactics, I'm sure they've been in hot water before."

Jasmine nodded. "Maybe we need to search the Internet more creatively."

Sandy grinned. She and Jasmine each turned to their computers and dug, sharing search terms to avoid duplication. Within fifteen minutes, Sandy whooped. "I don't believe it!"

"What did you find?" Jasmine practically fell over her desk trying to lean close enough to see Sandy's screen.

"I should have known," Sandy said. "It all goes back to last year in Seattle." She tilted her screen to show Jasmine an archived report from the *Seattle*

Times. "This is an article—a teeny, tiny little article—that mentions how Ranger Properties won a lawsuit against a consumer rights group that wasn't happy with one of their developments in Bellevue, Washington. This is dated the same week I met Jake in Seattle. The week he was there celebrating wrapping up a big case with his workmates."

"Okay, it's a start, but we can't be sure that it was Jake's firm representing Ranger Whatchamacallit."

"That's what I thought until the last sentences. Allow me to read them to you." Standing and assuming her best imitation of a lawyerly courtroom posture, she drawled, "'My clients are pleased with this outcome and look forward to renewing their relationship with the owners in the Remington Estates community. Although the evidence clearly showed that Ranger Properties was in no way at fault for their difficulties, the company will be reaching out to help homeowners find solutions.' Guess who they were quoting."

Jasmine hooted. "Jake Manning."

"Ding, ding, ding. We have a winner! That's why you get to go be the big boss in Harlem." She hit "print" and then whipped the article off the printer so she could show Roberta. "I'm going to go figure out what we should do now to put Jake and his evil shadow corporation on the ropes."

"I'll fish around and see what else I can find about this Ranger company," Jasmine said. "I bet we find an interesting and not-at-all-flattering trail leading from their door straight to the River Oaks Landing misinformation campaign."

Two minutes later, Roberta finished scanning the article with a sardonic smile. "Ah, cynicism. I wouldn't cling to it if I weren't right so often about this kind of thing."

"You're not cynical," Sandy contradicted her. "You have way more faith in corporations and congressmen than I do. A cynic wouldn't have been able to channel so much funding to this organization without a core belief that people do the right thing."

"Shh. You're exposing my gooey caramel center. I keep that under wraps."

"What next, boss lady?"

"Dig for more information on Ranger Properties."

"Jasmine's already working on it. I'll go help." She headed toward the door.

"Keep something in mind, Sandy." She turned to hear Roberta out. "You won't find everything you need by the hearing, but if the zoning commission decides to revoke our permit, there may be another way to win this battle.

Very few rulings handed down are more final than the ones delivered by the court of public opinion. However, we don't have forever to get this resolved. We're going to lose the grant if we don't have the center open by the fall. Fight hard."

"I will."

"Do. But don't do anything too awful to Jake Manning."

Sandy laughed and headed back to join the search for dirt on Ranger Properties. Despite Roberta's caution not to expect too much in the next few hours, she was determined to walk into the zoning hearing fully armed and ready to battle. She'd been frustrated with Jake before for not seeing the importance of the New Horizons annex. At least she had believed he'd had good intentions toward his clients' well-being. Now? She smothered a disappointment in him that verged on aching. She didn't know what Ranger Properties was up to in the long run, but all signs pointed toward no good, and she hated that Jake's hand was the one keeping their whole scheme on course.

Chapter 21

SANDY STOOD OUTSIDE THE BUILDING on Fourth Street and drew a deep breath. She was a half hour early. Nothing short of a tranquilizer dart would calm her now, but she did her best to bring her racing nerves under control. A couple dozen supporters stood on the sidewalk and carried hand-lettered signs with slogans like "New Horizons gave me a chance—Give them one!" and "I deserved a new lease on life and the annex does too!"

Jasmine had organized this part of the operation, and Sandy was impressed as she greeted everyone. They were all New Horizons graduates, and they stood, many with their children by their sides, looking cheerful but determined as they gripped their placards. All of them were dressed professionally, and Sandy knew their impact on the opposing side would be profound.

She made her way inside to the council chamber, glad to find it nearly empty. She dropped her tote bag on the front row to save herself a prime seat and slung her coat across the back of the chair.

She tugged her suit jacket into place. Her chocolate brown suit was the most expensive thing she'd ever owned, but the exquisite tailoring was utterly worth it. A strand of antique glass beads draped her neck, and spiked heels completed the look. She knew the outfit hit the right balance of professional but approachable because she had agonized over it the same way she had over every element of the evening ahead.

Humming with nervous energy, she busied herself leafing through her notes, anxious to make sure she had every detail committed to memory. Slowly, the tension receded. She had done her best, and *that* would secure a New Horizons victory.

The chamber door opened to admit a small group of people, no one she recognized. She glanced at her phone. Twenty minutes to go until the hearing started. No sooner had the door clicked shut than it whooshed open again, this time admitting a couple of welcome faces: Cindy, a middle-aged store cashier who was in their retraining program, their lab assistant Geneva, and a couple of other clients she knew well.

Sandy greeted them, glad to see them, but she was still attuned to the entrance, bracing for Jake's arrival. She didn't have long to wait. With little more than ten minutes to spare, he strode in wearing one of his Hugo Boss suits and carrying an expensive attaché case. He led the River Oaks contingent to some seats across the aisle from her, settled them in, then headed for her.

One part of her brain, the small part that was fair to a fault, whispered that she couldn't criticize his expensive suit or perfectly coiffed hair, considering the time and money she'd spent on the same things for herself. But she overrode that fair part by reminding herself that this was Jake Manning, a guy who represented a morally bankrupt development company while pretending to embrace high standards and integrity.

She knew better than to put any stock in his warm smile. No one smiled like that and meant it only days after storming out of a fight. His seemed tainted with a practiced charm, and his confidence read more like arrogance. She frowned, and his smile slipped, concern clouding his eyes.

"Sandy?"

"Jake."

"The protestors are a nice touch."

She didn't answer. An awkward silence ticked by while he waited for a response. She shrugged.

"Besides the obvious, is there a problem?" he asked, his tone neutral.

"By obvious, do you mean the fact that we wouldn't even be here if it weren't for you and your . . . *clients*?" she returned in the same bland tone.

His brow furrowed. She could tell he couldn't read her, and that pleased her since a trial attorney should be an expert at doing just that. "I'm sorry it's coming to this," he said, and he did sound sorry.

"Why? I would think this is exactly what you want. This whole evening is about slowing us down."

"Us," he repeated. "You keep taking this personally."

"As opposed to you, who are here to rack up more billable hours versus really giving a rip about your clients?"

His jaw tightened, and she waited for him to unload. He didn't. His tone grew cooler than she'd ever heard it, lacking any emotion at all. "It must be nice to be so right," he said. "I'm sorry you have a problem with me earning the money I deserve for the job I do."

"I couldn't care less about what you earn. I just think it's lame when you act like it matters what happens to River Oaks with your little speech about protecting their families and their hard-earned investments."

His lips thinned, and his grip on his briefcase tightened so that his knuckles grew white.

She smiled. Good. First blood. Jake Manning may have spent years showboating to gullible jurors and railroading other lawyers, but she refused to be intimidated. She would stand up to anyone—big-shot cocky lawyer or an angry neighborhood mob—for the little guys. Or in this case, for a bunch of underrepresented women.

A cough at her elbow startled her, and she turned to find Bertie from the meeting standing there looking uneasy.

"Hi, Bertie," she said, hoping her smile didn't show any strain.

"Hello," Bertie said. "Jake, can I talk to Sandy?" It sounded almost like she thought she needed his permission. Jake must have sensed that too because he looked at the dainty woman in surprise and nodded.

"Of course," he said. "I'm going to go say hello to the rest of the group."

Bertie drew Sandy off a bit, far from Jake's earshot. Her tight grip signaled her distress, and Sandy placed her own hand on top of Bertie's wrinkled one to comfort her.

"What's wrong, Bertie?" she asked, her voice low.

"I couldn't sleep last night," Bertie answered with a quaver. "I kept thinking about how you said those young men came to our neighborhood and gave us false information. It bothered me."

"I'm so sorry," Sandy said. "I didn't want anyone to lose sleep over this."

Bertie shot her a sharp glance. "Haven't you?"

After a pause, Sandy gave a slight nod.

Bertie tugged her down into a chair and leaned even closer. "I Googled your center," she said. "I thought if I did a bit of research, I'd find it was like that awful CHEP outfit that came in and tricked us."

Sandy smiled, both at the image of this wizened woman navigating the Internet like a pro and the certainty that a Google search would only work in New Horizons' favor. "And what do you think now?"

Bertie squeezed her arm again. "Your program isn't like that at all," she said. "I feel terrible."

"What do you mean?"

"I'm worried now that Jake will win this hearing tonight," she said. "He's been very effective at convincing us that it's a bad idea, and the early information people received riled them badly." She sighed. "The more I read last night, the more sure I was that your annex is necessary, and I don't see it hurting our neighborhood at all. It's wrong to stand in the way of a good program like that. I'm disappointed in myself for not doing my own research earlier."

Sandy patted Bertie's hand. She too wished that more of the River Oaks neighbors had checked into the facts, but there wasn't anything she could do about it now. Had she been with New Horizons during the site scouting, she would have made sure to reach out to the neighborhood first, to educate them about the annex and help them feel comfortable with this program as part of the community. To be fair, it had never been necessary to run a public relations campaign for a New Horizons expansion because they'd never run into resistance like this before.

With Jake playing earnest crusader on their behalf, Sandy could understand how so many of the homeowners had been sucked into a misguided cause. She bore them no grudge; she would divide it between Jake and Ranger Properties once she could prove a connection.

In the meantime, she had a remorseful senior citizen clinging to her arm as if Bertie could communicate all her regret through that grip. "Bertie, it's okay. If anything, I'm so grateful you took the time to dig around and look for the truth on your own. Please don't be too hard on yourself."

Bertie sighed again. "I wish there was something more I could do."

"There is. Look at these women," she said, indicating the demonstrators filing into the seats around them. "Your neighborhood should have every chance to benefit from their hard work. If Jake Manning wins this thing tonight, it will be your chance to start talking to your neighbors and telling them the truth about us. We still have a shot if we win over public opinion. Would you do that?"

Bertie nodded. "I can do that," she said, sounding resolved. "And I'm sitting on *your* side."

Sandy laughed. "I'd love that, but if you really want to help, you can go sit with your neighbors and start setting them straight. And if you want to, you could maybe boo every time Jake Manning stands up to talk."

She loved the twinkle in the little woman's eyes when she smiled back. "I'll take care of that young man. You leave him to me." She hopped up from her chair with remarkable spryness and headed to the other side of the chamber. She marched straight up to Mr. Stanich, and Sandy almost pitied the man. He was about to be bulldozed by a five-foot-tall elderly woman on a mission, and he had no idea it was coming.

If only she could catch Jake in a similar blindside tonight. New Horizons needed a win.

Chapter 22

·

THE DOOR BEHIND THE COMMISSIONERS' desk opened, and five men filed in. Sandy knew three of them were appointed by the mayor, and the remaining two slots were filled by the architect of the Capitol and the director of national parks. Those two worried her the most.

Jasmine slipped in as the chairman called the meeting to order. Sandy waved her into the seat next to her, and they rose for the Pledge of Allegiance. Her mind blanked halfway through, and the first pangs of panic licked at her gut. This was bad news for her carefully memorized presentation.

Fighting for calm, she found the words again in time to proclaim "and justice for all" extra loudly to help bolster her determination. That's what she was here for: justice for the overlooked. She could keep it together for them. She took her seat again, feeling better, but offered her thousandth silent prayer that she could pull this whole thing off.

The night's business began. The commission heard two appeals to allow for building new businesses. One they approved; the other they tabled for another four weeks pending construction details from the petitioner.

All of that information sat in Sandy's hand, but she wouldn't need it; the annex required no changes to the exterior of the property. The only reason they needed a permit in the first place was that the shopping center was zoned for commerce but they were a nonprofit educational organization. The commission had approved it months before. It had all been smooth sailing until Jake had filed his injunction.

Sandy knew that on paper his objection sounded reasonable. That's why she had worked so hard with Jasmine to put a face on the annex that reflected the women they were serving. Hearing real-life stories from the women who lived them was calculated to destigmatize these mothers' "criminal pasts," soften their listeners' hearts, and ultimately change their minds.

Failing that, Sandy had distilled weeks of research on crime statistics for all the New Horizons centers to prove it was a nonissue. A convenience store was more likely to invite crime in a neighborhood than one of New Horizons' centers would. They would win that argument.

But this historical landmark wildcard Jake held . . . that scared her.

Only one more ruling remained for the commission until her turn. She sat without hearing as two gentlemen wrangled over an air-rights issue. Every second of the next fifteen minutes felt like its own minute as time dragged. Finally, the chairman opened the River Oaks text amendment for discussion. Jake smiled, took his spot at the podium, and delivered a polished overview of the group's concerns.

He spoke with eloquence, which was no surprise. But he also spoke with passion, and that surprised Sandy a lot. She couldn't work up that kind of emotion unless it was something she really cared about, and she wondered what it said about him that he could fake it so easily. She cataloged each emphatic gesture, each time he gripped the edge of the lectern to make a point, each time he leaned forward, apparently swayed by his convictions. She tallied each of these things . . . and then she marked them against him, big black marks that cemented in her mind what a duplicitous rat he really was with his phony performance.

She watched his audience. The commissioners maintained the same neutral expressions they had through the prior appeals. When Jake had wound down his narrative of all the ways in which River Oaks stood to lose when the annex opened, he led into his next point, the one Sandy had dreaded.

"The District of Columbia has long been at the forefront in fighting to keep its historical identity intact," he began his final pitch. "A central location for some of the greatest moments of our nation's history, this city has a sacred responsibility to preserve its character and spirit against the eroding forces of unchecked development and the plague of urban decay."

She could see that he'd caused a ripple with a couple of the commissioners. The architect of the Capitol looked more alert. She fought not to fidget.

"Sometimes the past fades so slowly that it's gone before we realize what we've lost. The face of any modern city changes, and in the quest for progress, we don't always give priority to some of the quieter values that define a city's character."

Where was he going with this? She saw others' faces and hated to admit that she felt the same curiosity she saw mixed in with their puzzlement.

"River Oaks Landing, the development in question, was installed almost twenty-five years ago, and it's showing every sign of hard living during that time. It's rundown and outdated. The Landing itself replaced a mess of businesses that added no value to the community for decades before that. Liquor stores serving as graffiti magnets, derelict gas stations and rundown repair shops, dingy corner groceries . . . the list of tenants in that spot is long and undistinguished as far back as buildings have been there."

Confusion nagged at Sandy. This didn't substantiate historical landmark status. He seemed to be indicating that the Landing had always been an unremarkable piece of real estate, a finding supported by all of her research.

Jake paused and gave each commissioner a measured glance. "However, until the turn of the last century, that plot of land represented the heart of a vibrant community as a park designed and landscaped by none other than Robert Magnus under a commission from President Ulysses S. Grant. President Grant wanted the landscape architect to establish a space within the District boundaries to rival the grandeur of New York's Central Park. He envisioned Magnus's work heralding a renaissance in Washington DC, launching it as a major cultural center on par with New York and San Francisco."

Sandy sat, stunned. She'd spent all her time tracking down a history of the *buildings* that had occupied the square mile surrounding River Oaks Landing and had found nothing of historical significance. She was aware that a park had sat there for some time but had had no idea it was a Robert Magnus project. She knew his name well from her liberal arts studies as an undergrad. He was nearly as well known as Frederick Law Olmsted, the genius behind Central Park.

Furthermore, she had no idea it had been installed by presidential decree. If Jake's facts were correct, there was more trouble ahead for the annex. Big trouble.

The cadence of Jake's voice slowed, signaling the wind-up for his big finish. "For too long, we have prized the value of progress over heritage. There is a way for these things to coexist. Reclaiming River Oaks Landing and reinventing it to reflect the purpose it was first designed to serve is a rare and precious opportunity. The people of the District deserve to see their history reclaimed from the concrete and aluminum-siding eyesore it has become."

Sandy's own background in liberal arts studies had sprung from a need to connect with history and beauty since her mother had rarely stayed anywhere long enough for her to grow roots. It went against Sandy's nature to advocate for a mediocre strip mall if it was replacing something as rare as a Robert Magnus landscape park. And yet, the Landing was the only viable option for New Horizons in that part of the city. There was no way she could let her aesthetic ideals trump the needs of these women. She couldn't let the commission do that either.

She exchanged a glance with Jasmine as Jake fielded questions from the commissioners. She didn't need words to convey how damaging his speech had been. She could see in Jasmine's face that the other woman recognized the problem. The majority of the commission's questions stemmed from this historical landmark claim. She'd hoped that when she heard Jake's evidence, it would sound flimsy at best. Instead, it sounded credible. The emotional appeal he'd made for civic pride worried her even more. How was she supposed to debate that?

The commission questioned him for several more minutes, and as she listened and Jasmine feverishly took notes to research further, Sandy prayed. She prayed for clarity and the ability to find the words to make the annex a reality for the women who needed it so badly.

When the chairman finally excused Jake to be seated, he called for anyone else who wanted to address the issue. Sandy stood and walked to the podium with nothing in her hand. She left every note, statistic, handout, and brochure she had painstakingly compiled on the seat behind her. She opened her mouth and heard herself say, "I love the work of Robert Magnus."

It was true. She did. The rest of her argument took shape. "I studied him in college, and his philosophy of integrating the natural beauty of a landscape space with the needs of the community that surrounded it was pure genius. It's only fitting that he would have been commissioned to design something in the nation's capital. But in the excitement of this discovery, there are key things we must not lose sight of."

She took a deep breath and hoped her thoughts would stay coherent and sound that way to everyone else. "First, this park has been lost to history for a long time. We don't have a true sense of the original scope of the project or the role it played in the city's identity. To become a historical landmark, it has to meet certain criteria, and we don't have nearly enough information to know if it does. While it's an exciting prospect, we can't overlook other factors when deciding the future of that property."

Reaching far back into her memory banks, she mined for details she had learned in her junior year of college. "Choosing Magnus to design the park says a lot about what President Grant valued and gives us a clue about the right path to take here. It's true that River Oaks Landing is currently an undistinguished strip mall, but opening a New Horizons annex there is a far better fulfillment of President Grant's intentions than denying us a lease."

This caused a murmur, but with her back to the audience, she couldn't determine whether it was skepticism or curiosity. She continued, the words coming to her even faster.

"The whole point of Robert Magnus's work was to take a natural resource in the community and develop it to the point that it became self-sustaining while reflecting the community's values. It's a metaphor for what New Horizons does, only our natural resource is invaluable: it's people.

"The annex will take women who are separated from River Oaks by a few geographical blocks but also by a mountain of life experience. That mountain is made of disappointments, setbacks, and failures, but countless women are ready to stand at the foot of it and take the challenge of conquering it. The New Horizons annex is like a base camp, ready to equip them with tools and guides so that each of these women can reach a pinnacle of success they've never experienced before."

She turned to survey the women who had shown up that night to speak about the power of rising above their circumstances, and she drew courage from their faces. She took some time to explain the history and purpose of New Horizons and noticed with satisfaction the looks of interest and respect in the committee members' faces as she spoke. She drew a steadying breath and gave her last, best argument. "That doesn't come at the cost of this neighborhood's peace of mind. I have reams of evidence about what the statistics Mr. Manning quoted to you really mean. Rather than dump it all on you now, I think it's best that you hear from the statistics themselves about how getting a second chance has changed not only their lives but also their communities. That's what this is about, really. The annex *will* mean change but a change for the better."

She sat down and waved to a tall black woman named Gwen, who took her place at the stand. Jasmine slid an arm around Sandy's shoulder and hugged her. "No one could have done that better," she whispered.

Maybe not, but Sandy hoped it was enough. She settled back to listen to Gwen's compelling story of overcoming an incredibly hard life and becoming a paralegal with a salary that had freed her family from the welfare cycle. More compelling was how she now mentored young women at the local junior high school.

She tried to gauge the effect Gwen and the three women who followed her had on the crowd. The commission once again wore neutral faces. In the

River Oaks side of the audience, she noticed a few expressionless faces but also several interested ones. That heartened her, and she dared to steal a glance at Jake to see how he was reacting to all of this. She wasn't sure what she expected, but it wasn't the earnest attention he paid to each speaker. He leaned forward, his eyes never straying to study the commissioners, never darting around to see if he still had all the River Oaks people on his side. He just . . . listened.

When the last woman sat down, nervous but beaming, Sandy stood once more at the podium. "In conclusion, we respectfully ask the commission to consider the short report being handed to you now that addresses the specific concerns Mr. Manning has raised."

Jasmine passed a small stack of reports to the clerk, who handed one to each commissioner.

"Above all, we believe in the power of partnership and clear communication. With the commission's permission, we would like to provide any interested River Oaks residents with the same information."

The chairman nodded, and Jasmine distributed copies of the report to anyone who raised a hand. Sandy was relieved to see that nearly everyone took one.

After thanking them for their attention once more, she reclaimed her seat and waited for their decision. The chairman addressed the rest of the commission. "Is there any further discussion on this before we vote?"

"Yes, as a matter of fact," the architect for the Capitol said. His nameplate identified him as Dennis Beamons, but Sandy could think of him only as The Architect. "As intriguing as the possibility the complainants have raised is, we couldn't make a decision about this without a great deal of additional information. Mr. Gleason, wouldn't this fall under your purview?"

Mr. Gleason sat in the national parks director spot. He nodded. "Yes, my office will have to investigate further. Mr. Manning, we'll need any information you've discovered relating to this property. Please see that copies are sent over with the open of business tomorrow."

Jake stood. "Absolutely, sir. I'll have my secretary send you everything as soon as she gets in."

"Good," the chairman said. "We'll need to table a final decision until we meet in two weeks. All information regarding this matter must be in our possession at least a week prior to that for it to be considered in our decision. Ms. Burke, we would welcome any further information you want to submit regarding the annex."

"Thank you, Mr. Chairman," she said. "We'll make sure you get the facts."

The chairman adjourned the meeting and dismissed everyone. The commission members filed out, and then the hearing chamber stirred to life, the quiet whispers growing into full conversations as the people around her provided their own color commentary on what it all meant. Sandy skirted the angrier-sounding debates. Instead, she made her way to Gwen and the other women to thank them again for being brave enough to speak up.

Gwen hugged her. "Is this historical park thing a problem? It's been gone for years. Why does it matter?"

Sandy shrugged. "We'll find out how big the problem is in two weeks, I guess. But in the meantime, I'll be very busy figuring out everything I can about that park."

Gwen hugged her hard once more and then let her go. "I know you will, lady. That's why you're good for the center. Roberta's a smart woman to hire you."

Sandy smiled, but her heart dipped. She had given her best, but she didn't know if it was good enough. Maybe Roberta hadn't been so smart at all.

Jake approached her, not looking nearly as scared as he should. "That was quite a speech you gave," he said. She heard admiration in his tone.

"Same to you," she returned, minus the admiration.

"I'm surprised you were able to turn up that Robert Magnus information in your research," he said. "It took a team of paralegals a few weeks to unearth that."

"It didn't come up in my research. I studied him as part of my liberal arts bachelor's program."

His eyes widened. "Wait, you came up with your whole Magnus rebuttal on the fly?"

"Yes." Her tone was cool, maybe a few degrees warmer than arctic.

"Wow," he murmured so low that she instinctively leaned forward to hear him better. "You're full of surprises."

Refusing to get sucked into any of his cat-and-mouse garbage, she stepped around him. "I need to go thank some more people," she said.

"Sure. And I hope you don't mind me talking to any of these ladies here." He indicated the dozen or so women who had shown up to support New Horizons.

"Of course not," she said.

Several minutes passed as she met and visited with a number of the River Oaks homeowners, answering questions they had about the crime report or addressing concerns some of them expressed about leaving a strip mall standing on a historical site. She offered them all a standard answer: they shouldn't worry until the facts emerged.

As the crowd broke up and drifted toward their cars and homes, her anxiety escaped in one long breath. She grabbed her belongings and headed for the door. Jake reached for her, but she rerouted to avoid him and slipped past his outstretched hand. Pausing at the door, she looked at him over her shoulder and shook her head.

He mouthed something before turning to give Mr. Stanich his undivided attention. She wasn't positive, but it looked ominously like, "Tomorrow."

Because that was all she needed—more Jake.

Chapter 23

"I HEARD YOU WERE FANTASTIC last night," Roberta said when she walked into the center midmorning. She'd been tied up in a breakfast meeting with one of their corporate sponsors.

"That's an overstatement," Sandy said.

Roberta shook her head. "Just when I think I've got you trained, you prove you have more to learn. Take *every* compliment you're due, Sandy. Especially the sincere ones."

Sandy gave a slight smile. "All right, then. It's true: I was fantastic last night. I'm fantastic all the time."

Her boss laughed. "Lesson number two: don't take more than the compliment that's given. Although I'm sure you're right."

Grinning, Sandy stood and followed Roberta back to the office. "How did you hear about last night already?"

"Oh, I had a few e-mails waiting when I checked my Blackberry during the CEO's speech." Roberta shook her head. "He's a nice man, but trust me when I say he didn't make it to where he is because of his masterful oratory." Her exaggerated yawn emphasized her point.

Sandy slid a file over, and Roberta skimmed the two typed sheets inside. "Robert Magnus? Should I know who he is?" she asked.

Sandy shrugged. "Not unless you had about a million humanities classes. He was well known in his time, but very little landscaping endures compared to other forms of art."

"Poor man," Roberta tsked. "He was making topiary sculptures when he should have been carving statues. Shrubs don't really stand the test of time, do they?"

"No. But good or bad, enough of his designs have lasted to make him a credible threat to the annex." Sandy leaned back. "I'm going to spend as much time as I can trying to research Jake's claim. Jasmine will handle the admin stuff today and try to track down a connection between Ranger Properties and River Oaks between tasks."

"Can you guys handle everything between the two of you?"

"We have to," Sandy said, unwilling to admit how much their one-week deadline for the commission was going to tax them.

"Maybe not," Roberta said. "Tap the human resource side of your brain and see who we can pull in from the field to help on this for a few days."

"You want to pull someone in?" Sandy hadn't even considered it because they tried to leave as much of their field team to work in the community as they possibly could. It was one reason that she and Jasmine usually had the front office to themselves.

"I'm open to the idea. Better yet, what do you think of Karina Mills?"

Karina was nearing the end of her executive assistant course and was performing well. Her quiet demeanor made her hard to get to know, but she did exceptional work, and Sandy liked her. "She's a good student. What do you have in mind?"

"Let's have her finish out her coursework in an internship for us. I have every intention of hiring an assistant for you, but I don't have the budget for it until Jasmine transfers. You have final say over who you want working under you, but I think you should give Karina a shot for a few weeks. At the very least, she can take some of the busywork off your hands while you chase down all this information for the zoning board."

"That sounds like a great idea. I'll call her now."

Karina was thrilled with the opportunity and promised to be there within a couple of hours. For the rest of the morning, Sandy jumped and then mocked herself every time the phone rang or the front door chimed. When Jasmine stared at her strangely after she flinched when the door opened to admit Geneva, Sandy offered a weak smile. "I'm keeping an eye out for Karina," she said. But in truth, she was waiting for Jake to make good on his threat of "tomorrow."

Despite her nerves, she managed to do a little more research into the Magnus park. Emphasis on *little*. Google was surprisingly quiet on the subject. After an hour of fruitless clicking, she pushed her chair back with a sigh. "I can't believe I'm about to do this," she announced.

"Do what?" Jasmine asked.

"I'm going to the library."

"Library? Never heard of it."

"It's a building full of books. I think we have a large-ish one around here somewhere."

"Nothing on the good old Interwebs, huh?"

Sandy shook her head. "Not really. I'm going to take a brain break and get Karina's desk ready. Maybe I'll have a better idea of where to look when I hit the Library of Congress later."

She jumped when her phone suddenly blared "Crazy Train."

Jasmine eyed her but didn't comment any further on her skittishness. "Your mom's ringtone is funny, but I'm not sure it's right," she said instead.

"Mind your own business," Sandy replied without any heat. "It's my passive-aggressive coping mechanism."

"My ex-husband earned himself a death metal ringtone, so I'm not judging. But I don't think your mom is crazy."

"Uh, did you forget the great Mystic Crystal in the Cupboard Incident?"

Jasmine grinned. "Who could forget your booty sticking out like that?"

"I was really thankful for Spanx that day," Sandy said solemnly.

"Your ma is kooky but harmless. I like her. You should go easier on her."

Normally, Sandy would have spit out a defense about all the instability she'd experienced as a child, bouncing from one town and school to the next, one of Magdalena's boyfriend's houses to another, one commune to the next. But the woe-is-me pity party didn't seem worth throwing for once. She'd been in charge of her life since she left for school at eighteen, and it had turned out pretty well so far. She couldn't exactly preach the gospel of Changing Your Life and Putting the Past Behind You to women every day if she wasn't buying into it herself.

"Okay," she said, surprising herself. "You're right. Magdalena hasn't been so bad on this trip. I'll call her and invite her to lunch with me."

Jasmine nodded her approval.

"But I'm not changing her ringtone."

"Baby steps."

Sandy called Magdalena back and wandered over to the minifridge in search of yogurt while she waited for her to pick up. She was debating between key lime pie and a healthier but less tempting fruit-on-the-bottom option when Magdalena answered.

"There's something wrong with your cat."

"Good morning, Magdalena."

"I mean it. There has to be something seriously wrong with its chi."

"Cats have chi?"

Her mother's sigh was long-suffering. "*All* living things have chi, Sand Dollar."

"And what's wrong with Larry?"

"What isn't?" her mother said, her tone surprisingly wry.

"Point taken."

"It's nesting on my favorite tunic. I don't even know how it found it."

Sandy stifled a laugh. She'd lost a couple of sweaters that way. "*It* is a she. Maybe she's molesting your shirt because you called her an *it*."

"No. It's her chi."

"Fine. It's her chi," she said with an eye roll and grabbed the key lime pie yogurt.

"Don't roll your eyes, Sand Dollar."

"I wasn't."

"I could hear it in your voice."

Sandy had no idea what to say to that. "Well, I was calling to see if you thought you could navigate the Metro well enough to come up to the center. Maybe we could do lunch or something."

"Yes, I can figure it out," Magdalena said. "Then after lunch I could stay and do some more filing."

"Actually, I was thinking maybe you could help me with a project I have today at the Library of Congress," Sandy said. "It should be full of mind-numbing research and dusty books, but if you're really good, I'll let you play on the microfiche machines."

"The what?"

"Never mind," Sandy said. "You're coming up?"

"I'll be there in an hour."

When she hung up, Sandy experienced a pang somewhere on the left side of her rib cage, a feeling she'd learned over the years to associate with guilt. It had taken as little as an invitation to lunch and the library to make Magdalena happy, a sad commentary on how much attention her mother was used to getting from her only child.

She squelched the pang with a bite of key lime yogurt. It wasn't like Sandy hadn't been an afterthought to her mother's whims and fancies during her childhood, and she'd turned out fine. Magdalena could take it, since she had spent so many years dishing it out. When the same spot under her rib cage flared up again, she decided it was indigestion, not suppressed guilt, and chased the yogurt down with kiwi-melon-flavored fitness water.

She picked up the phone to call Jessie to fill in the details on the sparse text messages she'd been reduced to since Magdalena had arrived in town, but the front door chimed, and Karina walked in. Sandy welcomed her warmly. The girl would have to dive into the deep end this week, but Sandy knew she was capable, or Roberta wouldn't have recommended her. They were stocking Karina's new desk with supplies from the office cabinet in the back when Sandy heard the door chime just before noon. She hustled to the front to find Magdalena staring at a blank wall.

"That needs something," she said, pointing at the bare wall.

"As soon as we have some extra money lying around, I'll origami it and do a modern-art installation made of extraneous dollar bills."

"Sandy," Jasmine called her name, the scold in her tone obvious. "It's good to see you, Magdalena."

"You can't miss her," Sandy muttered beneath her breath.

"You said we weren't staying in the office, so I didn't worry about the dress code," her mother replied serenely. She wore a bright blue peasant blouse, embroidered vividly around the neck with . . . vegetables? . . . and peacock feathers embellished the hem of her full cotton skirt. Real peacock feathers. A sparkly floral pattern bedazzled her black ballet flats, but they had nothing on Magdalena's head, which she'd wrapped in a violet paisley scarf. It caused the unbound curls behind it to bounce wildly with her every movement.

Sandy didn't say anything else. It wouldn't pierce her mother's obliviousness, and besides, she'd seen her mom in brighter colors. "Did you have any problems with the Metro?" she asked instead.

"No, but I don't know why you're so worried about me people watching in the mornings. Lots of people watch me too, you know. I don't think it's as big a deal as you think it is," Magdalena said.

Sandy started to point out that they might have been trying to process the indescribable, er . . . fabulousness of her mother's getup when she caught Jasmine's eye. Jasmine pointed a finger at her in warning, and she bit her tongue.

"Maybe you're right," she said. She could feel Jasmine waiting. "And that's a nice color on you."

Jasmine nodded her approval. "Bossy," Sandy mouthed. Her office mate smiled.

Karina knew the routines well enough already that Sandy had no problem leaving her to man the front on her own. "All right, Magdalena. Let's grab some lunch." She gathered her purse and laptop and gave Karina some last-minute instructions. "We're going to eat at Louie's and then head over to the Library of Congress. I can't take any calls there, but text me if something comes up. I'll get back to you right away. Ask Jasmine if you have any questions, or Geneva if Jasmine's busy."

Karina nodded. She lifted her chin and smiled, but her fingers tapped a jittery rhythm on the desktop.

"Relax," Sandy said. "You're going to be great. It's my business to know stuff like that, and I can tell."

"Thanks," Karina said, more confidence showing in her expression. "And thanks for the chance."

"You earned it." Sandy waved her cell phone at her new assistant to remind her she was only a text away and then led Magdalena out of the office.

They polished off some hearty salads at Louie's. Sandy didn't even roll her eyes when Magdalena made statements like, "Mushrooms are proof that Nature is a loving mother" or, "Candied pecans are almost as good for a spiritual awakening as the Kabbalah center I go to."

Kabbalah? Sandy didn't even ask. Why not add Jewish mysticism to her mother's New Age grab bag? They finished up their meals and set off for the library. Sandy figured that at a brisk pace, they could reach it within fifteen minutes and burn a few candied-pecan calories along the way. The nearness of everything was one of the things she'd always liked about big cities, from Seattle, Washington, to Washington DC. She loved the bustle and energy of so many people moving with purpose to do important things in tall, shiny buildings.

The Library of Congress was not tall or shiny but still grand. It was composed of three buildings, but Sandy's investigations told her they should start at the Jefferson building, a huge edifice in the Neoclassical style. Soaring columns and arcades of windows housed an unimaginably huge trove of books. Two staircases curved up toward the galley of entrance doors. She guided Magdalena up the nearest steps then froze at the top. Leaning against the column by the centermost door stood Jake Manning, scanning the crowds. She knew the exact instant he saw her. His eyes locked on hers, and he pushed away from the column, heading in her direction.

She muttered one of the curses she wasn't supposed to know anymore, and Magdalena looked at her in surprise. "What's wrong?"

"Nothing," Sandy said, forcing herself to stay composed. "But Jake's here."

"Oh good," her mother said, delighted. She caught sight of him and darted forward on light feet to meet him. "So good to see you! How fortuitous to find you here. I don't believe in coincidence, you know. Something cosmic aligned us to meet like this."

His good-natured smile at this pronouncement did nothing to quell Sandy's growing irritation. "This isn't cosmic alignment unless that's another name for Karina. I guess she mentioned I'd be here?"

Jake nodded to confirm. Disappointment shadowed Magdalena's face, but then she brightened. "You said there are *three* buildings to this library. It's still good fortune that you picked the right one."

"Is that what happened, Jake? You got lucky in three-card monte?"

He hesitated, clearly not wanting to deflate Magdalena, but then he confessed. "I guessed you were coming to research Magnus, right?"

Sandy knew she didn't need to answer. Why else would she be here?

"The Jefferson building is the most logical place to start," he explained to Magdalena. When her face fell again, he hastened to add, "But it was definitely lucky that I got here at the right time to catch you on your way in."

This seemed to make her mother feel better, but it only irritated Sandy more. "Why?" she asked. "Why catch me on the stairs instead of making a phone call? I'm on a tight schedule this week, and things like this put me off of it."

"I'm on the same schedule," he reminded her. "But I wasn't sure I could get in touch with you once you got into the building, so I hustled over."

"And you did that because . . ."

"There's no reason for you to do the research."

That brought her up short. "What do you mean?"

"I mean that I'm willing to share everything our paralegals came up with on Robert Magnus and his park."

She wavered between astonishment and suspicion. "I don't understand why you would do that."

He shrugged. "You'll eventually find what we did anyway. I figure if I make you waste a week in the process, it'll only tick you off more."

True.

She studied him skeptically. "You give me the Magnus research and you get . . . what?"

"You mentioned that you were going to pursue your conspiracy theory about who's funding the River Oaks case. I'm asking you to wait until after the hearing to do that."

He glanced at the people skirting around them to get into the building. "I'd rather not explain here if I can help it. Could we go somewhere and talk? Maybe I could buy you ladies ice cream or something."

"I like ice cream," Magdalena said.

"What do you say?" he asked Sandy.

She frowned. She didn't want to go anywhere with Jake. "The price for your info is that I can't look into whoever is backing River Oaks? I can't agree to that."

He drew Magdalena and her to the side. "I know how this looks, but let's go somewhere else so I can explain this to you. For once, please withhold judgment, Sandy. I promise you that you don't have all the facts right now."

"No kidding," she gritted out between clenched teeth. "And it looks like you don't want me to get them either."

"Sandy," Magdalena said, her tone firm. "You are making a scene out here. We'll go with Jake, eat some ice cream, and if you don't like what he says, we'll come back here and dig through books."

Sandy eyeballed her. "You just want ice cream, don't you?"

"Yes."

"Fine." She turned to Jake. "I'll hear you out, but only because my mother gets very fixated on ice cream, and she'll be useless for the next hour now that the idea is in her head. But fair warning, my patience is short, so don't test it." There was no need to show how interesting she found his proposal. She had no doubt he was up to something sneaky, but maybe it was something she could use to her advantage.

"Got it. Let's go."

Neither of them said anything for the next three blocks, but Magdalena filled their silence with her chatter about the people they passed on the sidewalk; she paid no attention to the deep, uncomfortable silence between her daughter and Jake until they reached a Baskin-Robbins. "I want my ice cream before you two start fighting," she said.

Sandy took a seat at one of the dinky tables and watched her mother zigzag back and forth between the cases on either side of the register, oohing and aahing over each choice. "She could take awhile," she warned Jake.

"That's okay," he said. "What are you going to get?"

She sighed like she was doing him a favor by ordering. "I'm going to need two scoops of butter pecan to think straight."

He was up in a flash and back a few minutes later with her order. Magdalena was still hovering over the choices, asking for samples of nearly everything.

Sandy took her first bite and nodded at him. "All right. So far, you trying to stall my research says I'm on the right track. And I'm wondering if maybe the Magnus information isn't that valuable if you're so ready to give it to me."

He shook his head. "You really are ready to believe the worst about me, aren't you?"

"Have I been wrong? You *are* in this way deeper than you let on at first, and you *are* being funded by someone besides the River Oaks group. All signs point to Ranger, which is probably a very bad thing, even if I haven't found much proof of corporate wrongdoing. *So far.* What should I believe?"

"The truth, which is what I've told you," Jake said, masking the hint of surprise that had shown in his eyes when Sandy had mentioned Ranger. "I'm working like crazy to make this all benefit the greatest number of people, and I really think I can do that." He looked at her with such an open and honest expression that she almost bought it. Then she remembered the tidy pile of facts stacked against him.

"Who's included in this 'greatest number of people'? You keep mentioning that, but what does it mean?" She frowned down at her dwindling ice cream, dismayed it had disappeared so quickly.

"I can't tell you that right now, but I'm asking for some trust." A note of pleading shaded his voice. She'd never heard that tone from him before.

"I'm not going to make that leap without some kind of guarantee." She shrugged. "This deal you're working on—or whatever it is—can you promise that if I wait a week to publicize a definite link between Ranger Properties and this zoning dispute, it won't hurt the annex?"

"Yes." He held her stare without flinching.

She chased the last of her ice cream around the bowl, trying to listen to her instincts. Even though he waited quietly, she still found his nearness unnerving. Intrusive thoughts nagged at her. What if he was telling the truth and she couldn't cast him as a villain in this drama anymore? It would be harder to defend against him personally if they had nothing left to fight over professionally.

She couldn't sort through her internal tumult under Jake's intense scrutiny. "I need to think about it this afternoon," she said. "I'll give you an answer by tonight."

"That's fair. Thanks for even considering this."

Magdalena wandered over then. "I want mocha swirl and blueberry cheesecake and rainbow sherbet. I can't decide."

"Get a triple scoop, and then you don't have to," he said as he guided Magdalena back toward the ice cream.

She beamed at him like it was some kind of genius solution and then placed her order, managing to change it only four more times before she was done. When her mother reached the table with her dangerously tilting ice cream cone, Sandy stood. "Thanks for the dessert, Jake. I'll call you later with an answer."

"Good," he said. "I'll be waiting."

Once he left, Sandy dragged her mother out of the store and headed back toward the Library of Congress. Whether she took Jake's deal or not, she couldn't waste an afternoon of research. Wondering if she even remembered how to find a library reference number, she snuck a look at her mother's triple-scoop ice-cream cone and made at least one firm decision.

"That looks awful, Magdalena," she said.

"I know. Would you like some?"

"Definitely." She may not know exactly what to do about Jake's cease-and-desist request, but this she knew for sure: ice cream never faileth.

Chapter 24

"I DON'T LIKE THIS," MAGDALENA announced. "These federal cutbacks must have included a layoff for whoever is supposed to dust these things." She waved at the pile of nearly twenty books surrounding them on their worktable.

Sandy grinned at the tart observation and conceded that Magdalena might be right. The online card catalogue search they had done returned hundreds of leads on Robert Magnus, but each one evaporated into a puff of book dust when they tracked it down. Sandy tried to squelch her frustration, but it was hard to race down dead ends and make no progress. Jake had been clear that his team had turned up useful information. Knowing it was in the library and being no closer to finding it made Sandy as cranky as Jake had accused her of being earlier.

Her mother dragged another book toward herself and leafed through it in search of an index. She tried to wave the resultant dust cloud away but ended up coughing as it hovered stubbornly over its leather-bound home. She sighed, and Sandy gave in.

"Okay. We're done."

Magdalena brightened. "You found something?"

"No. I'm going to take Jake's offer. I need to spend my time sifting through what he's already found, not wasting the whole week figuring out where he found it."

"We're leaving, then? I think I just saw my own aura change colors. It's a happy pink now."

"Go wander around out front," Sandy suggested. "I'll straighten these books up then join you."

Her mother needed no more urging. Ten minutes later, Sandy joined Magdalena on a bench outside, where she found her staring at a squirrel.

"What are you doing?" she asked.

"Communing with nature. It can be done even in a concrete jungle."

"All right, nature lady. Time to hit the office again."

Magdalena waved a reluctant good-bye to her puzzled squirrel friend, and she and Sandy headed back to the center. Karina didn't appear too overwhelmed when they got back. After a gentle reminder that her whereabouts were to be disclosed on a need-to-know basis and that Jake would *never* need to know, she turned Magdalena loose in the filing room and picked up the phone to accept Jake's deal.

"Hi," he said. The warmth in his voice sent a tickle down her spine.

"Hi. I'm going to take you up on your offer."

"Good," he said. "You won't be sorry. I'll bring everything over tonight."

"Bring it over? Wait, what? Can't you just send me a couple of e-mail attachments or something?"

"Nope. I want you to have the same access to the information that I did and know that none of our copies have been messed with or altered in any way. That means I'll be at your place with three large-ish boxes later, like around . . . dinnertime?"

She hesitated. "I don't know about that. I haven't spent much time with my mom this week because of the hearing. I figure I'd better do that tonight."

"Doesn't sound like you're very excited about it." His tone held no judgment, only an observation.

"I'm not. I don't know what to say when it's only the two of us. Seems like almost everything leads to a fight."

"A fight about what?"

She considered how to explain the complicated dynamic then wondered why she bothered. It wasn't his business. "Stuff," she offered, finally. "We fight about stuff."

"That's a clear 'butt out,'" he said. "Sorry. I wasn't trying to be nosy."

"I don't believe you," she said. "I think you're one of the nosiest people I've ever met. It must be that cross-examination instinct you lawyer guys are born with."

He laughed. "Believe it or not, I'm not like this with everyone. It's one more special quality you bring out in me."

His tone may have started out light, but the soft way he ended made the joke sound like a confession. She wasn't immune to the effect.

She realized he was waiting for some kind of response, so she cleared her throat. "I'll take your word for it, I guess."

"So. How do I get this information to you since inviting myself to dinner didn't work?"

"Let me check with Magdalena," she said. "If she's okay with it, you can go ahead and drop by around dinnertime." *What are you doing?*

"Are you sure?" He sounded concerned. "I don't want to interrupt your bonding time. I know she's leaving soon."

Sandy dropped her head to her hand and listened to herself like she was eavesdropping on someone else's conversation. A crazy woman's conversation. "No, it's okay. She likes you, and I need those boxes."

He didn't say anything again, and she felt herself coloring. "Never mind. Maybe one of the overworked interns you guys keep locked in the office closet could run them by in the morning."

"Wait, no. I'll come to dinner tonight," he said. "I was just surprised."

"Why?"

"It's not that easy to get you to hang out. It's usually a bigger fight."

"I'm tired of fighting," she said before she could second-guess herself.

"Me too."

She didn't want to dig any further into her confession, so she mumbled something about seeing him later and got off the phone. She stared at it until Jasmine heaved an annoyed sigh, and Sandy realized she'd been tapping her pen against the desktop. "Sorry," she said.

Jasmine nodded.

Sandy looked at the different tasks laid out in her "In" tray and the backlog of e-mails she had to go through. Her brain froze.

"Jasmine, I'm going to step out to make a phone call."

"Okay."

She snatched up her cell phone, headed halfway down the block, and perched on a large concrete planter before dialing Jessie. She'd been interrupted the last time she'd tried to call her, so getting out of the office for a minute to find peace and sanity was her only option.

Jessie picked up on the second ring. "Who died?"

"Why would you ask that?"

"Only something major could get you on the phone."

Sandy shook her head. "No one died. Magdalena's here though."

"You mentioned that in one of your texts. That's why I quit calling a couple of days ago. I figured one high-maintenance person was enough for you right now."

"You think you're high maintenance too?" Sandy asked with a laugh. "Yeah right. What's the opposite of high maintenance?'

"Uh, low maintenance, duh."

"I'm losing my mind."

"No, I am, with all this wedding stuff. That's what turned me high maintenance. I don't know how it happened. One day I'm doing my thing, killing it at work, hanging out with Ben, and the next, I have decision paralysis over colored napkins."

Sandy winced. "You need to go on a honeymoon or something."

"You're telling me. I just have this wedding to get through, but somehow I've managed to convince myself that it's not going to happen if I have blue napkins instead of teal."

"In your defense, blue napkins would look bad against the bridesmaids dresses."

A long sigh came from the other end of the line. "Finally, a voice of reason."

They were drifting into one of their silly banter sessions, but as much as she could use the laugh, Sandy needed advice even more. Or not even advice—more like clarity.

"I'm sorry I haven't been here to support you through the drama of the serviettes."

Jessie laughed. "I'll live. How did the hearing go?"

Sandy caught her up on the latest developments, from her discovery that Jake was in the zoning mess deeper than she'd thought to the deal they'd made for her to temporarily back off. It felt so good to have her friend listen, interjecting only to ask a couple of perceptive questions. When she finished her recap, silence met her from Jessie's end of the line.

"Jessie?"

"I'm here."

"What are you thinking?"

"I think . . . that I heard a lot in what you didn't say."

"I don't know what that means."

"A month ago, you were ready to crush him because he dared to exist after not calling you last year when you met at The Factory."

"I wasn't that mad."

"You were, Sandy. I was there, remember? Don't answer this, but think about why he had such a lasting impact on you after only one night."

"I—"

"Seriously, don't answer. You're only going to say something I won't believe, and I'll have to waste this conversation on a lecture."

Sandy grinned. "Yes, ma'am."

"Anyway, a month ago you're ready to crush him, and now you're inviting him over to dinner on some manufactured excuse about boxes. And what really blows my mind is that in between, it seems your suspicions of him were right all along. He's doing something shady with this group that's suing to stop the annex, but despite all that, he sounds like he's more under your skin than ever."

"You did not hate saying that. You liked saying that."

"You're right. I totally did. Did I pretty much cover the facts?"

"Kind of, but I think you're screwing up their interpretation." Sandy knew she sounded sulky, but she couldn't help it. Just because she prided herself on being up-front and honest did *not* mean she enjoyed being transparent, not even to Jessie, and Jessie was getting awfully close to the mark.

"Explain it to me, then. How should I be interpreting this?"

Sandy, having no answer, stayed silent for a beat too long.

"Ah ha!" Jessie crowed. "I wish you were here so you could see my victory dance. It's kind of awesome."

"Is it the one where you look like a chicken with a seizure disorder? Because that's not so awesome."

"Trust me. I look good. Being right does something for a girl, you know?"

"You're not right."

"You just told me a ten-minute story of all the things he's done that should send more red flags flying than a bullfighting doubleheader, and you're not mad. Instead, you invited him to dinner with your mother. What does that tell you?"

"That I had no idea bullfighting even did doubleheaders."

"Sandy, Sandy, Sandy."

She sighed. "It tells me that having Magdalena here has scrambled my common sense, I must have a vitamin deficiency that affects normal brain function, and I should call Jake and cancel."

"No way!" Jessie nearly hollered. "He definitely needs to come over. *And* you guys need to have an evening where you talk about anything besides zoning hearings and River Oaks. Have you had any conversations in the last two months that have *not* been about those two things?"

Sandy was silent again so she could avoid handing Jessie more ammunition, but her silence was confession enough.

"Wait a minute. You have! You've had conversations about other stuff. Like what? No holding out." As much as Sandy didn't want to fuel more speculation on Jessie's part, she couldn't resist the urge to confide in her. The whole point of calling her had been to get an objective perspective.

She grimaced and then gave in. "Okay, here's the thing. We've talked about *us* quite a bit."

"There's an 'us' with the two of you? Yes!"

"No! I mean, Jake always talks about us. He's always trying to dig into things instead of just letting them be." The sulky note crept back into her tone.

"Like what? Come on, woman. This is like pulling teeth. I promise to give you my platinum-rated objective opinion if you will just, for the love of all that is chocolate and good in this world, *spit it out!*"

Sandy laughed. "All right, all right. Jake sees *us* as some kind of work in progress. I don't see an *us* at all, so most of our conversations are about whether *we* even exist."

"That was super deep."

"I know, right? I don't know why he can't kick around in the shallow waters like everyone else." She straightened. "That's it. I'm definitely calling to cancel dinner."

"I forbid it. A noncombat dinner is the best thing you could do right now."

"Have I been the only one listening to me talk during this conversation? What I hear me saying is that I have evidence that Jake is up to no good. Meanwhile, I had some sort of weird mind warp where I thought now would be a good time to overlook that and invite him to hang out with my lunatic mother. You're supposed to jump in and talk me off the crazy ledge, Jess."

"Uh-uh. I'm ready to push you over. You've always had great instincts about people, and I think they're right this time too. They're drawing you toward Jake for a reason. If he's promising you that it's going to work out, you should give him a chance to prove it. It's a leap of faith. Take it."

Sandy pulled the phone away from her ear and tapped it against the concrete planter while she thought. She could hear Jessie's voice sounding tinny as she called, "Hello? Sandy?" but she ignored her. A leap of faith? It wasn't something she did easily, and she was supposed to do that for Jake? To trust that he was telling her the truth about wanting to do the right thing?

She brought the phone back up to her ear. "That's a big ole leap."

"I know."

"What if I'm wrong? I was the first time at The Factory."

"No, you weren't. You thought you had an amazing connection, and you were right. It's held up after a year apart, through political maneuvering and across major professional differences. That's powerful."

"Um, I don't like it when you put things in perspective."

Jessie laughed. "It's scary when you think about it that way, huh?"

"Heck yes," she admitted. "There's so many ways he's wrong for me. That we're wrong for each other. This whole attraction to him doesn't make any sense."

"You've always been the most impulsive dater I know. What happened to the fun-at-any-cost approach?"

"I don't know," she said. "It changed when I started coming back to church. It's like I need something more than entertainment to keep me in a relationship. I'd rather sit and have an interesting and real conversation with someone once a month than a pointless date every week." She stopped and re-evaluated her own words. "Wow. When did I turn into such an old-lady fun sucker?"

Jessie laughed again, like Sandy knew she would. "You're not old or a fun sucker. Welcome to being real."

Sandy responded by blowing a raspberry, which set Jessie off again. When she calmed down, she picked up the thread of her interrogation again. "One more question, Sand Dollar."

Sandy growled.

"Just answer me this. What are you so afraid of?"

"You sound like Dr. Phil," Sandy said, but her friend's point had found its mark and was needling her uncomfortably.

"Answer the question."

"No."

"At least think about the question. In the meantime, don't cancel dinner with Jake. Promise?"

"I promise," Sandy said, sounding as if she'd never been less excited about anything. And yet . . .

Although she'd never admit it to her friend, she'd never been so glad to be bullied into something, ever.

Chapter 25

SANDY SURVEYED THE TABLE AND decided it was good. She wasn't going to pretend to be a domestic goddess. Setting the table with matching napkins and an edible meal marked a major milestone. Eyeing the casserole on the center trivet, she wondered if Jake was expecting anything fancy. It was hard to cook impressive vegetarian meals for carnivores.

And it was just plain hard to cook. She caught the faint, acrid whiff of burnt beans in the air and scrounged up an old T-shirt to shove on top of the ruined pan in the garbage.

Satisfied that the tell-tale burnt odor was contained, she examined herself in the mirror over her entry table. Her vintage snap-front shirt peeked open at the neck to reveal a lace-trimmed tank, and skinny jeans accentuated her figure.

Well, jeans and the Spanx. Stupid ice cream.

Jake's firm knock sounded on the door.

"Hi," she said as she opened it, glad she'd formed the word before she'd caught a full glimpse of him. He looked . . . hot. Like forget-to-breathe-for-ten-seconds hot. She half wondered if he'd mugged the best-dressed mannequin in an H&M display. His striped button-down shirt struck just the right note with his dark jeans. He wore a pair of Jack Purcell sneakers, and his dark hair looked as casually tousled as her own. She wondered if it took him as much time as it did for her to look like he'd put in no effort at all.

"Hi," he said and leaned in to kiss her cheek before she could think fast enough to decide if she wanted to move out of the way or not. "I brought dessert." He held up a paper bag from a local bakery as he showed himself into the kitchen.

Magdalena emerged from Sandy's bedroom, where she'd gone to dress after helping with dinner. Her simple white T-shirt made an interesting counterpoint to her outrageous skirt. So many glass beads and other sparkly embellishments encrusted the ankle-length crinkle fabric that Sandy could barely make out the vibrant, almost violent orange of the material underneath. Yet, it somehow worked.

Sandy shook her head and followed Jake into the kitchen.

"What's dessert?" she asked.

"Not telling," he said as he lifted several white bakery containers out of his bag. "I'm holding dessert hostage so you don't throw me out early."

"How evil of you."

"Maybe. What's in here is pure sin."

She cocked her head. "You just guaranteed that you'll be staying until I eat whatever that is."

"That's what I thought," he said with a grin and then began rummaging for space in her fridge so he could store his boxes.

"It's good to see you, Jake," Magdalena said. "You bring such a nice energy with you."

"Thank you," he answered, like it was a normal compliment.

"We cooked," her mother continued. "I once almost converted to the raw foods movement because the kitchen disrupts my chi, but I'm glad I didn't. This dinner will be good."

"I'm sure it's delicious."

"It is," Magdalena said and then drifted out to the living room.

Jake caught Sandy's eye, and his lip twitched, which forced her to smother a laugh. Really, what was the point of being annoyed with her mother? If Jake could see the humor in Magdalena's antics, then she could too.

Dinner went well. Sandy had to admit that what her mother lacked in culinary skill, she made up for with the fearless application of spices. The eggplant casserole had a delicious kick to it that prompted Jake to declare he didn't miss the meat at all. When Magdalena got up to clear their places, he waved her back into her chair.

"I'm on dish duty," he said. "I'll handle it while you guys eat dessert."

"Oh, no thank you," Magdalena said. "I think I've had enough sugar today. If you don't mind, I need to find a quiet space for my spirit to occupy. I'm going to Sandy's room to meditate while she's not using it. Is that okay, darling?"

"Sure. Just don't light any incense near my closet. I don't want to go to work smelling like patchouli."

Magdalena wandered off, and Sandy turned her attention to Jake, watching hungrily as he staged dessert. Watched the dessert hungrily, that is. Whatever he was sliding onto the plate looked amazing in the way only layers of pastry, cream, and chocolate can.

"What is it?" she asked when he set it down in front of her.

"Heaven."

"I guess we'll see," she said, "but I think I believe you."

"No, I mean the name of the dessert is 'Heaven.' I have a slice of Paradise and two pieces of Nirvana if you're still hungry after Heaven."

He watched with interest as she chewed. It didn't help her self-consciousness. And then the full impact of the dessert hit her, and she ignored everything else but the bliss of the next three bites.

"Well?" he asked.

She tapped her fork lightly against her plate. Pretending to be deep in thought, she asked, "Do you think it's possible to love and marry a pastry?"

Jake laughed, and she noticed again his even and perfectly shaped teeth. Then she mocked herself for noticing. *Snap out of it.*

He let her enjoy the rest of her treat in quiet, not interrupting with conversation. It was true that he often had a lot to say, but at the same time, he never blathered just to hear himself. She supposed she would have to give him credit for that. When she was done, he pushed another plate toward her, this one bearing something gooey and chocolatey.

"This is Paradise," he said.

"No thanks." She shuddered. She refused to regret the first pastry, but there was no way she was succumbing to a second one. Not unless she could get her yoga attendance back on track. At this rate, she'd be rolling into her next class as one big blob of cream-fed cellulite.

She took a deep breath to clear the sugar haze in her brain and then let it out slowly. See, that was yoga. She could do this. She focused on Jake again. "Thank you for bringing the Magnus files."

He shrugged. "Just keeping up my end of the deal. I hope you find what you're looking for."

"Why wouldn't I?" she asked, suspicious again.

"No reason. Relax. I'm not sure what angle you're planning to take, that's all."

"Angle," she mused. "Why do I have to have an angle? Maybe I just want to verify the information you presented at the hearing on Wednesday."

"You think I would falsify something like that?"

"No," she admitted. "But I wonder about your interpretation of the facts."

"Fair enough." He was quiet for a moment. "Could we not talk about work?"

"Isn't that why I invited you here?"

He studied her. "You aren't mad anymore."

She sighed. "No."

"And despite your complete lack of faith in me, I'm not mad at you either. I tried to be, but I can't, and I don't know why. I've given up trying to figure it out. *Now* can we talk about something else?"

"Like what?"

"Anything else. Please? I'm so sick of this case right now, and I don't want to waste an evening on zoning when that's all I think about all day long. Or almost all I think about." Even though he murmured the last part, she heard it and couldn't mistake his implication.

She shifted. "We can talk about something else."

"Okay. I pick vacations."

"Vacations?"

He nodded. "Yep. Where would you go if time and money were no object?"

He was going to pretend like all the issues at work didn't exist? Fine. She'd play along. "Spain. What about you?"

She watched as he mulled over his answer and then settled on the Baltic States. Curious about that choice, she encouraged him to elaborate and then listened and analyzed him. The set of his jaw changed when he talked about something he loved, like travel. His eyes crinkled more at the sides too. She'd bet that in a few years' time those crinkles would become laugh lines. They gave his face character.

His mellow energy relaxed her the way yoga did when the stretches stripped away the stress of the day. It was so opposite of the way she normally felt around him. Instead of being keyed up for a confrontation, she found something inside of her unwinding and gentling.

Her brain warned her to be on guard against him, whispered that he had slipped past her defenses too easily, but she ignored it. She followed impulse more than logic. In fact, Jake's rejection the year before had flipped a switch in her and made her far more cautious and analytical about dating. Before that, she'd rarely considered the consequences. Jessie had accused her more than once of being careless with people's feelings, but Sandy never saw it that way. In Sandy's mind, she had always figured that if she wasn't emotionally invested, the other person couldn't be either; if there was something between two people, *both* of them would know it.

She'd believed differently after that night at The Factory. She'd always scoffed at the notion of love at first sight, but she'd left the restaurant that night feeling changed somehow. In the three hours she and Jake had spent absorbed in each other, she'd experienced a tiny internal seismic shift. She'd pushed her carefree flirt aside so that a more thoughtful, real Sandy could connect with Jake. The air between them had hummed. Occasionally their shoulders had brushed or their knees had bumped softly beneath the bar table while they talked, or sometimes a subtle lean-in had made the other person wonder if it was imagined. That was it, and still, after she'd left, electricity had thrummed along her nerve endings when she thought about him.

That night, they had found more things they had in common than ways they differed. She'd woken up the next morning near drunk with giddiness. She'd thought she couldn't wait to talk to Jake again.

Only . . . he'd never called.

She could look back at that period in her life from a distance and appreciate some of the positive change that had come out of it. But she could also look across her table at Jake Manning, the catalyst for all of it, and wonder what kind of new havoc he would wreak if she let him in.

Jessie's earlier observation played through her mind. *You thought you had an amazing connection, and you were right. It's held up after a year apart, through political maneuvering and across major professional differences. That's powerful.*

Ignoring it for the past couple of months hadn't diminished it. Continuing to ignore it felt like a waste of time, so where did that leave her? Leave them? How could that connection not have been obliterated by time, distance, and the stupid zoning hearing?

"And that's when I declared blueberries my mortal enemy for life."

She glanced up, startled.

"Oh, *now* you're paying attention?" Jake teased. "Where did you wander to?"

She shook her head. She couldn't explain what she didn't understand, even if she wanted to, which she didn't. "Sorry," she said instead. "It's been a long week. I think some of my brain cells are paralyzed."

"It's better than atrophying."

She jumped up from the table, eager for some space. "Good word. I'm going to give you a prize." She fished around in her kitchen junk drawer. Okay, one of her kitchen junk drawers. A minute later, she was back at the table. "Here's a sticker for having an excellent vocabulary."

He took it from her, and she saw him fight a smile. "This is a stamp."

"No, it's a reward."

"It looks an awful lot like a twenty-two cent stamp. I don't think they've printed those since I was in high school."

"See? That means it's old and rare and super valuable. You should go pawn it tomorrow."

"Cool. How much do you think I could get for it?" he asked.

"I bet at least twenty-two cents."

"Wow. Add that to the change on the floor of my car and I think I might be able to upsize my next Slurpee."

"It pays to be educated," she said, her voice serious. "It's the principle that New Horizons is founded on. We're improving lives, one upsized Slurpee at a time."

He laughed, and she watched the crinkles deepen around his eyes, smiling in return without thinking about it. He caught her eye, and his laugh faded into a return smile. He stood and drew her into a hug. She let him. He didn't say anything, just stood there with his arms wrapped around her, and she was okay with that.

More than okay.

"This is what I wanted this evening to be," he said.

She pulled back a bit to stare at him. "One long hug? How long? Because my legs get tired after awhile."

He rolled his eyes and tucked her head back under his chin. "That's the smart mouth I know and love."

She froze.

So did he.

He cleared his throat. "I didn't mean it that way. I meant that—"

"Forget it," she said. "I know what you meant." She pushed on him gently but enough to break the embrace. "Don't you have some boxes for me?" Best to change the subject before the silence grew too awkward.

"Maybe."

She eyed him. "Maybe? Isn't delivering those boxes how you wrangled an invitation to dinner?"

"I do have the boxes, but if I surrender them to you, are you going to make me leave?"

"I guess not," she said. "But I might make you hang out with Magdalena. I don't want to be the world's lamest daughter and ignore her for her whole visit."

"That's cool," he said. "Why don't you go lure her out of your room, and I'll drag the boxes in from my car."

Sandy tapped on her bedroom door and stuck her head in. Her mother had lit all the lemon candles and was sitting cross-legged in the middle of the room, breathing deeply. It seemed a shame to interrupt her meditation, but between wanting to make sure her mom felt included and also needing a buffer against Jake, she called her name softly. "Magdalena?"

Her mother didn't stir.

"Magdalena?"

One eye cracked open slowly to survey her then closed. Sandy heard a long sigh, and then Magdalena opened both eyes and stood, rippling up from the floor like a reverse waterfall. It was a neat trick.

"Yes, daughter?"

"I feel bad that you're hanging out in here all by yourself. Why don't you come out here with Jake and me?"

Her mother waved a hand, the gesture calling to mind an aimless leaf on a breeze. "Oh, no. You two go ahead and enjoy each other."

Deciding not to ask for clarification on her mother's definition of "enjoy each other," she cleared her throat and said, "We'd love it if you joined us. I'd especially love it if you did."

"Hm," Magdalena replied. "We'll see."

She brushed past Sandy and entered the living room, where Jake was stacking the last box of documents inside the door. "Hi, again," he said. Then he looked past Magdalena to smile at Sandy, who felt her toes curl.

Then she frowned. Magdalena hadn't returned his greeting. She stood halfway between him and Sandy and studied them with a long, searching look. Her eyes glazed over, and she gave the air a delicate sniff. Jake's gaze shot to Sandy, who interpreted it to mean, "What's she doing?" She answered with a shrug. It was Magdalena. Who knew?

Magdalena took a couple of steps toward Jake and then waved her hand around his head and shoulders a few times as if testing the air currents in his part of the living room. She said nothing and then drifted toward Sandy and did the same thing.

"Magdalena?" Sandy asked. "What are you doing?"

"I'm going back to meditate." Her voice reflected the dreamy quality in her eyes. "I need a more soothing energy. Everything out here is . . ."

"Just fine," Sandy hurried to complete her mother's sentence before anything embarrassing could come out of her mouth. "Go on back and enjoy your trance or whatever." She placed a hand at Magdalena's back to usher her out more quickly, but Jake stopped her.

"No, wait," he said. "What were you going to say, Magdalena? Everything out here is . . . what?"

"So fraught," Magdalena said. "Spiky, frenetic energy. Good, but not soothing. And it's definitely flowing strictly between you two. It's not a welcoming energy. Not hostile, you understand."

"I understand," Jake said with a solemn nod.

Sandy glared at him.

"But it's intended for only you," Magdalena repeated. She sniffed once more. "I detect positive love ions."

Sandy flinched. "I think it's the lemon candles."

"No." Magdalena drifted back to the bedroom without another word.

When the door closed behind her mother, Sandy braced herself before turning to face Jake. "She, um, likes a dramatic exit."

He grinned.

"What?" she demanded. He didn't say anything. He stood there with the same goofy smile plastered on his face, watching her. She sighed. "You can't put much stock in what she says, Jake. She thinks she's psychic and believes in numerology."

"Oh, I don't know. My mom's about the most down-to-earth person you'll ever meet, and she believes pretty strongly in mother's intuition. Maybe Magdalena has hers really dialed in."

"Yeah right. You need practice for that, and she barely took on the mommy title a few years ago."

"Really?" he said. He took her hand and drew her to the sofa next to him then wrapped an arm around her. "Tell me more."

She lost her train of thought while she enjoyed the feeling of being nestled next to him.

"Sandy?"

"Hm?"

"You were going to tell me about you and your mom," he prompted.

"I was?" She gathered her thoughts but stayed where she was with her head tucked into the warm hollow between his neck and his shoulder. He smelled like something spicy and delicious. Finally, she strung a few words together that made sense. "Magdalena has spent most of her life and all of my life trying to figure out who she is. She chases every new spiritual fad in the headlines and wanders from one spiritual adviser to another."

"Was that hard on you as a kid?"

She nodded. "Yeah. It meant moving from place to place while she tried to figure out where she belonged. She'd convince me that we'd found the commune or town that was the perfect fit for us. She'd throw herself into it like she'd lived there her whole life, and then when I relaxed enough to feel okay about putting down some of my own roots, she'd get distracted by a swami or a new philosophy somewhere else, and then we were off again."

"And it tore your baby roots right out of the ground, huh?" His voice was full of compassion. "That must have stunk."

"Yeah." She remembered the lost feeling she'd constantly harbored throughout her childhood, the uncertainty that was part of her daily fabric. "The moving was hard, but she sent so many confusing messages too. Like when I was little and she didn't want me to call her mom, wait, no, *do* call her mom."

"But you didn't."

"Nah. It took too much energy to keep up with all the mind changes. You saw her order ice cream. That's about how committed she is to any one world view. I just stuck with what I knew." She chewed her lower lip for a minute. "Okay, honestly, there's maybe a little bit of payback in calling her Magdalena instead of Mom."

"Can't blame you," he said, and she detected a smile in his voice. "What about your dad? I never hear you talk about him."

"There's nothing to say. He left when I was three. I guess he couldn't handle Magdalena's instability. He sent money whenever he had it, and by the time I was twelve, he was paying our bills. I guess he does well with his business. He's an import/export guy, which is about as specific as people who describe themselves as consultants ever get. But whatever. He never came around."

That used to eat at her, him never showing up. When she was younger, she would spend hours making him cards for every holiday, sure that if she decorated it prettily enough, he would accept the invitation she included in each one. "You should come and visit, Daddy. I'll show you my new Madame Alexander Doll," or some variation. Eventually, she quit sending the cards.

Jake stroked her hair and said nothing while she wandered down memory lane. She sighed and burrowed further into his embrace. "He called when I was thirteen," she said. "It was the first time I remember hearing his voice after he left. He wanted to get to know me, have me come out and spend time with him, but he'd married some lady who already had three kids, and I wasn't into the idea of showing up to play Cinderella." She pushed a wayward curl off her forehead and then pulled it straight in front of her, separating it strand by strand. It was easier than focusing on old memories.

"Was that the last time you talked to him?"

She shrugged and separated another strand from the curl. "He quit trying to call when I was eighteen. He paid for college though. And he sends cards," she admitted grudgingly.

"How do you feel about that?"

"Fine," she said. "It is what it is. I'm glad he didn't keep pushing for a relationship or whatever. Best case scenario, it would be awkward. No thanks."

Jake stilled the fingers worrying at her hair and tucked the tortured curl behind her ear. "I'm sorry he wasn't more of a standup guy," he said.

"It's not your apology to make." She said it without heat. "Besides, maybe he would have been. He just asked for a second chance too late."

He tilted her chin up so he could look her full in the face. "What about me? Is it too late for my second chance?"

Chapter 26

SHE FORGOT TO BREATHE. HE watched her intently, the naked truth of how much her answer mattered exposed in his eyes.

Mistaking her speechlessness for reluctance to answer, he turned toward her more fully. "I know the timing seems bad on this. A smarter guy would wait until everything calmed down before trying to date you. But when I saw you at church that Sunday, I knew that not calling you back after The Factory was an even bigger mistake than I'd realized."

She shot him a glance.

"Yeah, I figured out I was an idiot for not calling you in Seattle when you were still on my mind two weeks later. And a month later. And another month after that. I pulled my phone out fifty times a day and thought about it. Look," he said and shifted so he could fish his phone out of his pocket. He scrolled through the display and handed it to her. She saw her name on the screen with her Seattle cell number underneath it.

"Why do you still have my old number?"

"It's kind of symbolic. Until I found you a couple of months ago, it was a ten digit reminder of how stupid I was to let you get away." He sighed and slipped the phone back into his pocket. "I was trying to do the right thing by not getting involved with you when I thought you weren't Mormon, but I still couldn't shake the nagging feeling that I should have called. Now . . ." he trailed off then laced his fingers behind his head and leaned back to stare at the ceiling.

"Now . . . what?" she asked.

He squinted. "Did you know you have money stuck to your ceiling?"

She poked him. "You were saying?"

"Now I pull that number up on a semiregular basis to remind me that there's a good reason for not giving up every time you tell me to get lost."

"I've never said get lost."

"Yeah, you have. It sounds like, 'It doesn't make sense to date you right now' and 'You're a corporate snake,' but it pretty much means the same thing." His mild tone took any sting out of his words.

"Then why bother?"

He kept his gaze on the ceiling but smiled as he reached over to touch her curls. "Do you think your hair is deflecting everything I'm saying?"

She gave a halfhearted swat at his hand.

"I told you, I knew I never should have let you get away in Seattle. I should have asked more questions, somehow figured out that the religion thing wasn't an issue. I don't think it's a coincidence that our paths have crossed again. There's something bigger at work here. I'm not going to stand in the way."

"Like what? Fate? You sound like Magdalena now."

"Fate?" he mused, still smiling. "I guess that's one word for Him."

She shook her head.

"What?" he asked. "Are you willing to say we both ended up in Washington DC at the same time as a fluke?"

"I can't figure you out. On the one hand, I have all kinds of evidence that you're doing something underhanded for Ranger Properties with the River Oaks claim, and then you're sitting on the sofa talking about God. Does not compute."

He shifted to face her, propping his head on the arm still resting on the sofa back. "Do you think I'm corrupt?" He pinned her with his gaze.

She searched it, looking for signs of discomfort that would reveal he had something to hide, yet knowing she wouldn't find them. His eyes were clear and calm. She forgot what she was looking for, lost in his gaze. They darkened, and the calm disappeared as his gaze grew electric. He leaned closer, and even though he gave her plenty of time to move, she didn't. She stayed right where she was and met his kiss. Heat flooded her as his lips pressed against hers with perfect, unbearable force.

When he drew back long enough for her to breathe, he smiled, and she learned that her knees could buckle even if she was sitting. He leaned in again, and she brought her fingers up to rest lightly against his lips before they could touch hers again.

"No," she whispered.

Jake drew back slightly. "No?"

"No, I don't think you're corrupt."

Then she closed the gap between them.

When Larry landed on her lap with a graceless thump, Sandy experienced her first moment of true appreciation for her pet. Somehow, Jake's kisses were managing to rearrange the properties of time and space in a way that unnerved her—when she eventually came up for air, because she didn't always remember to. She gave her cat a light thank you pat. Larry shot her a glare and hopped down from Sandy's lap, her work done.

Sandy climbed to her feet and headed for the kitchen.

"What are you doing?" Jake asked.

"I'm pretending I need something from the kitchen while I try to get my act together," she called back. She opened the fridge. "Now I'm going to rearrange stuff while I get my head on straight."

"This is why I like you."

"Why? Because I have more of my mom's nuttiness than you thought?"

He didn't answer until he was standing in the kitchen entrance. "No. Because you shoot so straight. There's no guesswork with you."

"Hm. I don't think I've ever felt less mysterious," she joked.

"It was a compliment."

"I don't deserve it." If anything, the last hour had proven that she'd been lying to herself about what she wanted since the second she walked away from him at church a few weeks before. All the games, the verbal slaps, the flirting, the accusations . . . all of it was meant to increase her distance from him, and it had nothing to do with zoning issues or professional differences.

It was fear, pure and simple. When he never called after The Factory, Jake had touched a nerve she'd thought had been cauterized after the last unanswered valentine she'd sent her dad when she was ten. She had shoved that raw need to be acknowledged and loved by her distracted mother and absent father so far under her armor of independence that she'd nearly forgotten how much it hurt.

Oh no.

A bubble of laughter escaped her, and Jake stared at her strangely. "You okay?"

But the laughter gripped her now, and she couldn't stop it, even as she gasped for breath.

"Seriously, Sandy. Are you all right?"

She gasped out an explanation in between semihysterical giggles.

"I'm fine." More laughter. "I just realized Magdalena was right. I think I have a wounded inner child." She sat down right where she was, on the floor in front of the open fridge, and laughed until her sides hurt.

Jake stood staring down at her, concerned. "Should I go get her?"

He turned to go, but Sandy regained enough control to call out, "No!" He turned back around.

"Don't get her. I'll be fine." A few last shudders of hilarity worked their way out in delirious hiccups. She gestured for a hand up, and he helped her to her feet. She took advantage of his help and leaned in to steal a quick kiss. "I said I trust you. On the sofa. We were sitting there, and I said, 'I don't think you're corrupt,' but I meant, 'I trust you.'"

His eyes gleamed. "I like that."

"It's kind of a big deal that I said that."

He folded his arms across his chest and leaned forward until his forehead touched hers. "Good. I'm taking it as a very big deal. So what happens next?"

"I have no idea. I've never gotten this far before. Do we have to decide right now?"

He took her hand and guided her to the dining table again then disappeared back into the kitchen only to reappear with a slice of Paradise. He set it down in front of her and took a seat. "This is going to require more fuel."

She groaned but picked up her fork and sank it into the rich pastry. "Can we eat this and not have a define-the-relationship talk?"

"This is good," he said, pressing his thumb down on a flaky crumb that had escaped the fork. "But not good enough to get you off the hook. Answer the question, Miss Burke. What happens next?"

She shook her head. "I'm not kidding when I say I don't know."

"Okay," he said, settling into the chair and stretching his legs in front of him. "Let me backtrack to a different question, then. Instead of what happens next, tell me what just happened."

"What do you mean?"

"I mean, how did we go from you yelling at me on the Library of Congress steps this afternoon to you deciding that you trust me tonight?"

She studied the mosaic tile in the tabletop and considered what to tell him. She wasn't sure she knew the answer herself. Maybe it was Jessie's admonition to take a leap of faith. Or maybe it was realizing that of all the people who had walked away from her in her life, Jake was the one most adamant about coming back.

She raised her head and met his eyes. "Call it instinct. I'm trusting my gut."

"Your gut, huh?" He grinned. "I was aiming higher. Like maybe the heart region."

Her stomach gave a giddy flip. "One step at a time," she teased. "You've already got my lips. Let's start there."

"Fine. For now."

She stared at him and drummed her fingers impatiently.

"What?" he asked.

"I meant let's start there *now*."

And after he finished laughing, he did.

Chapter 27

SANDY LEANED AGAINST THE DOORWAY to her closet and considered the dress in her hand. The deep purple was a good color for her, but she wanted something more springlike. She wished she was the type of girl who owned a lacy, frothy, ruffled, floral confection of a dress, because that suited her mood this morning. Whatever she picked, she needed something to add a little color to her cheeks after a late night on the phone with Jake.

She collapsed on her bed in a heap of happiness. She'd had a perfect weekend with him, and now, in one more hour, she would see him at church. She didn't want to look haggard, especially since on the inside she felt as wired as she had over her first crush in junior high.

Magdalena poked her head around the door. "I want to go with you."

Sandy pulled her purple dress over her face to block the argument she'd been having with her mother for most of the morning. "No."

"I'm going to call your priest and tell him you're not meeting your recruitment quota."

"What are you talking about?" Sandy shifted the dress out of the way so she could give her mother the evil eye.

"Well, you didn't go for a mission so you didn't get any recruits there. And now you won't bring me to church, so you're missing an opportunity here too. You'll get in big trouble for that."

"Recruits? Do you mean converts? We don't have quotas. And you're still not coming with me."

"I don't understand you at all."

"No kidding," Sandy mumbled, but her mother pretended not to hear and warmed to her campaign.

"For years you've said I don't understand your religion, and now that I want to go learn about it, you won't let me. I've always shared my beliefs with you."

"Shared? That's how we're going to characterize your attempts to brainwash me since childhood? Ha!"

"Hey! That's not very Christian."

Sandy gaped at her mother. "You have no idea what Christianity is!"

"Exactly!" her mother cried like it was the "Eureka!" moment she'd been waiting for Sandy to have. "How am I supposed to learn if you won't take me with you?"

Sandy groaned and buried her head under the dress again, which was now so badly wrinkled that she couldn't possibly wear it. She didn't know what bee had crept into Magdalena's metaphysical bonnet this morning, but the woman would not give up this notion of tagging along. If she'd believed for one second that Magdalena was sincere in wanting to learn about the LDS faith, she'd have said yes. But Magdalena had come to church with her once before when she earned her Young Womanhood recognition medallion, and it had been a disaster. Magdalena had ambushed her Laurel advisor after sacrament meeting with a fifteen-minute rant about modern feminism and the evils of a male-dominated priesthood.

Sandy plucked the dress away and sat up to face her mom. "You know why I don't want you to go. I trusted you once, and it was a nightmare. I'm sorry, but I'm not taking you." She wouldn't sacrifice her last refuge from Magdalena just because her mother was playing the guilt card.

"Maybe I'll go by myself, then."

"You don't know where it is. Besides, we meet for three hours. You hate sitting still that long."

"I would do it for you, Sand Dollar." Her mother's tone was sweet. "Whether you realize it or not, I'm trying to do what's best for us, but if you don't want to take me, I'll check with the girls downstairs."

Brooke would find it a total hoot. Sandy had to put a stop to this.

She took a deep breath. "Mom," she said, hoping to soften Magdalena up. "What is this about?"

"I want to learn about your religion."

"No," Sandy sighed, "you don't. Tell me what you really want."

Magdalena wandered over to the dresser and picked up one of the lemon candles. She inhaled deeply then set it down and fiddled with a couple of the perfume bottles Sandy kept on top. She sniffed one of them and sprayed some on her wrist, mumbling something under her breath.

"What did you say?"

Magdalena turned around and crossed her arms over her chest. It was an unusually defensive posture for her. "I want what Jake has."

Sandy wrinkled her brow. This conversation was making less sense as they went. "An expensive car and designer suits?"

"Don't be ridiculous."

"It makes as much sense as anything you've said this morning."

"He stole my aura!"

"Wha . . . ?"

"I've been working so hard all week to help you balance your chi and create some cosmic harmony in our relationship. The aura between us has been orange for years."

"That's bad?" Sandy guessed.

"It's not good. Pink is best. Pink is a happy, healthy aura. I finally got our aura to peach a couple of days ago. A couple more days and I could have gotten it to pink, but Jake stole it."

"Jake is walking around with a pink aura?" Sandy asked, distracted by the mental picture.

"No," Magdalena snapped. "Pay attention. Your aura together is pink. Separately he's a purple. It's a virile color. Every time you've been around each other all week, you've made a bright red. Energy, conflict, potential. But now, suddenly, it's pink. And you and I are still peach." She whipped back around and toyed with the perfume bottles again.

Sandy felt like she should do something to reassure her mother but had no idea what. She sat on the bed, stumped. "I'm sorry." She offered the apology tentatively, not sure that's what Magdalena wanted. "I thought you *wanted* me to hang out with Jake this weekend."

After their peace summit on Friday night, she'd wanted nothing more than to make up for lost time. She'd checked with Magdalena before inviting him over on Saturday. Her mother had insisted not only that he come over but that the two of them not worry about including her because she wanted to balance her chakras with deep meditation. She'd shooed them out of the house and seemed pleased when Sandy returned later that night and reported that they had spent a great afternoon at Rock Creek Park, followed by a fantastic dinner of Chesapeake crab at a local dive. Sandy had capped the night off with a couple of hours of Animal Planet with Magdalena and then talked to Jake until the early hours of the morning after he called to say good night.

"I want you to follow your bliss, Sand Dollar. But I've spent years trying to heal the hurt I've done you, and you keep me out. Jake makes a mess of things, and you forgive him in one night. He gets the pink aura, and it's not fair!"

Nonplussed, Sandy sat staring at her frustrated mother with no clue about what to do next. As Magdalena's words sank in, one key point bubbled out of her confusion. "Did you say you wanted to fix how you hurt me?"

Magdalena sniffed and nodded.

"You've never said anything like that before. You've never even acknowledged that you've had anything to fix. I feel kind of . . . stunned."

"Guru Hamir told me years ago that clinging to regret was a way of keeping our spirits chained to the past, and I should let go of all regret." She crossed to Sandy and climbed onto the bed. "Maybe that's true for some people. But I don't think it's true for me. Or, at least, I don't think ignoring regret is the way to let go of it."

She dropped her head and stared down at her lap like it was a magic looking glass that would deliver her the words she was searching for. "I went with a friend to a retreat two years ago, where the main speaker talked about guilt and forgiveness. And she talked about restoration, about making things whole again if you break them. I realized that if your blocked chi was interfering in our relationship, I had probably blocked it."

It was a remarkable insight for Magdalena and much closer to the truth than she usually got with her New Age buzzwords. Sandy didn't say anything, not wanting to interrupt a rare flash of clarity for her mother.

"Anyway," Magdalena continued, "I realized I needed to make things right with you. And I've been trying to be in your life like I wasn't when you were a kid. But I guess I don't know how to do it, because you and Jake are pink, and we're still stuck at peach." Sadness clogged her voice. "What do I do, Sandy? How do I make this better? Is it too late?"

Sandy didn't answer. Her thoughts and feelings chased each other in a dizzying circle while she tried to figure out where to fit in Magdalena's confession and plea. It wasn't until she heard another sad sniff that she realized Magdalena was crying. As expressive as her mother had always been, Sandy could never remember her crying. The tears shocked her.

"Don't cry. Really, don't." She hopped up and searched for tissues, settled for a wad of toilet paper from the bathroom across the hall, and raced back to hand her mother the crumpled bundle. "It's okay," she said, helpless to know how to reassure her mother and surprised that she wanted to.

"Is it?" Magdalena asked. "Sometimes I think it's never going to be okay. I've been working at this for two years!"

"It might have helped if I knew you wanted me to forgive you."

"I didn't want you to dismiss this as another fad. I thought maybe actions would speak louder than words this time. I was so sure if I worked at it long enough, you would see how much I want to fix our relationship. Haven't you noticed anything different about the last two years?"

"Now that you've pointed it out, I do," Sandy admitted. From the time she had graduated high school until recently—two years ago recently, as a matter of fact—their relationship had been distant in every sense of the word. Sandy usually spent holidays and vacations with friends rather than going home. "Home" hadn't meant anything anyway. Magdalena had called every few months when she remembered she had a daughter, and Sandy had sometimes bothered to pick up. Then Magdalena had started inviting her to different retreats or inviting herself to Sandy's place for a visit.

At first Sandy had ignored most of these invitations too, but Jessie had convinced her to let Magdalena come around. Without fail, her mother drove her crazy, and without fail, Jessie always managed to convince her that Magdalena wasn't that bad before her next visit. Sandy had even taken up her mother's offer of a spa weekend, the one and only time she'd ever accepted Magdalena's invite. It had not gone well, thanks to the self-help charlatan running that particular retreat. His approach to "liberating" Sandy from her "modern baggage" had been decidedly more hands-on than she was okay with. More like handsy. Blech.

After that, they had sunk into a pattern where Sandy rejected a handful of Magdalena's invitations to hit some New Age hot spots and then, feeling guilty, caved when Magdalena wanted to come see her. A few stressful days later, Magdalena would leave, and they'd start their routine all over again. It didn't occur to her that Magdalena was trying, in her own misguided way, to fix their relationship.

"I don't know what else to do," Magdalena said, verging on a wail. "Jake is practically ruining your career and you'll date him, but I try to share life space with you and you can barely stand to have me around." She swiped at her eyes with the toilet paper.

"Jake isn't ruining my career," Sandy said. "And I didn't know you were trying to share my life space. I thought you only came around when you ran out of other interesting places to go."

"I'd go anywhere for you."

She meant it; Sandy could tell, and she softened. Or softened further. Despite the bad timing of her mother's visit and her exasperation at Magdalena's antics, Sandy'd gotten kind of used to having her around. There was something to be said for having her mom waiting for her at the end of a long work day, waiting to greet her the only way she knew how. Maybe as a kid she'd never come home to fresh-baked cookies and a glass of milk, but it was nice to have Magdalena light candles and heat up tofu.

"Okay," Sandy said, uncertain of how to navigate this new territory. "I'm not sure what to say."

"Say you don't hate me. Say there's a chance you'll forgive me one day."

Sandy slowly nodded. "I didn't like having to be the adult as a kid. While you tried to find yourself, I got lost in the shuffle. When Dad took off, that left me with no one. It wasn't an easy way to grow up."

"I'm so sorry. I don't know how to be a regular mom. I never felt adequate. I figured if I found the right path to enlightenment, it would help me be a better person and parent. It didn't work out like that though."

Sandy said nothing, because it was true.

"One day I turned around, and you were gone. I mean, you were in the same house with me, but you were checked out." Magdalena dragged a hand through her hair, badly disarranging it and not caring. "You had a whole new family when you joined your church. It seemed like you were doing fine. I was still looking for me, so I just let it go." She rose to her knees and reached out to touch Sandy's face, stroking her daughter's cheek with a feather-light touch. "If I had any idea how many years that would cost me with you, I would have held on so tight."

Sandy reached up and took Magdalena's hand, the one caressing her, and, wrapping it in her own, brought their joined hands down to rest in her lap. Emotion she couldn't name overwhelmed her, and she waited for the tightness in her throat to subside before she tried to speak. Even so, her first attempt failed, and she cleared her throat before trying again.

"This is the craziest weekend ever," she said, with a small laugh. "Everything is inside out. I'm suddenly dating the guy I hate, and the mother I wanted twenty years ago just showed up. I don't know what to think."

Magdalena squeezed her hand and offered a tiny, hopeful smile.

"All right, Magdalena." She exhaled deeply, trying to breathe out all the confusion she'd been harboring. "I don't know how to do this, how to make us better, but I'd like to try."

Magdalena beamed. "I'm so glad." She swiped at another tear.

"Well. Uh, where do we start?"

"Maybe you could call me Mom."

"Mom." Sandy tried it out, saying it honestly instead of as a gambit to soften her mother up. "I can do that."

"Good." Magdalena pulled her into an embrace, not one of her fluttery specialties but a full-fledged hug. "And one more thing. Can you change my ringtone?"

Chapter 28

"WHAT WAS THAT FOR?" JAKE took his eyes off the road for a quick glance at her as Sandy heaved a deep, dramatic sigh.

"I don't know," she said. "I don't know if that's a sigh of relief or a bummed-out sigh." They had dropped her mom off at the airport and were driving back to Sandy's place.

"It could be both, right?" Jake asked.

"Yeah, it could." In the past, it had been all she could do to refrain from shoving her mother's luggage onto the airport curb and laying rubber in her hurry to escape. While she was glad to have her own space back, Sandy suspected it might feel the tiniest bit empty when she returned to it this time.

"I like your mom."

"Me too," she admitted. "Don't tell her I said that."

When they pulled into her driveway, she started to climb out of the car, but Jake stayed put in his seat. She shut her door again and turned to face him. "What's up?"

He took her hand, absently brushing his thumb over her knuckles. "How are you feeling about this week?"

"In terms of . . . ?"

He smiled. "Tomorrow the zoning death match starts up again. Are you okay with that?"

She shrugged. "*Okay* is maybe not the right word. But it is what it is."

"I can't wait for this whole mess to be over. I'm tired of having it hang over us."

"To tell you the truth, as much as I hate that you're on the other side, I kind of like seeing you in action."

His eyes gleamed. "Is that a fact?" He leaned toward her and growled, "Speaking of action . . ."

She laughed and pushed him away. "Yes, that's a fact. I like knowing that you can earn an honest living and you're good at what you do." She sobered for a minute. "It is an honest living, right?"

"Are we going there again? We can if you want to."

"No." She leaned forward to offer him a quick kiss. "It's fine. I said I trust you, and I do." She smiled when he squeezed her hand. "Do you want to come up for a little while? I'm sure Larry will be happy to see you."

"Larry, huh? Tempting, but no. Thanks to a certain gorgeous redhead, I'm running short on sleep this weekend, and I don't know if you heard or not, but I have a deadline on Wednesday with the zoning commission."

"I had no idea."

He smiled. "Should we pretend there's no such thing as work when we're together until this whole stupid mess is over?"

"I vote yes."

"It's unanimous, then," Jake declared. "We don't talk work until the final decision of the commission is in, and then we pretend the whole thing never happened."

"Just call me the queen of denial."

"It's not just a river in Egypt."

"Boo." She poked him for his corny joke.

"Ow." He narrowed his eyes and then leaned forward. "First, I'm going to be a gentleman and come open your door for you. Then I'm going to make you pay for that."

"Make *me* pay? I'm not the one torturing people with lame jokes."

"That's it. Payback starts now."

She scrambled from the car and ran for her stairs, laughing too hard to maintain much of a lead. He caught her around the waist as she reached the first step and startled a happy shriek out of her.

"Gotcha."

She turned and wrapped her arms around his neck. "Yeah. You do."

* * *

Sandy stared at the conference table, puzzled. She had laid out every piece of documentation in the three boxes Jake had delivered and skimmed through all of it. She had no doubt that she now had the exact same information he had when he put together his argument for historical preservation status, but it left her with far more questions than answers.

First, Jake's argument to the panel had implied that the park Magnus was commissioned to design was intended to rival Central Park in New York.

The few specifics she could locate on the park indicated that the capital city project was on a far smaller scale, equal to the size of one city block. There was a letter to Robert Magnus from a man named Jacob D. Cox, whom Google identified as the secretary of the Interior under President Grant. The letter referred to prior communications about the park and noted that the president was pleased that Magnus had accepted the commission.

Sandy didn't suppose people often said no to the president when he asked for anything, no matter the president or the assignment. Still, details about the park were scant. Beyond the size, she could find nothing describing what it should look like except for a single sentence in Secretary Cox's letter that mentioned looking forward to the result of Magnus's "creative endeavors with much anticipation."

Even after spending three days reviewing all of the research, the only new and pertinent information she had was that at one point, a Magnus park had been intended for an area that might *possibly* have been where the strip mall now stood. At best, it was a modest, bordering on inconsequential, side project for someone of Magnus's professional stature. Even if reams of evidence suddenly surfaced that put the park in the dead center of River Oaks Landing, there was no reference point for restoration or details about its original appearance or function.

Despite seeing Jake nearly every night that week, she hadn't brought up River Oaks once. Their growing closeness aside, Sandy had no doubt he was as committed to winning his case for his client as she was for New Horizons, and she didn't expect him to offer pointers any more than she would.

She eyed her watch. The zoning commission needed any additional written arguments and evidence supporting or opposing the historical landmark status by the close of business today. It gave her five hours to wrangle the research before her into some kind of report that would discredit the claim that the park should be restored.

At best the evidence was inconclusive. She guessed Jake was getting the big bucks because he would be able to finesse the few existing facts into some kind of irrefutable argument in favor of restoration. That made sense for the neighborhood; the River Oaks people would probably delight in seeing the strip mall razed in favor of a landscaped green space. However, the neighbors weren't paying Jake's bills, and it made no sense for Ranger Properties at all. If they were planning to develop the area, they would lose an entire city block to the park if it was restored. That represented significant income that could be generated by everything from building new homes to opening an updated retail space.

The whole strategy was a no-win endgame. If the zoning commission ruled for restoration, everybody lost. The annex wouldn't open, and Ranger couldn't develop the area for their own profit. Sandy couldn't figure out what Jake was up to, but she reminded herself that she had decided to trust him. He said he was working out a solution that was best for everyone, and she was counting on that. In the meantime, she would figure out what case to make for the annex and somehow get it typed and submitted before the deadline.

She settled in for an intense afternoon.

* * *

A chickpea fell off of her plate, and she smashed it with a fork before scooping it up and returning it to the edge of her plate.

"Sandy?"

"Hm?"

"Remember me? Jake? Your date for the evening? You doin' okay?"

She glanced up to find him smiling at her, a faint glimmer of concern in his eyes.

"I'm fine."

"You sure? You're abusing your dinner, and I don't think it deserves it."

"Yeah, sorry. I'm distracted, I guess."

He watched another chickpea fall off of her plate. "Is it something you want to talk about?"

She shook her head. "Can't. It falls under the heading of stuff we're pretending doesn't exist."

"Ah. How about if I come up with a subject of conversation, then?"

"Go for it."

He pushed his plate aside and leaned back in his chair. They were eating at her place again, some takeout from a nearby Indian place, and the smell of curry hung in the air. "I'd like you to meet my family," he said.

She'd met the families of past boyfriends plenty of times but usually because they lived in the area and it was a casual drop-in for dinner. Meeting Jake's family meant something different.

"They're coming to town?" she asked, stalling while she tried to sort through her feelings.

"No."

Her head shot up. Jake's parents and most of his siblings lived in the Chicago suburbs. This was definitely a next-level commitment. "Oh." It was the only thing she could think to say.

He watched her closely. "I was thinking that next week after the final hearing is over, I could cash in some of my frequent flier miles for a pair of tickets, and we could spend the weekend at my parents' house."

"I can't," Sandy said, still reeling from the implications.

His jaw tightened. "Thanks for thinking about it at least."

She stared at him, surprised by his sarcasm.

"Sorry. That was supposed to come out funnier than it did."

"I didn't mean that I can't, like I don't want to. I'll be in Seattle next weekend for Jessie's wedding. I'm a bridesmaid."

His face relaxed. "I forgot about that. Sorry for jumping to conclusions."

With a shrug, she returned to showing her chickpeas who was boss to avoid eye contact with him. "It's okay. I did."

"Did what?"

"Jumped to conclusions." She smashed another chickpea.

"About what?"

"Your invitation. I may have read into it." Another chickpea bit the dust.

"Sandy."

"Yes?"

"Look at me."

She tore her eyes away from her chickpeas and met his.

"What did you read into my invitation?"

She met his eyes again. "That it seems kind of like a next step."

"Are you okay with that?" The lines around his eyes looked deeper than normal.

She gave up on her meal. Her appetite had vanished. A trip to the kitchen bought a couple of extra minutes to consider her answer. If she listened to reason, then going to Chicago so soon made no sense at all. They still had a lot of things to figure out about each other before she could be sure she wanted to get all attached to his family. That's what her head said. But her gut . . .

If she assumed the warm glow there wasn't heartburn from the curry, then she had to admit that all of her instincts were telling her to go for it, to take another leap of faith.

Walking back to the table, she stopped behind his chair and leaned down to wrap her arms around him. She dropped a kiss on the top of his head. "Yeah, I'm totally okay with that."

He reached around and pulled her onto his lap for a hug. "I'm glad. I thought I blew it there for a second."

"No. We're good."

He pulled her tighter then leaned his head against hers. "Good. Then all we have to do is make it through that stupid hearing and we're set."

Chapter 29

"ON YOUR MARK, GET SET, go!"

Sandy grinned at Jasmine's joke as the commission members filed into the hearing chamber.

"Seriously," Jasmine said, nudging Sandy. "Run up and start talking so fast in the microphone that Jake never has a chance. Your infatuation isn't making you soft, is it?"

Sandy rolled her eyes. She'd admitted to Jasmine that she and Jake were dating and had regretted it ever since. Her friend delighted in teasing her about fraternizing with the enemy and hatched at least a dozen jokes a day. "Have some decorum, woman."

"No, you," Jasmine returned with a nod toward an approaching Jake. "Don't go getting all gooey and embarrassing."

"Don't worry. We do that on our own time."

Jasmine pretended to gag, and Sandy ignored her. "Hi," she said, when Jake reached them. This was their first on-the-job interaction since they'd officially started dating, and she couldn't wait for the hearing to be over so they could put it behind them.

"Are you ready?" he asked.

"As I'll ever be."

"I'd better watch out, then." He smiled, and she returned it.

She wanted to come up with something more personal to say, but it wasn't the time or place, especially not with Jasmine's eagle eye watching. Jake nodded and gave a polite hello to Jasmine, who returned it coolly. With a final amused smile for Sandy, he returned to his side of the room to wait for the hearing to start.

Sandy turned to stare at her coworker, exasperated. "He's not the devil, I swear."

Jasmine scowled. "I'm not going to ask if you've checked for a tail or not. What about sprinkling him with holy water? Have you tried that?"

"Mormons don't have holy water. Unless root beer counts," Sandy added as an afterthought.

Her friend's face grew serious. "Look, jokes aside, are you sure you can trust him?"

"Yes." There was no hesitation in her answer. She had spent two weeks letting her guard down further and further with Jake, and it felt good. There was a sense of ease between them unlike anything she'd ever known in a relationship before. She'd had this kind of openness in her friendship with Jessie, but even with her, she'd never shared some of the things she had with Jake. Despite paying for it the following days at work, they'd spent several late nights on the phone in conversations that meandered through every corner of their lives, learning about each other, discovering each other.

"You've shown excellent judgment other than your questionable taste in men. Although he is obnoxiously good looking," Jasmine conceded. "I'll take your word for it that this is going to be okay."

"It will be," Sandy said.

It felt odd to be so sure when she had no idea what his plan was. Because of client confidentiality, Jake hadn't elaborated any more on his assertion that he was working on a solution that benefited the most people, but that had to include the future clients of a New Horizons annex, or it couldn't be a true statement. Tonight she would finally see what he'd been up to, although she couldn't see how anything short of him retracting the claim of historical landmark status could help either of their causes.

A few more observers straggled in, but it was nothing like the crowd of two weeks before, since tonight the commission's decision would be final and the only people permitted to speak would be the designated representatives of New Horizons and the River Oaks group, if asked.

The clerk stood and called the meeting to order, and then the chairman took over. Just as before, the commission heard several disputes and requests ahead of theirs, and Sandy only half listened as she reviewed her statement in her mind. She'd spent several more days combing through the research on Magnus and had put together the best argument she could. If the committee saw things her way, Ranger Properties would be the only loser in the scenario, and she could not care less what they wanted. Jake would have to settle for a victory on behalf of the neighbors who were his client of record anyway.

Over an hour dragged by before the chairman called for item J, the vote on the annex. As it stood, the annex was already approved. Now the decision would be whether or not to revoke their permit.

"The panel will now vote on River Oaks versus New Horizons, an agenda item that was tabled at our last meeting pending further investigation. On the first claim that the proposed annex will negatively impact the crime rate in the River Oaks community, do any of the commissioners wish to speak?" He surveyed the other four people at the council table, and they shook their heads. "Then we move to a vote. All in favor of revoking the permit, vote aye."

Sandy held her breath. This was the first major hurdle they had to clear. The first commissioner spoke a clear nay into the microphone. Good. One down, four to go. When the second no came in opposing the claim, she snuck a peek at Jake. He didn't seem too concerned. When the final unanimous vote came in denying his claim, he looked unperturbed. She was glad but puzzled. She didn't want him to be upset, but he was taking it far better than she would have. Maybe he'd trained himself to keep a poker face after all his time in the courtroom.

The chairman directed the clerk to enter the result into the record and then addressed the second part of the claim. "The River Oaks group asserts that the parcel of land currently occupied by the River Oaks Landing shopping development is a historical landmark based on records dating back to 1872. Both parties have submitted their research. Have all members of this panel reviewed the evidence and arguments?"

This time, everyone nodded yes.

Satisfied, he leafed through a few papers in front of him, skimming quickly. "Do any of the commissioners wish to speak?"

The architect of the Capitol, Dennis Beamons, lifted a finger to catch the chairman's attention. "I have a couple of questions," he said. "I would direct these to Mr. Manning."

The chairman waved Jake up to the lectern, and Jake stood, looking confident as he waited for Mr. Beamons' questions. Sandy had a feeling this is where she'd finally glimpse his strategy. He'd need to walk a delicate balance between still defending his clients' interests and subtly discrediting the viability of restoring a long-forgotten park—a reversal of his previous claim—but Sandy was sure he could do it. The River Oaks group would eventually forget their concerns when the annex opened and the neighborhood realized the women posed no threat. After all, they weren't paying the bills;

Ranger Properties was, and they would not be happy to have that land locked up and unavailable to develop.

Mr. Beamons fired his first question. "Mr. Manning, the only documentation you submitted to substantiate the existence of a Magnus park was a letter from Grant's secretary of the Interior referring to Magnus as accepting the commission. Do you have any evidence that the park was ever built?"

Good, Sandy thought. He had been handed the perfect out. She smiled at Jasmine, who had obviously grasped that this worked in their favor.

"There are no schematics on record," Jake began. "But I think we've found sufficient evidence over the last week through additional research to prove that it existed."

Jasmine shot Sandy a puzzled look, and Sandy could only crinkle her brow in confusion. There hadn't been anything in the research she'd received from him, which left her as clueless as Jasmine.

"I need to request the commission's indulgence for not submitting this earlier," he continued, "but the information surfaced only in the last few days."

Sandy didn't know what new information he had, but she had a sick feeling in her stomach that told her it wouldn't do her side any good. She stood and cleared her throat. "Mr. Chairman, I apologize for interrupting, but I think you were very clear in your directions during the last hearing that all evidence was to be submitted a week ago. It's inappropriate for Mr. Manning to bring it up now."

"I understand Ms. Burke's concern," Jake said easily, "but this isn't a court of law, and this council has some leeway in this instance. It would be a mistake to issue a decision without all of the facts, and that's what I'd like to provide you with."

What is he doing? Jasmine mouthed. Sandy shook her head, frustrated. She didn't know.

The chairman nodded at Jake. "Go ahead, Mr. Manning. I don't appreciate you bringing this up so late in the game, but you're right. What new evidence have you uncovered?"

Jake waved to a middle-aged woman who had accompanied him to the hearing. Sandy assumed she was a paralegal or office assistant. "With your permission, Mrs. Layton will pass out a short outline of what we discovered this week." When the chairman nodded, Jake continued. "All of our research about this park focused on the information available through public records and the documents at the Library of Congress. As you know, we found some evidence that a park had been intended for that spot, but it wasn't compelling. I began to wonder if we were looking at the wrong records. We checked with the Capitol Historical Society. As you know, they're a nonprofit group that keeps records not of interest to the larger institutions like the Library of Congress. These records include things like photos and correspondence between ordinary citizens documenting day-to-day life."

Although she still wasn't sure where he was going with this, the pit in Sandy's stomach opened wider. This didn't sound like he was letting the historical park argument fade quietly away. If it didn't, then it would be the annex that faded instead. Her shoulders tightened, and tension crept up her neck.

"We discovered one journal and one packet of letters from a Mrs. William Rigby, whose husband worked for the War Department. She wrote regularly to her sister in Richmond, Virginia, and the letters are now on file with the Historical Society." His assistant stood again to pass another paper out to each commissioner. "Mrs. Layton is now distributing photocopied excerpts from three different letters in this collection. The originals can be made available by the Society on special request."

The chairman interrupted. "We'll review these fully, but in the interest of time, what's the gist?"

"The letters refer to the afternoons she spent with her children at a park near her home, a park designed by Robert Magnus. She didn't know much about him. She calls him a 'fancy Chicago gentleman who designed the shrubbery.' She thinks it's an odd job, little more than glorified gardening. But I'm going to quote her here. She writes to her sister, 'Still, I look around at this little piece of Heaven and cannot deny that it is several steps above ordinary and perhaps worth all the fuss that was made when the park finally opened last year. It just grows more beautiful as new plants and flowers blossom and reveal themselves, and I'm disposed to think more generously of that fancy gardener.'" He paused to let that sink in.

One of the other commissioners cleared his throat. "It's a nice piece of history, Mr. Manning, but it doesn't specify that this Magnus park was on the disputed land parcel."

Jake smiled. "The letter itself doesn't, but its envelope does. If you refer to the last copy in your packet, it's a reproduction of the envelope this letter was in. She mentions in one of her letters that she needed only to walk a quarter of a mile east of her home to reach the park. Her return address, when matched with a street map of the time, shows that she was taking her children to a park situated exactly where the strip mall is now."

Sandy sat stunned and unmoving. The evidence he presented wasn't a slam dunk, but it was damaging. Extremely so. And not only because it significantly strengthened his historical landmark claim. With his presentation, delivered in such a calm and measured tone, he had effectively launched a grenade at her plans for the annex *and* their relationship itself. It was almost as if she could feel the concussion of the explosion as her trust in him disintegrated. The sound of her own heartbeat was so loud in her ears that she missed the next few exchanges between Jake and the commissioners.

The chairman thanked him and then excused Jake to his seat, and as Jake turned, he caught her eye. He offered her a cautious smile, clearly uncertain of her reception. For the first time that night, she saw his confidence waver when she didn't return the gesture. She remained stone-faced because she didn't know what to think or feel besides a growing sense of betrayal. She stared at him long and hard before she deliberately blinked and returned her attention to the chairman.

He clarified a procedural point for his clerk, but he soon turned back to the microphone and called her name. "Miss Burke, you're here representing New Horizons, correct?"

"Yes, sir," she managed to confirm around the lump in her throat.

"Do you wish to speak any further on this issue?"

"Yes, I do." She climbed to her feet slowly. She had no idea what to say other than, "Jake Manning cheated, and you shouldn't let him win, or the universe will implode." But she couldn't say that. When she reached the lectern, she gripped the sides and paused for a minute to collect her thoughts.

"Miss Burke?" the chairman prompted her.

"Yes, sir." She fought the urge to shoot a panicked look at Jasmine, and blocking Jake and the pain that threatened to swallow her whole, she focused on the annex. "As I stated in the previous hearing, I don't question the need to preserve the important elements of our nation's history. But the key word is *important*, and that's a matter of interpretation. At best, the anecdotal evidence points to a small park, almost a folly of a landscape architect who left no copy of his plans for this park and didn't make mention of it in his personal or business journals. That alone raises questions about the true value of this park. How much could it have mattered if it was so easily lost to time?" She took a deep breath, knowing that the outlook for the annex was grim. She groped for the right words to save it, but the sense of calm she'd had when speaking here two weeks before had evaporated, and she battled the wave of hurt from Jake's betrayal. She bet he would try to explain it away as "just business," but he had deliberately withheld information that would torpedo her case and hadn't had the decency to warn her. When she heard one of the commissioners shifting in his seat, Sandy offered her last argument.

"It would be wrong to trade the future of the women this annex is intended to help for the past—a questionable piece of the past at that. There is no way to determine the true value of that park in a historical context because it didn't impact anyone enough for them to have saved it or done more than mention it in passing in some old letters. There is also no way to determine the value of the women who need this annex or their potential, because they're priceless. Without a record, it would be impossible to restore that park to its former state. Without the annex, it will be nearly impossible for these women to change their futures. We respectfully remind you that it is their futures that hang in the balance on this decision. Furthermore, it won't benefit the community at all to restrict this land so that it can't be used to generate revenue for anyone. You can't let property become more important than people." She stopped and then gave a single nod to indicate that she was done. She didn't dare speak and reveal how close to tears she was. When she took her seat again, Jasmine lifted an eyebrow and shrugged as if to say, "That's all you can do."

"Thank you both for your input," the chairman said. "Normally, we would vote on granting a permanent injunction against the New Horizons annex, but this is a special case. Because this disputed park is in the District boundaries, if it is in fact a historical landmark, it will fall under federal protection and become the responsibility of the director of National Parks. He will determine whether his office will grant historical landmark status. Director, are you ready to issue a decision at this time?"

Sandy could feel Jake's eyes on her, but she refused to even look at him, instead focusing all of her attention and energy on the director, willing him to keep the annex alive.

He leaned into the microphone and announced his decision. "After careful consideration of the evidence submitted last week and the new evidence submitted this week, we have made a decision. Miss Burke, I am deeply sympathetic to your cause, but although it is flawed, there is too much evidence supporting the existence of a Magnus park at the River Oaks site."

Sandy felt sick. The rest of his words reached her as if they were coming down a long tunnel. She barely noted Jasmine's hand gripping her arm.

"Our office is charged with preserving our national heritage, and I'm afraid that in this case, it will be at the cost of the annex. Mr. Chairman, the Parks Department finds that the River Oaks Landing site shall be granted provisional historical landmark status pending a further investigation of the park's original appearance and function to be conducted by my office. All businesses currently located there may continue to operate until a decision about restoration has been reached. There will be no new development or licenses granted for businesses in that location until our investigation is complete."

Her head spun, and Sandy fought the urge to lean over and place it between her knees like she used to do when she got dizzy in middle school PE.

Theirs was the last issue on the agenda, so in a matter of minutes, the chairman had adjourned the meeting, and the commission filed back out through the door leading to their offices.

Jasmine hadn't said anything, but she turned to Sandy and gave her a hard stare. "Do not blame yourself for this, girl. I know you're going to try, but it isn't your fault, so give that idea up right now. No one could have gotten up and made that argument as well as you did. This is not your fault," she repeated.

Sandy swallowed, trying to dislodge the disappointment caught in her throat, making it hard to swallow. "It wasn't good enough. I trusted that Jake had handed me everything I needed, and I didn't ask any more questions. I should have kept looking. I should have been prepared for this."

Jasmine shook her arm. "Stop it right now. Jake's firm has a massive number of secretaries and associates scurrying around brainstorming stuff like this. You're an army of one, and regardless of what the real Army says, sometimes it isn't enough. Even if you had thought of this, there's no way you would have had the time or resources to uncover what they did. Besides which, you're still new to town and don't have these kinds of connections yet."

"That's no excuse. He's new here too."

"Yeah, but his fleet of office droids isn't," Jasmine pointed out. She sighed. "Look, I understand why you're upset, but don't beat yourself up. Roberta isn't going to be upset with you, and I'm definitely not. It will take time, but we'll find another place for the annex. You can hold your head high."

Even though she knew Jasmine never said things just to hear herself talk, her sincerity wasn't much of a salve at the moment. Sandy felt like a raw, exposed nerve, and every part of her throbbed with hurt, inside and out. Beyond the sting of losing the hearing, a deep and growing pain crowded her chest. And yet, there Jake was, making his way toward her through a small crowd of well-wishers. She could see the hope-tinged smile on his face, and her stomach clenched. Did he really think forgiveness would be that easy?

She stood to gather her things. She wanted to be on her feet when she dealt with him and not give him the slightest edge over her. He'd already taken so much advantage of her that the scope of his manipulation made it hard for her to breathe.

"Sandy," he said, and it made her skin crawl to hear him say her name in the same sweet way he had for the past two weeks. She didn't trust herself to speak, so she turned to meet him with a flat stare and said nothing.

"Can we talk?" he asked.

She shook her head and shoved a copy of the evening's agenda into her Coach bag. Jasmine intervened. "You got what you wanted. Their decision is final. There's nothing else to say, so why are you standing here trying to say something?"

"I understand that you're upset—"

Sandy's head shot up. "No. You don't. If you had the faintest idea of how I feel, you wouldn't be standing here trying to talk to me right now." She shouldered her purse strap and stepped around him. "I'm going home. Congratulations on your victory." She couldn't keep the bitterness out of her voice as she called the last part out over her shoulder.

"Sandy—" he called after her, but then she heard Jasmine start in on him again, and she hurried toward her car, grateful for the escape. She was pulling out when she saw him burst from the building and head toward the parking lot at nearly a run. She ignored him when he tried to wave her down, and she gunned the engine toward home. She spent every one of the twenty minutes it took to get there fighting to keep her mind a merciful blank. A few tears escaped, and she dashed them away. Every time a hot wave of anger at Jake or shame at her gullibility threatened to drown her, she focused on the white lines on the road ahead and nothing more.

She walked through her door exhausted. Even Larry fled when Sandy returned her sulky stare with a glare far more fierce. She collapsed onto the sofa and stared at the ceiling, studying the dollar bill. She put every ounce of her dwindling energy into trying to decipher the serial numbers on it and shut out everything else.

She had no idea how much time had passed when she heard an urgent knock at the door. Sure it was Jake, she ignored it. Thirty seconds later, the pounding came again, but she heard Brooke's voice calling to her through the door, not Jake's. "Sandy? Are you okay? Open up, please. I heard you come in, so I know you're home."

Sandy debated ignoring her, but the pounding continued.

"I need to make sure you're okay. Open up, or I'm busting out the key you gave us."

Sandy gave in, dragged herself to the door, and opened it.

"Are you all right?" Brooke demanded. "Your mom called and got me all worried, so I told her I'd come up and check on you."

"My mom?"

"Yeah. She said she'd been trying to reach you for an hour, but your phone was off. She said you had a big night, and she should have heard from you by now. What's going on?"

Sandy turned around and headed back to the sofa. She just wanted to be left alone to stare at her ceiling until her eyeballs couldn't take it anymore. Brooke stood over her, waiting for an explanation, so she thought of one that would appease her.

"I'm fine. I had a rough night at work. I'll text my mom and let her know I'm okay. Thanks for checking on me."

Brooke regarded her uncertainly but finally nodded. "Let me know if there's anything I can do for you," she said and then closed the door quietly behind her.

Sandy had dropped her handbag on the floor near the sofa before collapsing, and she leaned over to fish her phone out of it. When she turned it on, her voice mail alert chimed, and the screen informed her that she had twelve messages waiting for her. Knowing most of them were Jake trying to explain something that couldn't be defended, she ignored them and tapped out a quick message to her mother to reassure her with a promise to call tomorrow. A text came in from Jake before she could even hit send on the message to her mother, but she ignored it and turned the phone off again.

She didn't even bother with her laptop before heading to bed. She had no doubt it would be full of more messages from Jake, and she didn't have it in her to listen to one more lie tonight.

Chapter 30

SHE NEARLY TRIPPED OVER JAKE the next morning. He was waiting outside of her door when she opened it to leave for work. Despite being impeccably dressed in a charcoal suit, he looked as haggard as she felt. Good.

"Go away."

"I want to talk to you."

"No." She headed down the stairs and toward the sidewalk in the direction of the Metro stop. He stayed on her heels and tried again. "Did you get any of my texts?"

"I don't know. I didn't look," she said, stone-faced. "I didn't pick up voice mails or my e-mails, so don't ask about those either." She picked up her pace, and he matched it.

"I want to explain. I know what that looked like last night, but there's more to it than what you saw."

That stopped her. "What do you think I saw, Jake?"

He stuck his hands in his pockets. "It probably looked like I sold you out and withheld information from you."

"You're right. It did. *Because you did.* Please stop following me." She spun around and hurried toward the train, cursing the four-inch heels she wore and wishing for once she'd adopted the hideous practice of wearing running shoes with her business suits.

He didn't listen, instead staying right behind her again. "That's not what it was."

"So you didn't withhold information from me?"

"No."

She stopped again to stare at him in disbelief.

"I gave you everything we found at the Library Congress at the time we had it."

She waved a hand dismissively in the air. "And yet this whole other stack of information from the Historical Society never made its way to me. It's my own fault. I should have learned my lesson a year ago. You don't do what you say you're going to do. You didn't then, and you don't now. The more I think about it, the less it surprises me."

"That's not true."

"Careful. You're not in a position to call me a liar."

"I'm not calling you a liar!" He ran his hand through his hair, obviously not for the first time. "I didn't have any of that information until after I'd already dropped off the library research. I wasn't withholding anything."

"Then why was last night the first time I heard about it?"

"Nothing was stopping you from going out and getting the same information," he said, his voice level.

"Nothing was stopping me except I don't have fifty people ready to jump and do my bidding when I snap my fingers, and you know it. You should have warned me about that new research, Jake. But that's not even the worst part of this." Her voice wobbled, and tears stung her eyes. "The worst part is that you made a promise and broke it."

His carefully composed expression cracked. "I didn't, I swear to you. I'm going to keep every promise I made."

"Really? What about your promise to do the best thing for the most people? I thought that meant *everyone* involved, but since we lost any shot at opening the annex, I guess you really meant you'd do the best thing for the most of *your* people. I'm such an idiot," she said, fighting a sob.

"I know it looks that way, but there's more to it. I'm asking you to have faith in me just a little longer."

That startled a laugh out of her. "You want me to trust you? Then tell me that you're going to make the annex happen. Tell me that you didn't lie about that."

He put his hands on her shoulders and squeezed lightly. "I'm working on something."

She shrugged him off. "Yeah. You're working on Ranger Properties' dime. What are you planning that could possibly make up for this?"

He hesitated then looked regretful. "I can't say anything, Sandy. I promise I'll tell you when this is all worked out, but I'm working hard here to make the right ethical choice."

"I'm so over this, Jake. I know I'm not a big enough pawn for you to have dated me just so you could win the hearing for your client. But I think you planned on winning for them regardless of what's actually right and figured dating me would be a nice bonus." She swiped a hand at a tear that tried to fall. "Congratulations. Don't call me again. I'd say it's been real, but it hasn't. At all."

She headed for the train again and heard his footsteps behind her. She sped up, and he did too. Desperate to escape him before he could see her cry, she slipped off her shoes and set off at a run. She didn't care how crazy she looked, barefoot in her business suit, her hair probably out of control. She wanted to get away from him, to outrun the pain she felt every time she looked into his face. It hurt to realize that the laugh lines around his eyes that she had come to adore, the quick twist of his lips he couldn't stop when he was amused but trying to keep a straight face, were all part of his carefully rehearsed charm. It was smoke and mirrors and had been all along.

The footsteps behind her slowed and then faded. He was letting her go. She reached the train barely in time, the doors closing as she slipped in, and slid back into her shoes. She dashed away the tears that slid down her cheeks and struggled to compose herself. She sensed the surreptitious glances from the other passengers who were watching her as she stood there sniffling but trying not to. Who knew that when a heart broke, everything in it came out through the eyes?

* * *

"You heard?" Sandy asked as soon as Roberta walked into work.

Her boss nodded and waved her back toward her private office. "I heard," she confirmed when Sandy sat down. "The commission shut down the annex. Is that why you've been crying?"

Sandy winced. She'd tried to cover the tear tracks and repair her make-up but not well enough, apparently. "Not exactly," she said. She didn't want to get into her boyfriend troubles with her boss. Crying was unprofessional enough.

"Good," Roberta said, her tone brisk. "It's bad luck that we picked a property that Ranger wanted. This whole mess started before you got here, and I threw you in to clean it up. None of it was your fault, and I don't want you blaming yourself for it."

"It's generous of you to excuse me, but I have to take some of the blame."

Roberta eyed her thoughtfully. "Do you mean because of your connection to Jake Manning?"

Sandy flushed. "Yes."

"Do you feel that compromised your performance?"

"I know it did," Sandy said. It killed her to admit it. "I misplaced my trust in him, and it hurt us."

Roberta didn't say anything for a moment; then she sighed. "As I understand it, he gave you a copy of all their research so you could save time. Then it turned out he didn't give you everything after all. Is that right?"

Sandy nodded. "Pretty much. He gave me everything he had as of the commission's deadline, but he introduced critical new information last night, none of which he shared with me."

"I understand why that's frustrating, but that new information wasn't part of his deal with you, was it?" Roberta's tone stayed neutral, and Sandy couldn't tell how she felt about the whole mess.

"It wasn't, but let's ignore the fact that it was a deliberate choice to mislead me. The bigger issue here is that my relationship with Jake clouded my judgment. If I hadn't decided to trust him so completely, I might have been thinking more critically and found that information myself. I let myself get lazy."

Roberta outright laughed. "There's no way you're lazy. You've put in incredible overtime, and I know you're salaried, but I'm going to find a way to compensate you with time off." She tapped her finger against her desktop several times before she continued. "As for clouded judgment? Maybe," she conceded. "But I doubt it. Let's remove Jake as a factor. If you had found all the Magnus research on your own and filed your report with the commission on time, would it have occurred to you to keep looking for the information Jake's team eventually turned up? Would you even have thought to check for unofficial historical documents like that?"

As much as she wished she could claim that kind of creative problem-solving, Sandy had to answer honestly. "No, I wouldn't have."

"Me neither. Mr. Manning taught me a new trick on this one, and I'm a very old dog." She held up her hand when Sandy started to protest. "I am. I've been around a long time. This whole dispute is new for us. We've never faced this kind of zoning opposition before. And beyond that, consulting the historical society was a stroke of genius. I don't think his claim will hold up long term, but it was enough to shut down our request, and that's all he needed to do. We'll have to move on to a different solution, and that leaves the playing field uncontested if Ranger Properties is willing to wait. And they will," she said. "They really want that property if they're willing to go to all this trouble."

Sandy studied Roberta, trying to figure out why her boss was letting her off the hook. Roberta correctly interpreted the look and smiled. "You're thinking an outcome like this would have gotten you fired anywhere else, right?"

"Well, yeah."

"That's because you're too used to corporate America. Typically, your boss would be looking to make you a scapegoat if a project failed. Lucky for you, that's the opposite of everything New Horizons stands for," she teased. "We're about empowering women because we have faith in them, and this is a safe environment for them to take risks even if the outcome isn't successful. I extend the same courtesy and faith to the people who work here, not just the ones who train here."

Even in Sandy's misery, Roberta could impress her. She had a lot to learn from this woman and said so. "I kind of figured I'd have grown out of this kind of idiocy by twenty-seven."

Roberta grinned. "You're still a baby. And to be clear, you may have a legitimate claim to idiocy over your Jake problem, but as far as the job and annex problem goes, I have no complaints. Understood?"

Sandy gave a reluctant nod. She was glad Roberta was being so cool about everything, but she knew it would be a long time before she could forgive herself.

"All right," Roberta said. "Let's move on to a little housekeeping, then." They discussed Karina's job performance and Sandy's impending time off for Jessie's wedding. Sandy kept her composure and offered thoughtful solutions when they reviewed their transition plan after Jasmine relocated to the Harlem office, but inside, she felt hollow and bruised. Sandy stood when they were done, ready to return to her desk, but Roberta called to her when she was halfway out the door.

"Sandy?"

"Yes?"

"There's this movie called *How Stella Got Her Groove Back*. It's old, and I know you probably haven't seen it, but it's about this woman who's beaten up by love and how she finds her way back to a happy place."

Sandy nodded to show she was listening, but she had no idea where this was going.

Roberta smiled. "I'd love a sequel, maybe, *How Sandy Got Her Sass Back*."

For the first time since the disaster of the night before, Sandy offered a real smile in return. "I'm so pigheaded that I think it's inevitable."

With a laugh, Roberta waved her out.

* * *

By the end of the day, her sass was still in short supply. She'd fielded calls all day from people who'd heard the news of the night before. Some were indignant, some were consolatory, but not one of them blamed her, and it made her feel guilty. She vented her frustration, hitting "Reject" on her phone extra hard each of the five times Jake called. She found equal satisfaction in sending his multiple e-mails to the recycle bin without opening them. She wasn't interested in whatever he had to say.

It proved harder to ignore him at home. A huge vase of stargazer lilies sat in front of her door. It irritated her that he thought flowers would accomplish anything. She grabbed the vase and marched it downstairs.

Shannon looked up and squealed. "Those are gorgeous! Who are they from?"

"Jake, and I don't want them, so is it okay if I leave them here?"

"Uh-oh. What happened?"

Sandy shrugged. "It's a long story, but I don't want to see him or his stupid flowers. If you see him coming, do you mind telling him to leave me alone? I know that puts you in an awkward position, but I can't deal with him right now."

"No problem," Shannon assured her. "I'll make sure he doesn't get past me."

Sandy, relieved by the promise, ran back upstairs and slipped into her yoga gear so she could catch the last class of the night at the studio. When she returned two hours later feeling heartsore but at least more limber, she discovered how determined Shannon was to keep her promise. As she rounded the house to take her private entrance, she found a sign affixed to the bottom of the stairs: "Stay Out, Jake!"

She spent the next hour on the phone reassuring her mom that she was fine and then explaining in an e-mail to Jessie what had happened. She wanted to discuss the whole mess as little as possible. The fewer people she had to run through the same conversation with, the better.

Friday was more of the same. The yoga had helped her sleep far better than the night before, but even though she woke with a clear head, her emotions stayed as muddled as ever. At work, Roberta instructed her not to start a search for a replacement site for the annex until after Jessie's wedding, so she spent the day alternately enduring condolence calls from New Horizons graduates and working with a new client to start her training.

She couldn't remember dreading a weekend so much. Two full days with nothing to do left way too much time for thinking. Friday night disappeared in a *What Not to Wear* marathon. Saturday she buried her thoughts by working through her backlog of novels, reading while she washed loads of the laundry she'd neglected for weeks. When that ran out, she spent almost two hours wandering aimlessly through a whole-foods warehouse. The idea was to find something new and challenging to cook to kill time, but as it turned out, nothing occurred to her by osmosis, magic, or otherwise. She gave up and grabbed a veggie hoagie from the deli to eat while she watched a Molly Ringwald marathon on cable all night.

Sunday she solved by attending an earlier singles ward on the other side of the city and then wasting the afternoon on two mystery novels that Leah had loaned her. By Sunday night, she was so desperate for something useful to do that she could practically taste Monday. She fell into bed, exhausted from the constant pressure of suppressed tears. Her mother called at least three times a day to offer reminders like, "Tears are your soul's way of purging psychic pain" and, "Crying helps you communicate your deepest needs to the universe." The last call had ended with her mom begging Sandy to cry, but she refused.

The pain cut so deep that she preferred to keep herself comfortably numb. Jessie called it emotional shock. Sandy didn't care what it was as long as she could keep a safe distance between herself and the hurt that had threatened to crush her in the long hours of Thursday night when Jake's betrayal had been fresh. She didn't want to go anywhere near that again.

Jake, of course, made it as hard as possible to keep him in lockdown. While he didn't show up again, three more flower arrangements did, and she sent several calls a day from him to voice mail. She had to empty her entire text message inbox twice, which she did with grim satisfaction, not bothering to read any of them. Even her Facebook account filled up with messages from him. She unfriended him, but he kept sending the messages anyway. She didn't read any of them. Her e-mail solution was the easiest; she blocked him.

She knew what he would say anyway, so what was the point? It would be some variation of an apology and a plea to give him more time. At least, that's what it would be if any of his texts or voice mails bore a resemblance to the six messages he had left with Karina on Friday before she started screening his calls.

Karina was already at work when Sandy walked in on Monday. Her assistant sheepishly waved a pink message slip at her. "Sorry," she said. "I picked up the phone without checking caller ID first."

"It's okay," Sandy said. She took the message and crumpled it on the way to her desk. "I'm sorry you're stuck in the middle of this."

"Don't worry about it," Karina said. "He might be persistent, but at least he's polite."

Sandy dropped the message into her trash can and turned her computer on. "I'm going to review field reports all morning and do exit interviews this afternoon. Unless a situation comes up involving fire, arterial blood, or structural building damage, hold my calls, please."

Karina nodded her understanding, and Sandy dove into her work. The front door chimed several times during the morning to admit employees and clients, but she ignored it, focusing instead on the reports. After a lunch of yogurt at her desk, she headed to the conference room for the first of her exit interviews. One of their executive assistant sessions had ended, and they had five women ready to enter the workforce. Sandy loved these exit interviews. The opportunity to chat with these women and hear what they had learned and how much hope they had for their new futures renewed Sandy like few other things could.

After the first two, her spirit felt the teensiest bit brighter. It was hard to be downhearted in the face of their optimism and excitement for whatever came next. It reminded her of why she'd taken the New Horizons job in the first place. The minor pay increase didn't in any way compensate for the crazy hours she worked, but the happiness on her clients' faces made up the difference. And then some.

She settled into her third interview with a sweet woman named Sharon, delighted to hear about the job offer she had received from a local real estate brokerage to train as their office manager. They were in the middle of reviewing the principles of active listening when the door flew open, and her head shot up. Jake stood there looking determined and slightly scary.

"I guess you didn't get my message," she said coolly.

"What message?" he barked. "You haven't returned a single call, text, or e-mail for four days."

"Right. That was the message."

He gave a short, sharp laugh. "Then yes, I did get that one."

"Obviously not, or you wouldn't be standing here." She touched Sharon's hand. "I'm so sorry, but I'll need a minute. Do you mind waiting outside while I take care of this?"

"Are you going to be okay?" Sharon asked, her voice anxious.

"I'll be fine. Why don't you go see if Geneva needs any help supervising the lab?"

Sharon shot a nervous glance at Jake before she nodded and skirted past him. He shut the door behind her.

"What are you doing here?" Sandy asked.

"I figured I'd catch you where you couldn't get away."

"Ah. How very stalker-ish of you."

His jaw tightened; then he forced a smile. "I like to call it being resourceful."

"Yeah, you like to call a lot of things something besides what they are."

He sighed. "I know you're still mad."

"Correct. Thanks for playing. Parting gifts are at the door. Bye."

"Can you give me a minute? Just one? I came all the way down here. It's the least you can do."

"I don't owe you anything, Jake. I want you to leave." She opened the folder in front of her and began leafing through the pages to signal the end of their conversation.

"Not until I've made my offer."

That got her attention. "What offer?"

"I have a client interested in sponsoring New Horizons. I want to discuss the terms."

What was he up to? she wondered. "If you think I'm doing business with you again, you're crazy."

"I don't think you can afford to pass this offer up."

"On the contrary. Your cost of doing business is way too high for me."

His face settled into an expression of challenge. "You sound pretty sure about that. Are you sure enough to bet sick amounts of money for the center?"

She hesitated. She had no idea what he was up to, and while she was sure it was no good, if on the off chance he did have an offer for the program, she didn't want to turn down much-needed funds because of their personal issues. She met his gaze while keeping her own expression blank. "My responsibility was to oversee the establishment and development of our new annex. We don't have a new annex anymore. Any other funding issues would go to our director, Roberta Jordan. She's out of the office right now, but I'll have her assistant call and schedule some time for you."

She pushed away from the table and pointed at the door. "Please tell Karina to send Sharon back again," she said by way of dismissal.

He eyed her in frustration. "That's it? You don't even want to know what my offer is?"

"I know what it is. It's some kind of bribe to get me to overlook every rotten and underhanded truth you revealed about yourself last week. No thanks. If you have a legitimate offer, then you need to take it up with the director."

He didn't have a play left that wasn't going to tick her off, and they both knew it.

"I'll schedule something with your director, then." He looked like he wanted to add something else, but he bit back whatever it was and turned toward the door. Just when she thought she was rid of him, he turned around. The bleak expression in his eyes caught her off guard.

"I'll do anything to make this right," he said. "But I can't chase you forever."

Sandy's eyes hardened. "Wow, Jake. You stuck it out for four whole days. I guess I'll have to live with that. Please leave."

"I didn't mean—"

"Leave," she said, and she couldn't keep a note of rising frustration out of her tone.

Hearing it, his shoulders slumped so slightly she wondered if she had imagined it. He hesitated for a painful half minute and then turned without another word and walked out. She was still staring at the empty space he'd left behind him when Sharon walked back in, concern written all over her face. "Are you all right, Sandy?" she asked.

"Sure, I'm great. Let's finish your interview, okay?"

Sharon, clearly unconvinced, followed Sandy to the table anyway, and they picked up where they'd left off, but Sandy couldn't calm her nerves after Jake's disruption. Even though Sharon graciously accepted her apology for her distraction, Sandy still felt bad—and mad that Jake had managed to ruin another day for her.

When Sharon left, Sandy headed back to her desk and examined her inbox. It was full of papers—forms she needed to sign off on, new applications to examine, even more field reports she need to vet before sending them on to Roberta. It was all necessary work, but since it represented the mundane part of her job, she had a hard time concentrating on it. She threw her pencil down in disgust just as Roberta walked in from one of her off-site meetings.

"Problems?" Roberta asked.

"No," Sandy said, quickly scooping her pencil back up. "Everything's great."

At her desk, Jasmine snorted.

"Is there something I should know?" Roberta asked.

"Jake Manning stopped by," Jasmine answered. "He won't leave Sandy alone."

Sandy scowled. "Sorry, Roberta. I had no idea he would show up here."

Roberta sighed. "Can I see you in my office?"

Sorry, Jasmine mouthed at her as she passed. Sandy shrugged. It wasn't Jasmine's fault Jake had shown up, and Roberta would have heard about it anyway.

"What's going on?" Roberta asked when Sandy closed the door behind them.

Sandy explained Jake's appearance but focused more on his offer of funding than on how inappropriate it was for him to show up at her office unannounced and uninvited. Roberta, intrigued by the possibilities of Jake's offer, quickly realized Sandy didn't have many details.

"I know you didn't invite him here, but you have to make it clear that he can't show up here without legitimate business. I know that was his excuse for coming here, but I also know it wasn't his real reason," Roberta said.

Oops. Sandy's distraction obviously hadn't worked. "I'm sorry," she said. "I'll find a way to make him understand."

"My guess would be talking to him might help so he's not compelled to pull a stunt like today."

Sandy stared, and Roberta grinned. "You're wondering how I know you've been ignoring him, aren't you? You're not the only one who listens to office gossip."

"Fair enough," Sandy said. "Excuse me. I need to kill Jasmine."

"Don't do that," Roberta said. "She only told me what's going on because she's worried about you." Sandy tried not to fidget while Roberta studied her. "I think Jasmine may have a point. I didn't lure you out to DC only to burn you out after three months. You're going back to Seattle this weekend, right?"

"Yes. I'm in my best friend's wedding."

"I know you weren't planning on leaving until Thursday, but why don't you go ahead and take off early? You're not starting any new projects until you come back anyway."

"I'm fine," Sandy protested. "I don't need any special handling."

"I know that," Roberta said patiently. "I'm not handling you. I'm rewarding you. I can't do it with money, but I can do it with time off. You did an exceptional job on the annex case, whether you see it yet or not, and you put in far more time than you had to. Take the extra time as a thank you."

Sandy hesitated. She didn't want to appear weak, but she had to admit that keeping busy with Jessie and wedding preparations sounded far better than hanging around here ducking Jake until the weekend. And the truth was she *had* put in a ton of overtime. "Okay," she said. "I'll take it. Thanks."

"You bet. Now go home."

Sandy didn't need to be told again. She said a quick good-bye to Jasmine and called Jessie on her way to the train. Jessie was delighted with the change of plans. Sandy used her phone to search for tickets on the Internet, and by the time she reached her Metro stop, she'd changed her outbound flight to a redeye into Seattle.

Four hours later, after a whirlwind packing marathon and bumming a ride from Leah to the airport, she took her first deep breath of the day and leaned her head back against her airplane seat. She always loved the exhilaration of takeoff, but there was no jet engine powerful enough to whisk her away from Jake Manning as fast as she wanted to go. She relaxed when the engines ignited. She couldn't wait to put him far, far behind her.

Chapter 31

"I can't believe you're letting me do this." Sandy grinned. "Who would have guessed a year ago that I'd be planning a girls' night out for the social introvert of the decade?"

"I know, I know; I was a pain. But I'm reformed, and that means having the traditional bachelorette experience. Um, Mormon style. So basically not a bachelorette experience at all." Jessie shot Sandy a warning look.

"I'm reformed too. Quit worrying, and hand over your phone. I need access to your contact list if I'm going to wreak some serious havoc."

Jessie plopped her Blackberry into Sandy's outstretched hand. "Whatever it takes to make you stop moping."

"I'm not moping."

"Then what word do you use for this?" Jessie pushed up from the sofa and slumped around the living room, staring off into space and heaving sighs.

Sandy laughed. "I haven't been that bad, have I?"

"No," Jessie conceded. "But you're pretty close."

"Fine. I'll get over myself. Now get out of here so I can call some people and arrange a surprise bachelorette party for you. Don't come out of your room until I say so."

Jessie didn't look like she minded being banished. She was probably in her room tying ribbons on her wedding favors and mooning over pictures of Ben, Sandy groused. Then she grinned. This is exactly what she had hoped would happen when she'd secretly signed her roommate up for LDS Lookup last year. She pulled out her laptop and opened her e-mail so she could access her Seattle list of friends. Her inbox contained several new messages, but only one was from Jake. It was the first one from him since the previous morning. That was practically a lifetime compared to the fast and furious pace he had rained e-mails down on her for the days before that. She opened one from Roberta marked "Urgent." It said simply, "We got new funding. Also, you should talk to Jake Manning."

Even though it excited her to hear they had more money coming, she decided the details could wait until she was in the office on Monday. As for Jake Manning, if Roberta made her, Sandy would call him when she got back. Otherwise, she was keeping her vacation as Jake-free as possible.

Coming to town early had definitely helped her stay busy and keep her mind off of him and the dull ache in her chest. Or it did while Jessie kept her hopping, which had been until bedtime all three days that she'd been here. Then her exhaustion weakened her guard, and the nights stretched far too long as she tossed and turned and tried to shut out her misery. She painted on a smile every morning and applied concealer under her eyes, but it hadn't fooled Jessie. Maybe Jessie only noticed because they were so close. Sandy didn't want anyone else speculating about her emotional state.

She shook off the creeping melancholy and focused on the party plans. She sent out an e-mail to all of her and Jessie's mutual friends to meet the following night at Tango, a nearby tapas restaurant in her old Capitol Hill neighborhood, and then scrolled through Jessie's phone and called anyone she didn't have an e-mail for. It would be a fun night, starting with good food and continuing with a limo ride downtown, where they could do the club crawl and hit some dance spots.

An hour later, she glanced at the clock and saw it was too late to call anyone else. Jet-lagged and sleep deprived, she dragged herself into her old room and crawled into bed, offering a silent prayer that she could get the sleep she badly needed.

* * *

The next morning she realized she should have been more specific with her prayer. She fell right to sleep only to spend the whole night having vivid dreams about Jake. She could remember only a couple of them. In one, she was a dog, and Jake made her roll over again and again and again, even though she barked to tell him how much she hated the dog treats he rewarded her with. In another, they were having dinner at a fancy restaurant, and he kept staring at a piece of toilet paper stuck to her shoe that wouldn't come off. She didn't bother trying to remember any more.

Doing her best to freshen up, she tended to her undereye circles and moisturized her dull skin; then she trudged out to find Jessie rustling up a breakfast of eggs and something that smelled spicy. Jessie waved her into a chair at the dining table and slid an omelet and homemade hash browns in front of her. Sandy smiled and poked at them with her fork.

Jessie said nothing for a while, eating her own food and watching her. Halfway through, she broke down. "Sandy, this is ridiculous."

"What is?"

"I've never seen you like this. It's crazy."

"What? I didn't sleep well last night, that's all."

Jessie studied her with a critical eye. "When *is* the last time you got a good night's sleep?"

Sandy shrugged. Maybe a week ago—the night before the hearing—but she didn't feel like admitting it.

"Maybe if you called Jake and had it out with him, you would feel better," Jessie said. "Or maybe if you called and listened, he might surprise you."

Sandy didn't say anything. It was at least the fifth time Jessie had made the same suggestion to give Jake a chance to explain.

"It doesn't add up," she had argued the first time Sandy had explained what happened.

Sandy had said simply, "Exactly. Turns out, it never did."

Jessie sighed when Sandy didn't respond. "All right. I'll drop it for now." She hopped up to clear the table.

"Remind me what's on the agenda for today."

"Today is all about throwing fits." Jessie grinned when Sandy's eyebrow crept up. "*Dress* fits. My sisters are all coming over so everyone can try on their dresses and my mom can make any last-minute adjustments."

"Great," Sandy said. "The only good thing Jake did for me was ruin my appetite this week. My dress fits again but barely."

Jessie scoffed. "It must be so hard to be a curvaceous size six. Poor baby." She ducked when Sandy winged a potholder at her. "I should have picked a hideous yellow that looks bad with your hair to level the playing field."

Sandy groped for another potholder or other handy missile, but the doorbell rang, and the door flew open to admit a gaggle of laughing, chirping women. Jessie's family had arrived.

* * *

"Whew!" Jessie collapsed on her sofa next to Sandy and admired her friend's toenails, which were now a soft, shimmery pink. After everyone had modeled their dresses and Sister Taylor had made a few minor tweaks here and there,

Jessie's sister Breanna had treated the group to manicures and pedicures at a nearby nail salon. The day had flown by, and it startled Sandy to discover that late afternoon had snuck up on them during their pampering. She studied her shimmery pink pedicure and decided it was totally worth it. Still, she was glad Jessie's family was at their hotel while she and Jessie took a short breather before diving into the evening's festivities.

"Where are you going to find the energy to get married tomorrow?" Sandy demanded. "I'm already wiped out."

Jessie laughed. "But you're always ready to party. You getting old or something?"

Sandy shook a fist at her without much conviction. "Yes. I got ancient." She dug a chocolate out of Jessie's candy dish on the coffee table in front of her and savored it.

"I miss you. You were the best roommate ever," Jessie said.

"I know. However, you're going to like the arrangements with your new roommate starting tomorrow. Fringe benefits and all."

"Don't say fringe," Jessie groaned. "It makes me think of the tacky negligee my mom bought me. I can't decide if it's a serious gift or not."

"It's hard to tell with her," Sandy agreed. Sister Taylor's dry sense of humor was near legendary. "If it's any consolation, I doubt she'll ask you if you wore it."

Jessie shuddered. "Good point."

They studied the ceiling for a while longer before Jessie broke the silence again. "Thanks again for being so incredibly bossy last year." She pointed to a picture of herself and Ben on the mantle. "If it weren't for your identity theft, I wouldn't even be getting married. I'll find a way to repay you someday."

Sandy shrugged. "It's true that I'm awesome and all-knowing. Also, you're welcome."

"Well, Your Omniscience, tell me what I should wear tonight."

"How about if you bring stuff out here and model it so I don't have to get up?"

Jessie, in a sudden burst of annoying energy, hopped off the couch and tugged at Sandy. "No way," she said. "It's time to go closet shopping. The night is about to begin!"

Sandy allowed herself to be pulled up. "It feels like backward day and we switched places."

"Nope, because if we had, I'd have your fashion sense, and I don't. So come help me."

Sandy loved the happy twinkle in her friend's eyes and resolved to catch her second wind. Heading down the hallway to Jessie's room, she called over her shoulder, "What are you waiting for? We've got a party to throw."

* * *

Sandy squinted in the dim light of the limousine, taking advantage of the debate flying around her to lean her head back against the leather seat and relinquish her role as the evening's social director. They'd been arguing for almost ten minutes, but Sandy figured one of them was bound to suggest something a majority would agree to. Her own pick of a dueling-piano restaurant had worked great until the lyrics had grown too crude and sent them scurrying for the exit—a single-file line of twelve embarrassed women threading through a tipsy crowd behind Jessie in her hot-pink wedding veil.

"What about the Owl n' Thistle?" someone asked.

"No way! I heard the bartender strips sometimes."

"Ew," Jessie said, which settled that.

"Is the comedy club still open?" Breanna asked.

"Yeah, but I want to dance," Jessie said.

"What about The Factory?" a girl at the other end of the limo called. "I know it's back in Capitol Hill, but it's always fun."

Jessie stiffened and darted a glance at Sandy, but no one else noticed, because they were all clamoring for The Factory. The girl who suggested it, Jessie's assistant, beamed at their reactions and tapped on the glass to tell the driver their new destination.

"Don't worry," Jessie said. "I'll tell them we want to stay downtown." She leaned forward to interrupt the others, who had transitioned into a colossally bad rendition of a Pink song, but Sandy stopped her.

"It's okay," she said near her friend's ear to make herself heard above the . . . singing. "It's the only thing they all agreed on. Let it go. I'll be fine."

Jessie watched her, concern etching a wrinkle in her brow. "You've already had a hard time this week. I'll pull a Bridezilla and demand to go somewhere else."

The offer tempted Sandy, but she shook her head. "It's fine."

Jessie hesitated but then nodded and leaned toward Sandy instead of the other girls. "Think of it as a chance to exorcise El Diablo."

Sandy mustered a convincing return smile.

Forty-five minutes later, she wished she would have taken the coward's way out and let Jessie be Bridezilla. The familiar sounds and smells of The

Factory flooded over her as she stood at the edge of the dance floor trying to identify Jessie in the churning mass of bodies. Sandy smiled to herself. Even her friend's bright-pink wedding veil had disappeared in the mix. Oh well. Jessie would have to come out for air or water eventually.

She wandered away from the dance floor toward the quieter part of the club near the billiards tables; without really meaning to, she drifted toward the corner where she and Jake had sat forever ago, caught up in the giddiness of instant infatuation. She remembered her amazement that night, how incredible it felt to click with a stranger in such an authentic way. She'd gone home with a head full of possibilities and hope.

It hurt so much worse now that she'd had two perfect, blissful weeks with him. It cut far deeper, and disillusionment throbbed behind her eyes and threatened to take the shape of hot tears.

A couple at one of the tables slid from their high bar chairs and headed in the direction of the dance floor. Sandy slipped into one of the seats and laughed at herself. It was the same spot where she and Jake had sat. How pathetic that she couldn't resist it. A cocktail waitress stopped and offered her a friendly smile.

"Can I get you anything?"

Sandy and Jake had spent their evening knocking back one of the club's nonalcoholic specialty drinks. Even as she chided herself for her own unhealthy compulsion, she knew she couldn't resist. "I'd like a—"

"Purple Haze."

She froze, recognizing the voice behind her. It was him. He continued, "Make it two, please."

The waitress nodded and left, and Sandy flinched as Jake took the empty seat across from her. Jessie stood behind him, looking nervous. He didn't say anything else, just sat and watched Sandy.

"Jessie?" she asked, too stunned to come up with anything else.

"Hear him out, Sandy. I did."

What did that mean? When had she heard him out? *What was going on?*

"What are you doing here?" Sandy demanded.

"I came to talk you. I understand if you want to run away again, but I'd love it if you didn't."

She didn't know how he got through Jessie, but her friend was the only reason Sandy didn't get up and walk out. She said nothing, because she couldn't trust herself to speak. Finally, she nodded at Jessie. Jessie gave her a quick hug.

"Sorry, but it had to be done. Just listen to him. Call it my repayment." She melted away, back toward the dance floor.

Jake moved a drink menu, a set of salt and pepper shakers, and a bowl of peanuts to the next table over.

"What are you doing?" she asked again, feeling like a broken record.

"I'm removing projectiles," he said calmly. He reached for his wallet, dug out a piece of paper, and handed it to her. She unfolded it to find a single-sentence note signed by Roberta: "Listen to him."

She crumpled it. "Boss's orders."

He dove right in. "I misled you, and I'm sorry, but I really thought it was the right thing to do in the moment."

She gaped at him. "When is lying ever the right thing to do?"

He shook his head. "I never lied to you. I misled you, and that may sound like I'm trying to rationalize, but I saw it as a clear and distinct difference. I would have done everything differently if I'd known how much this was going to hurt you, but this was not how it all played out in my head." He gave a short, sad laugh. "In my head, it all ended in happily ever after with me as the hero."

Sandy massaged her temples, trying to bring some order to the chaos in her brain. It didn't help. "If I hear you out, will you promise to leave me alone?"

He didn't answer at first. She could practically see his lawyer brain trying to find a loophole. After what looked like an intense internal struggle, he nodded.

"Then go ahead, Jake. Tell me how I got this all wrong. Tell me that you never misrepresented who your real client was or the true agenda behind shutting down the annex."

"My client really was River Oaks all along. Several of the residents there had legitimate concerns about New Horizons coming in, and at first, I did too." The waitress stopped by with their drinks, and he waited until she left to continue. "But I've been working with Ranger's in-house legal counsel as a consultant for four years now. They call me in when they want things handled discreetly. Groups have been known to protest a Ranger project just because it's Ranger."

"How can you work for someone so shady?" Sandy exploded.

"They're not shady. I know this company inside and out. They're sometimes sly in their approach to things, but it's only because they're trying to avoid the publicity that can drag their projects out forever."

"Do you not hear yourself? That reeks of rationalization."

"No, it doesn't. Let me give you an example of why they stay below the radar. Ranger had a great reputation until several years ago when Hurricane Katrina hit. They wanted to help with the rebuilding effort, so they made a decision to invest in new-home development in New Orleans. Everything was fine at first, but after about eighteen months, some serious issues emerged. Do you remember hearing a couple of years back about a huge drywall problem down in some of the southeastern states?"

She shook her head. It didn't sound familiar.

"Several large builders imported drywall supplies from China. That's normal, but Ranger's supplier had major contamination problems. Homeowners who received that drywall complained of respiratory issues. The government inspectors investigated and returned a report recommending that any home built with the tainted drywall should be gutted completely and rebuilt. The question was, who should pay."

He took a swallow of his drink and gathered his thoughts. "The insurance wouldn't cover it, federal aid for the homeowners got tied up in Congress, and the guilty factory in China folded up shop and went out of business. Ranger stepped in again to help, even though they weren't legally responsible. They replaced the drywall in their projects at their own expense."

He shook his head. "The New Orleans homeowners were grateful because no other builder offered to help, but when word got out that Ranger was a company with a conscience, things took a bad turn. Their name was linked with the drywall crisis through media reports that didn't give all the facts, and a very ugly perception of the company formed pretty quickly. They were slapped with claims and lawsuits from people who saw Ranger as an easy target. The company hemorrhaged money for months. That's when they hired our firm to consult on a strategy going forward."

"That's a sad story," Sandy interrupted, "but I'm not seeing the connection between Hurricane Katrina and the annex."

"I'm getting there," he promised. "But I really need you to understand how Ranger works. The strategy that our firm and their lawyers came up with was to keep the company's name out of the public eye as much as possible. The minute people found out Ranger was funding something, they either protested because they erroneously blamed them for the drywall problem in New Orleans or saw the company as a soft touch that they could sue for a quick settlement. River Oaks Landing is a perfect example."

"What I know is that they sent some goons to spread lies and scare some nice people about the big, bad, scary annex coming."

"At the time, we thought the annex was a blight," he admitted. "We knew about the CHEP scandal and figured we'd be doing the neighbors a favor by blocking your expansion."

"I don't understand," she said. "Even if you got us out, there were still several other tenants in that mall. What were you going to do about them?"

"Buy them out of their leases," he explained. "But it was much cheaper to simply block your annex from opening than to try to buy you out once you were in, and like I said, we thought we had grounds for an injunction."

"But you saw what New Horizons is. Why did you keep pushing the case?"

"Because I had a new endgame." He smiled. "How could I let the annex get phased out after knowing you and seeing your passion for it? I saw the good it did, and I thought I saw a way to get everyone what they wanted."

"I can't even figure out how Ranger Properties got what they wanted, much less New Horizons."

"The River Oaks people want peace of mind, New Horizons wants to expand, and Ranger wants to redevelop the area."

"At the expense of everyone else! It's wrong."

"I knew Ranger, even if they saw the positive statistics about New Horizons, would still feel like they were a better option for the long-term health of the neighborhood."

"How convenient for them since that world view also coincides with them lining their own pockets."

"They're a decent business, but they're still a business. That's what I had to work around. Arguing to keep the annex wouldn't do anything but tick off the partners at my firm. I convinced Ranger to let me try a new approach. Please don't throw your drink on me when I tell you this part," he said, possibly only half joking. "The historical landmark claim won't hold up to deeper investigation. I just needed to force an investigation to get your annex delayed. Ranger can afford to wait; I knew you guys couldn't."

He leaned toward her. "I'm hoping the end justifies the means here because that wasn't the final play. I had River Oaks happy. I cleared the way for the company to go in and develop when the historical landmark claim was denied. But that still left the annex. Maybe you didn't think you were getting through to me, Sandy, but you did. On so many levels. There's no way this could come out right if the annex was the only loser. I never would have taken the gamble if I thought I wouldn't win."

Confusion blunted her anger. "What's the win for us?"

"Ranger is always looking for ways to improve their image. I gave them one." He reached into the inside pocket of his leather jacket and pulled out a letter, which he handed her.

She unfolded it, and her eyes flew up to meet his after the very first sentence. "Ranger Properties partners with New Horizons for a bold experiment in social change," it blared. It was a press release dated for distribution on the following Monday.

"Roberta signed off on this already," he said. "Keep reading."

It outlined a major corporate sponsorship that would fund the new annex entirely, from construction to training new students.

She finally looked up to see hope written all over his face, but she didn't know what to say. She could accept that the annex was going to be okay, but it didn't change some key facts. She'd spent a week in a world of hurt, and she didn't know how to suddenly let that go.

"You still lied to me."

"No, I didn't. Not once."

She dragged a hand through her hair in frustration. "Stop with the lawyer semantics. If you're more comfortable calling it 'misleading,' then we can use that word instead."

"I only withheld from you what I legally or ethically had to. And even if I could have, I don't know if I would have said anything until I was sure Ranger would commit to this. I wouldn't have wanted to promise something I couldn't deliver."

"Why couldn't you have put this together before the commission's ruling? Then you wouldn't have had to resort to the historical landmark claim."

"That's the ethical problem. I had to represent my client's best interests, and that meant making sure that getting the property, even if it wasn't right away, was a lock. I couldn't divulge that strategy to you."

"But you could have offered us this deal."

"I wish I could have, but the company wanted the full PR benefits from partnering with New Horizons. That meant it needed to look like they were doing it out of corporate good citizenship and not because sponsoring the annex was the only way to get the land. They needed a clear victory so they'll look like even bigger heroes for offering the partnership anyway."

It was all beginning to make a convoluted kind of sense. "So the annex is going to open?"

"Yes."

"But not until the historical landmark claim gets sorted out. That could take a long time."

"Maybe not," he said. "I have some new paperwork to file with the zoning commission."

"And what's that?" she asked, slightly fascinated now.

"Turns out that if you do even more digging, there's not much to find on the Magnus park. We can document that. We already did, actually. We're going to present that to the Parks Department to help them facilitate their decision."

"How convenient for Ranger," she said with a wry smile.

"How convenient for River Oaks and New Horizons," he corrected. "Ranger plans to build a huge new shopping center there, but they want to make it a flagship design in their portfolio. They're going to try a more organic approach to development, designing a project that reflects the character and history of the community. A big part of that includes opening an arts center, and here's the kicker." He couldn't contain his grin. "The centerpiece to the whole design will be a tribute park to Robert Magnus, inspired by what it might have looked like, on the exact spot it occupied one hundred fifty years ago."

"Wow," she managed to say after mulling that over. "Just . . . wow."

He nodded. "Yeah."

"Ranger Properties is pretty smart."

"They're learning."

"They have a good lawyer."

Hope sparked in his eyes. "I try to be, but I'm more worried about being a good man. This is going to be a pretty hollow victory if I can't convince you that I am." He reached for her hands before catching himself and dropping his hands to the tabletop, still uncertain of her. "This has been the trickiest thing I've ever had to pull off professionally, but that stress is nothing compared to the pure torture the last week has been. It's killing me that you hate me so much right now, and I'll do anything to earn your trust back. Just name it, Sandy. Please. Tell me what I need to do."

She could see the pain mingled with the hope and the uncertainty in his face over which emotion would win out. She didn't mean to be so hard to read. Her blank expression was shock, nothing else. Her anger had fallen away after the first line of the press release, and the confusion had soon followed as he explained what he'd been up to. Now she felt . . .

Relief. Relief that he was the man she thought he was. And as she welcomed that relief, other emotions flooded in, feelings that were the direct inverse of all the ones that had caused her grief for the last three nights. She felt a bubble of something rising up from the place that had been a dark pit in her stomach for days. It tickled, and she recognized the soft flickers of happiness. Slowly, it spread, warming her as it rose until she couldn't contain the smile spreading over her face. "Okay," she said.

"Okay?"

"Yes. I'll tell you what you need to do." She slid her hand over to fit into one of his. "Forgive me . . . for doubting you."

"I understand why you did."

"I'm sorry anyway."

He squeezed her hand. "There's nothing to forgive."

"Thank you for doing what you did for the center."

"I totally believe those women deserve that chance, but truthfully, I did it as much for you as I did for them." He stood and walked around the tiny table to stand next to her. "I hopped on a plane as soon as I got the deal done with Roberta and harassed Jessie until she believed me and agreed to bring you here tonight."

Her mouth dropped open. "This was your idea? How did you even get in touch with Jessie?"

"I have Magdalena's number, and she gave me Jessie's. Then I called Jessie for two days straight and pleaded and begged and explained everything until she believed me."

Another small smile played around her lips. "And then you convinced her to drag me back here."

"Yeah," he said. "I did. It's the most important part of the plan."

"Oh really? How's that?"

He touched her cheek, his graze feather light. "My life changed forever here just over a year ago, but I was too stubborn to see it. I guess I've been hoping against hope that you would hear me out and give me another chance to fix a regret I've held on to ever since."

"What regret?" she asked, and she knew the huskiness in her voice betrayed how badly she wanted to know.

"I should have done this that night," he said, and he leaned down to kiss her, a searing kiss that she felt all the way down to her toes. When he lifted his head a lifetime later, he smiled down at her, a smile so full of promise it stopped her breath again.

"That night was the beginning of something amazing, and I walked away from it. I'm hoping that tonight is another new beginning. Is it, Sandy?" he asked softly.

With a smile, she pulled him down for another kiss. "This is going to be the best do-over ever."

About the Author

MELANIE BENNETT JACOBSON IS AN avid reader, amateur cook, and champion shopper. She consumes astonishing quantities of chocolate, chick flicks, and romance novels. After meeting her own husband on the Internet, she is now living happily married in Southern California with her growing family and a series of half-finished craft projects. Melanie loves to hear from readers and can be contacted at writestuff.jacobson@gmail.com or through her home page at www.melaniejacobson.net.